PET WHISPERER P.I.:

BOOKS 10-12 SPECIAL COLLECTION

MOLLY FITZ

Editor: Jennifer Lopez, Mistress with the Red Pen
Cover: TM Franklin

PO Box 873543
Wasilla, AK 99687

RETRIEVER RANSOM

PET WHISPERER P.I.

A dognapping turns into a kidnapping, which turns into... murder?

Octo-Cat and I have officially landed our first paying gig!

Our client? None other than the brand-new mayor of Glendale. You see, some disgruntled constituent just dog-napped the poor guy's golden retriever and will only return the purloined pooch when he agrees to resign his small-town position of power.

But little does our client know that while we search for his missing companion, we'll also be delving into his past to uncover the motive behind this sinister plot to push him out of office.

Woof, talk about drama!

Luckily, I've got the world's best talking cat on my side, which means I'm sure to land on my feet with this investigation... Uh, right?

1

My name is Angie Russo. I live in the Blueberry Bay region of Maine, and I can talk to animals. Thanks to this unique—but mostly secret—skill, I've taken to solving mysteries around town.

Usually my involvement happens because I have a tendency to wind up in the wrong place at the wrong time, but now I've also hung out my hat as a private investigator. And just because I don't have any clients, that doesn't mean I'm not good at what I do.

Or more accurately, that we're not good at what we do.

Yeah, my cat is my business partner, and we also get help from my quirky nan, her sweet Chihuahua Paisley, my lawyer boyfriend Charles, and even the handful of animals that live near our property—most notably, Pringle the raccoon who lives in a luxury tree fort in our backyard and is a tad addicted to reality TV.

Nan and Charles can't talk to the animals like I do.

In fact, I've never met another living soul who can, and I still don't know why I was blessed with this particular ability. All I know is that I got zapped by a faulty coffee maker, knocked unconscious, and woke up with a talking cat on my chest.

At first, I could only understand that one cat, but over time, my powers grew stronger. Now I can understand most animals, but occasionally I do still find a dud.

That same crabby tabby, Octo-Cat, wound up with me after we worked together to solve the murder of his previous owner. He came with a generous trust fund, a large coastal manor, and an endless string of color commentary about my life.

He has a girlfriend, a former show Himalayan named Grizabella. Their relationship is long distance and mostly sustained through my Instagram account. It's equal parts adorable, hilarious, and groan-inducing.

But, hey, a happy cat means a happy me.

And I have a lot to be happy about lately, especially since my bad luck often results in good outcomes. First there was the zap that gave me Octo-Cat, then Nan's impulsiveness landed Paisley in our lives, but those are nothing compared to the fact that a huge family secret had recently been cracked wide open.

Mom and I found out that Nan hadn't been completely honest about our family's origins even though she'd had more than fifty years to come clean. And, well, as awful as that whole thing was to discover, it also meant we were able to connect with long-lost family in Georgia, and thus I found the sister I never had in my cousin Mags.

She came for a visit over the holidays and that went well...

Mostly.

She still doesn't know my secret, but I think I'll tell her next time we're together. I probably should have told her before she returned home, but I was scared it would make her and the rest of our newfound family reject me.

I mean, did you believe me at first when I said I could talk to animals?

It's totally crazy, but also totally true and totally a defining feature of my life—and I wouldn't have it any other way.

That brings us to today.

We just celebrated the start of a new year. Normally I don't make resolutions, but this time I decided to do whatever it takes to finally get Octo-Cat's and my P.I. business off the ground. Even though we can easily live off his trust fund and Nan's retirement, there's a special brand of shame in having to be supported by your cat.

I mean, I have seven associate degrees.

At least one of those should be good for a job.

And a job is exactly what I'll have to get if my business doesn't take off this year. My boyfriend Charles said he'd welcome me back at the law firm anytime, and while I love him dearly, I always hated being a paralegal.

It doesn't matter, though, because I will succeed at this P.I. thing.

I'm too stubborn not to.

Besides, I'd really hate to let down my cat…

* * *

"This is so exciting," Nan trilled as we stood outside of city hall with a small crowd of other Glendalians to watch the incoming mayor get sworn into office.

Paisley barked merrily from within my grandmother's arms.

Octo-Cat had requested to stay home, given his disdain for crowds, and that was a battle I hadn't wanted to fight.

The mayor appeared at the top of the steps dressed in a fine navy suit with a light blue dress shirt and matching tie. At forty-seven, he was at least two decades younger than his predecessor. But while Mayor McHenry had been a family man, incoming mayor Dennison was a proud bachelor.

When asked about his singlehood by the press, he always said that his trusty golden retriever was more than enough family for him. Besides, less of a home life made it easier for him to give his full attention to making the humble town of Glendale the best it could be. Good answer, right?

As Dennison moved toward the podium now, a harsh boo rose from the crowd. Nan and I spun and saw a line of protestors holding signs that called for the new mayor to be ousted before he'd even fully taken up office.

"That's in poor taste," Nan hissed, shaking her head.

"Why does everyone hate him so much?" I whispered.

She shrugged. "Any time the party in office changes, somebody's bound to be unhappy about it. The whole country's a powder keg, so why not our town, too?"

I returned my gaze to Dennison, who stood stock-still with an unreadable expression. Poor guy. He'd won the election fair and square, yet he couldn't even enjoy this pinnacle moment in his career.

"What's going on, Mommy?" Paisley asked, wagging her tail in excitement, misreading the mood of the crowd.

I kissed her on the head and whispered, "Don't worry about it."

As much as I loved the optimistic little dog, explaining everything to her all the time often became exhausting—especially when we were in public and I couldn't speak freely.

"People of Glendale," the new mayor's voice boomed despite the continuing sounds of protest. "Thank you for electing me to serve as your mayor."

The boos and calls for him to resign grew louder.

Nan whooped and cheered beside me even though I knew for a fact she hadn't voted for him. She smiled at me sheepishly. "Poor guy. Someone needs to encourage him."

Now we both cheered.

Dennison's eyes met mine, and he nodded subtly before continuing. "I promise to do everything in my power to make these next four years prosperous and safe for all of us. Thank you."

He dipped his head, then disappeared back inside the building.

Octo-Cat would definitely be upset at having missed the drama of this day.

"Well, that was the shortest inauguration I've ever seen, and I've been to all of them since moving out here some forty years ago," Nan mused.

"I'm sure it will be fine," I mumbled. "People just need time to cool off after the election."

"Yes, because all of November and December and most of January obviously weren't enough," Nan responded after sucking air through her teeth.

We stood in place waiting for the crowd to disperse. Some of them did, but the protestors seemed to grow in number as they crept closer to the stairs outside city hall.

"Let's get out of here," Nan said, shaking her head sadly.

I couldn't agree more.

2

I sat in the enormous bay window of my home library sipping an oversized mug of English breakfast tea while watching the snow swirl past.

Octo-Cat sat at my feet flicking his tail back and forth to the tuneless hum of our mostly silent house. “You wouldn’t catch me dead in that mess.”

I lowered my mug and cuddled deeper into the woven afghan wrapped around my shoulders. “What? The snow?”

He scoffed at my apparent naivete. “Snow, yeah. You can’t fool me. It’s nothing but semi-solid water. No, thank you.”

“You know…” A smile crept across my face as I waited for him to turn toward me. “Maine Coons supposedly love water, and you are part Maine Coon, right?”

He always claimed to be, but we both knew that was a lie.

Octo-Cat’s eyes slitted and his tail stilled. “Yes,” he answered slowly, cautiously. "But I'm also part tabby. Tabbies don't like the water."

"Of course." I took another sip of tea to prevent a chuckle from escaping. Far be it from me to point out that Tabby was a coloration and not a breed. Everything Octavius said had to be taken at face value, lest we upset him.

He'd also gone to the Holiday Spectacular last month when the ground was covered in fresh snowfall and hadn't complained too much—at least not for him. It seemed we'd now crossed the acceptable level of snow since then. Either that or he was passing judgment on my less than stellar job keeping up with the shoveling.

Light clacking sounded on the floorboards, and a moment later Paisley appeared, tail wagging in its usual dark blur. "Hello, Mommy. Can I cuddle, too?"

Octo-Cat groaned and rolled his eyes when the Chihuahua jumped onto my lap.

"I wanted to say hi before Nan and I go on our run. Hi!"

I gaped down at her. "You're running in this?" The snow had to be twice as deep as she was tall.

She blinked wide eyes at me, confused by this question. "Why, yes. We run every day, come heck or high water."

"Water," Octo-Cat emphasized with a pointed flick of his tail. "Told you it was water."

Nan and Paisley had started their recreational running hobby on January first and had kept up with it every day since. That was my grandmother for you. She always had a number of hobbies going, usually at least one that was artistic and one fitness based. Often many more than that, too.

This month's commitment to running, however, seemed to be more about me than about herself. I often pointed out the fact my seventy-something Nan was in far better shape than twenty-something me, and that had become incredibly evident last month when we ran around downtown Glendale chasing killers, kidnappers, and more.

Apparently, I'd complained a bit too loudly and too often, because now Nan invited me to join her every single day—and I said "no" every single day.

Did she really think I'd be up for starting a new exercise regimen at the height of the cold season? Nope. No, thank you.

Sure enough, my worst fears were answered when Nan appeared about five minutes later. She was wearing a hot pink velour tracksuit and held a leopard print coat with a fur collar draped over one arm. "C'mon, we've got to get going a little early today. I have a quick stop-off to make before we hit the trail."

I doubted there was a trail, unless she'd woken up early to shovel one herself. A giant yawn pushed its way out from my chest as a massive shiver racked through my body. "You and Paisley have fun out there!"

"Oh, no. Today you're coming too," Nan insisted, reaching for my hand and attempting to pull me from my seat.

I ripped away as if she'd scalded me with her soft touch. "Ha, ha. Nice try. Today's answer is the same as it's been every other day you've asked me. Octo-Cat and I will hold down the fort here. See you when you're back."

"Nope. I'm not taking no for an answer this time." She crossed her arms over her chest and narrowed her gaze threateningly.

"Why not? You've taken it every other day." I was pushing my luck and I knew it.

She motioned toward the galactic space cats calendar that hung on the wall above my desk, then groaned and marched over to it. Flipping the page up, she pointed to a calico kitten flying through the stars in a giant cartoon taco shell. "It's the first day of a new month. February."

I stayed silent, accepting that the more I argued the harder she'd come down on me in the end.

Nan, however, refused to be dismissed. "You may have completely flubbed up January, but a new month means a new start."

"Can I maybe start in a warmer month?" I glanced out the window again. Everything was white—the ground, the sky, my reflection as all the color drained from my face in fear. She meant it this time.

I was doomed, but I still had to give my resistance one last ill-fated shot. "I don't have anything to run in," I complained and forced a sad look.

"Ahh, but you do." A giant smile lit Nan's face. "You'll find a new jogging suit that matches mine exactly. I also picked up some sport boots and thick wool socks. Everything's waiting for you in your room. Chop, chop. Like I said, we have a quick stop-off to make before hitting the trail."

Not even cute corn shell taco cats in outer space could save me now. I lifted my eyes to meet her, telepathically pleading for her to have some mercy.

It did not work.

"Five minutes," she said firmly and then began tapping her foot, already beyond the limits of her patience with me. "Then I'm dragging you outside, whether or not you're ready."

We both knew she'd push me butt naked into the snow if I took even a second longer. We also both knew that she was the stronger of the two of us.

I raced out of the library and up to my tower bedroom to get ready. Octo-Cat's smug laughter followed me every step of the way.

3

I gripped the handle for the passenger side door of Nan's little red sports coupe, but it didn't budge. Normally, Nan not only unlocked the car in advance but she also remote started it so the interior would be toasty warm by the time we took off.

"We're taking your car," she called from the porch as she locked up then descended with Paisley in tow.

My car, however, was not where I usually parked it.

Noting my hesitation, Nan pointed toward the far side of the house.

My breaths burst out in icy puffs. As much as I didn't look forward to running, at least it would make me warm. Right?

The moment I spotted my car, an indignant groan ripped right through me. My once-modest sedan had been outfitted with a hot pink snowplow. "What's this?" I screamed.

Nan passed by me, opened the door, and situated herself in the driver's seat. "For making the trail, of course."

Oh, of course. "Why is it hot pink?"

She shot me a proud grin. "Because that's my favorite color. You know that. I had it custom made."

"And did you put it on all by yourself, too?" I managed. Even though my grandmother was in fantastic shape, it was hard imagining her heaving this enormous thing around single-handedly.

She waved off my question with a deft swirl of her hand. "Don't be silly. I called Cal over to help."

Great. The next time I saw our favorite local handyman, he'd be getting a very stern talking to. I climbed into the passenger seat and buckled up.

Paisley immediately put her paws on the door and stared out the ice-covered window. I couldn't imagine she saw much.

"Why are we in the car? We don't need the car for running. We use our feet!"

Personally, I had other questions in mind. "Are you sure my car can handle this? There's a reason these things are usually on trucks."

Nan snorted. "This one's made of plastic instead of metal. I'm sure we'll be fine."

Uh-huh. Famous last words.

Besides, how else are we supposed to carve out our running trail?" She turned the key in the ignition and my tacky, made-over car sputtered to life. We jerked forward, then stopped again just as suddenly.

"What happened?" I demanded of my grandmother.

She ignored me and pushed down on the gas pedal again. Nothing happened this time.

"Huh. Well, it was working last night" was the only thing she said about that.

"Too bad. I guess no running for us today." I was already halfway out of the car and looking forward to a second cup of steaming hot tea in my favorite reading spot when Nan popped out of the car and called me to a stop.

"Not so fast," she called after me. "We'll take my car."

I kept going, so close to being free to return to my regularly scheduled day. "If my car can't handle that plow, there's no way yours can."

"Paisley, I'm sorry, but you'll have to stay here. The snow's too deep," Nan explained, returning to the porch and setting the Chihuahua down beside the electronic pet door.

The poor little dog whined and looked to me for help. "Mommy, tell Nan I want to come. I always come."

I didn't need to translate that. Paisley's whimpering and low-hung tail said it all. "I wish it was you instead of me, but Nan's right about the snow being too deep."

"Nonsense," Paisley cried, then bolted down the stairs and took a flying leap into the nearest snowdrift, disappearing immediately. Not even the tips of her giant foxlike ears showed above the bank.

I rushed forward and scooped her into my arms.

She was too shocked to do anything other than shiver. "Cold. C-c-c-cold!"

"We'll be back soon," I promised loudly, then whispered just to Paisley, "Seriously. As soon as possible."

She cried again as I set her back beside the pet door.

"Why don't you go see what Octo-Cat is doing and if you can help?" I suggested.

And just like that, her tail lifted and began to wag once more. She pushed through the pet door, barking happily and calling for our cat housemate.

"All good?" Nan asked, quirking a questioning eyebrow my way.

"With Paisley at least," I grumbled but followed her back toward the sports coupe and dutifully sank inside. This was going to be nothing short of torture.

"Where are we going?" I asked a few moments later when she still hadn't explained herself.

"A friend from my community art class needs some extra help. This weather really triggers the arthritis in her joints, and with her twin grandkids off at college this year, she has no one to walk Cujo."

I gasped in horror. "Cujo? I know we live in Stephen King's home state, but c'mon. What kind of name is that for a dog, given, well, everything Cujo did?"

Nan sighed but didn't turn to face me. "Big talk from someone who named her pet Octo-Cat."

I wanted to laugh but luckily held it together. "Please tell me he's not a Saint Bernard."

"No, he's a mutt. Husky mixed with something else. They're not sure what."

Well, we would find out soon enough.

And sure enough, even with the deep snow and icy roads, we were at Nan's friend's house five short minutes later.

"Wait here," she instructed, marching around to the back of the house and returning with an enormous fuzzy beast on lead a few minutes later.

She motioned for me to get out and join them. "Might as well start our run from here."

"Is that Cujo?" I asked, eyeing the dog hesitantly. He may not have been a Saint Bernard, but he was almost as big as one. His light blue—almost white—eyes made him even more unnerving to look at.

Nan chuckled. "Who else would it be, dear?"

"Stop looking at me like that," the dog said, reminding me that—oh, yeah—I could talk to animals.

"Like what?" I asked, voice shaking with equal parts cold and nervousness.

"A human who talks? Curious." Cujo breezed right past this revelation and answered my question head-on.

"Stop looking at me the way everyone does. Like I'm going to eat you. If the way you smell is any indication, you'd taste terrible."

He opened his mouth and panted in what I assumed was a self-aggrandizing laugh. "Look, I'm a working dog. That means I focus on the job that needs to be done, and right now, that's assisting your grandmother on her run."

"Fair enough," I answered, forcing myself to look away from his steely gaze.

"Hike! Hike!" Nan shouted and then took off at a pace I doubted I'd be able to match.

"Wait for me," I cried as she and the oversized husky tore through the snow-covered suburban street.

The day had just begun, and already I was more than ready to get it over with.

4

I'm pretty sure I almost died that morning.

Only almost, though.

Thankfully I managed to complete that wretched run without falling face forward into the snow like I feared every time my boot landed wrong on the poorly plowed street.

As much as I wanted to get in better shape, I didn't think sprinting through a snowstorm was the way to do it. Cujo, however, seemed to heartily disagree. During the entire half-hour ordeal, he barked encouragements to both me and Nan, acting as our own personal doggie drill sergeant.

"Pick up the pace! That's it! Let's go! Hike!" he shouted while tugging hard on the leash and forcing us all to move as fast as our feet could carry us.

When we finally returned to his yard, he gave me a long piteous look and laid his ears back flat against his head. "You didn't do a very good job today. We'll have to train much harder so that you're ready."

"Ready for what?" I barked back, already beginning to shiver now that we'd stopped moving.

"Whatever comes next," he answered—whether cryptically or dismissively I couldn't quite tell. I also didn't quite care, given my current level of exhaustion.

"Now that wasn't so bad, was it?" Nan asked once we'd both settled back into her car. She couldn't fool me, though. Even she had a hard time catching her breath after that muttsky-driven workout.

I laughed and leaned my head against the seat rest. Everything burned. Everything hurt. And I already knew Nan would force me to do the whole thing all over again tomorrow… and the next day… and the next day.

Working out with Nan would easily prove to be worse than a prison sentence. I just hoped warden Cujo's time with us would be brief. I much preferred Paisley's personal brand of encouragement—and her pace, too.

"Good effort out there today, dear. You've earned your sweets," Nan told me when we arrived back home. Still brimming with energy, she scuttled into the kitchen to pick up with some mid-morning baking.

I could have argued the senselessness of exercising when we would only use it as an excuse to pile back on double or triple the calories in desserts but knew that somehow pointing this out would only lead to longer and more intense workouts. No thank you!

I had just begun the now painful climb up the stairs to my library when the doorbell chimed overhead.

Ping. Ping. Ding bing, it sounded to the tune of "Eye of the Tiger," proving once and for all that Nan had planned today's forced fitness well in advance.

"Coming!" I yelled and then slowly turned myself around. Ouch, ouch, ouch.

"What happened to you?" Octo-Cat asked while effortlessly trotting down the stairs and thus throwing his ease of mobility right in my poor, tired face.

"Nan happened to me," I grumbled after drawing in a deep, ragged breath.

He raised a paw and chuckled. "Say no more."

The doorbell chimed again.

Octo-Cat's eyes glowed hot with judgment. "Well, aren't you going to get that?"

"Coming!" I shouted again and forced myself to hobble faster through the foyer.

When I flung the door open with a giant grin of relief, I found a familiar face staring right back at me from the porch. "Mayor D-D-Dennison," I sputtered in surprise. "To what do we owe the pleasure?"

Octo-Cat plopped himself down beside me, willing to brave the cold tendrils of air reaching in through the open doorway so that he could gain a front-row seat to whatever happened next.

The mayor removed his hat—an oversized Russian shapka—to reveal a messy head of hair. "May I please come in?"

"Angie!" Nan called as she hurried toward us, her gait completely unmired from that morning's workout whereas I could hardly walk. "Is that the mayor? Well, don't leave him standing out in the cold!"

She pushed past me and wrapped a motherly arm around Mayor Dennison's broad shoulders to usher him toward the living room. "Let's have a hot cup of tea to warm you up, then you can tell us everything."

"Nan," I interrupted. "He still hasn't told us why he's here."

"Perfect, then he can tell us over tea. Gossip always goes down easiest with a nice, steaming mug in your hands. Wouldn't you say?" Without waiting for either of us to respond, she returned to the kitchen, leaving me to make awkward small talk with the mayor at least half the town of Glendale never wanted.

"Got a lot of snow out there," I mumbled like an idiot. It was February in Blueberry Bay. Of course there was snow.

He nodded, smiled, glanced toward the kitchen.

I didn't want to ask about politics since I already knew there was some contention there, but I also knew better than to ask about the purpose of his visit before Nan returned with the tea.

Luckily, Paisley camc frolicking to our rescue, hopping right up onto the mayor's lap. "I smell a doggie!" she trilled, wagging her tail curiously.

"She likes you," I said with a grin. "Are you a dog person?"

Octo-Cat hissed somewhere from the other side of the room. He didn't even like that question to be asked, let alone answered.

"I have—well, had—a dog," the mayor answered with a wistful sigh. "Actually, that's why I'm here. I—"

"Oh no, you don't!" Nan hurried back into the living room, balancing a small serving tray with three cups of tea and all the fixings. "Not without me."

Our visitor cleared his throat and folded his hands in his lap while Nan served. When at last we were all seated comfortably with our beverages and snacks, my grandmother motioned for him to continue. "Now you may continue."

"I came because I heard you're a private investigator," he said to Nan, completely ignoring the mug that she'd handed to him.

She chortled at this. "Not me. Her."

She pointed at me, and I waved awkwardly.

"Okay, either way. I need to hire you to help me." He glanced pointedly in my direction.

"What seems to be the problem?" I asked, feeling oh so professional in that moment. Here I was, a proper investigator being called in to help the man who held the top political official in all of Glendale. It didn't get any bigger than this for a small-town P.I.

But then he spoke again and shattered my newfound delusions of grandeur. "My dog, actually. He's gone missing."

I choked on my tea, which led to an awkward coughing fit. "Your dog?" I asked hoarsely. "What? Did he run away?"

"No," he said firmly. "Marco didn't leave on his own. He was taken."

Nan raised a delicate eyebrow. "What makes you so sure?"

"Because the kidnapper left a note. A ransom note." After delivering this news, the mayor finally took a sip of his tea, much to Nan's satisfaction.

I sat back against the couch. My body remained tired, but my mind zoomed to life, a million gears all clicking at once.

Maybe this could still be a fascinating case, after all.

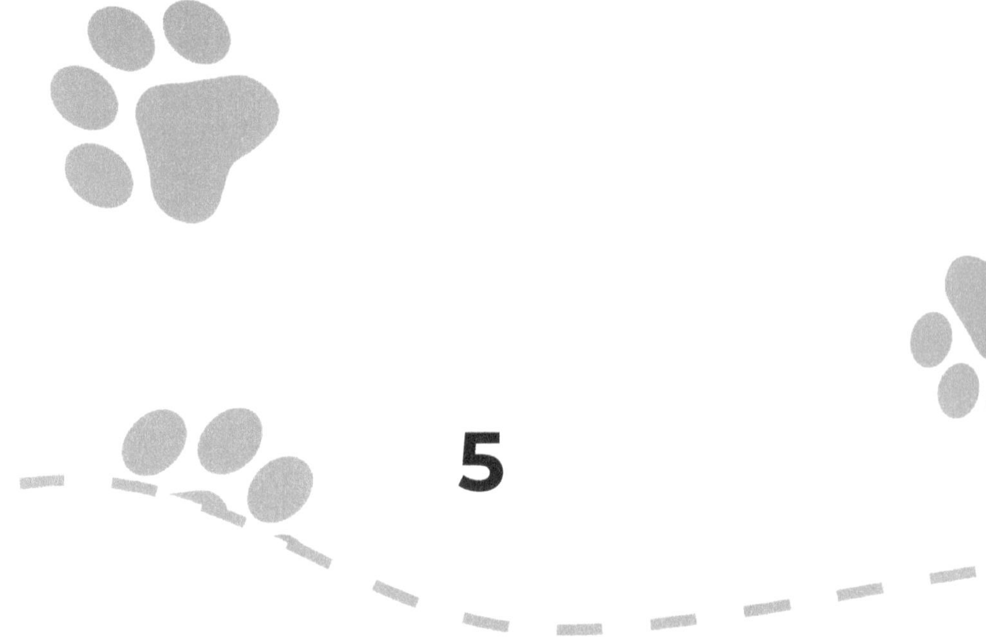

5

“I brought it with me,” Mayor Dennison explained, then withdrew the folded ransom note from his wallet. He handed it over to me, and Nan edged closer to read it over my shoulder, her lips moving as she soundlessly voiced each word.

The note was typed on a plain white piece of computer paper. The font was so large it filled the entire page with just a few harsh words: Resign. Or the dog gets it.

“Well, what do they mean by that?” Nan quipped. “They should have been more specific.”

For the first time, I noticed that the usually stoic mayor had tears in his eyes. “Do you really think they’d hurt Marco?” he asked, momentarily casting his gaze toward the floor.

I swallowed down the dry lump in my throat and said, “I don’t know,” rather unhelpfully. We still had no idea who they could be.

“Please find out who did this,” he begged, actually folding his hands and shaking them my way. "I'll pay. I'll pay whatever you need. Marco is the only family I have. We've been through it all together, and I can't stand the thought of anything untoward happening to him."

"Who would want you to resign so badly that they'd resort to dognapping?" I asked, forcing myself to remain focused on the facts.

At the same time, Nan blurted out, "Of course we'll take your case. Consider us hired."

He glanced back and forth between us, apparently unsure who he should address first.

Octo-Cat appeared from wherever he'd been hiding and jumped onto the coffee table right beside Nan's carefully arranged tea service. As he flicked his tail, he stared down his nose at the mayor, appraising our new client. "I don't know if I want to help find a lost dog," he said with a sneer. "This will forever go down in history as our first paying case, and it's about a stupid dog?"

Paisley whined and covered her snout with her paws.

But Octo-Cat continued unperturbed. "I mean, it's not even dead. We've been on a roll with the murders lately. Last time, we helped solve two murders. Two! Don't you see? A dognapping case is beneath us."

I shot my cat a disgusted look, wishing I could give him a firm tongue-lashing. Unfortunately, I had to ignore his sandpaper barbs as the mayor sat eyeing me intently.

"Yes, we'll take the case. In fact, it will be our top priority," I said with what I hoped was a reassuring nod.

"Yeah," Octo-Cat drolled. "Because we don't have any other cases right now."

I swept my hand across the coffee table and knocked him to the floor. "Bad kitty," I said emphatically, knowing I'd pay for it later.

"Do you have any pictures of Marco?" Nan asked before taking a long slurp of her quickly cooling tea.

"He's a golden retriever. Looks like a standard golden retriever, no unique markings or anything. I post all kinds of photos on my Facebook page, though, if you need them."

"Thank you. That would be helpful," I said, taking back over. I was the P.I. here, after all. "What we really need to talk about, though, is your enemies."

"My enemies?" he asked, taken aback. His jaw set in a firm, hard line, and his eyes turned colder than our tea.

"Clearly you have some if one of them would resort to ransoming Marco. But before we get into that, would it be okay for me to address you by your first name or do you prefer it to be more formal…?"

He shook his head, his normally placid expression returning just as quickly as it had left. "Yes, of course. Call me Mark."

It struck me then that I either hadn't heard his first name before or that I'd at least never connected the fact that he'd named his dog after himself, then tacked on one extra syllable. Mark. Marco.

"Mark," I said, forcing myself to keep a straight face. "Mark it is."

We all sat silently for a moment.

"Now, I know it can't be easy to talk about, but it's important. Given the show at the inauguration, your election has been quite controversial. Why is that?"

Although I didn't follow politics closely, I'd read the odd news report on this topic. Still, I wanted to get Mark's take on the situation to see what added insights he could provide.

He licked his lips and steepled his fingers before him. "The usual things mostly. The fact I'm a bachelor is a big one. How can a single man be committed to building a family community? they all ask." He scoffed at this, pausing briefly before he continued.

"And as you know, the vote was quite close. I won by hardly more than a percentage point. My opponent's supporters demanded a recount, but that was ultimately deemed a waste of taxpayers' money, and so I was sworn in."

I knew all this. The mayor had to be holding something back. Neither of these reasons were enough for someone to threaten harm to a lovable golden retriever, whether or not they disliked his owner. Golden retrievers were largely considered America's top family dog, and I'm sure it won back some points for the mayor that he had one.

Still, something wasn't quite adding up.

"Is that all?" I asked cautiously.

"That's all," Mark assured me with a quick nod.

Octo-Cat settled himself onto my feet, but not before giving my big toe a solid bite as punishment for my stunt earlier. "He's lying," the tabby informed me with a low growl.

I took a deep steadying breath, then focused my gaze back on the mayor. "Are you sure there's nothing else? No other possible reason for the kidnapping?"

"None," Mark insisted, smiling reassuringly in my direction.

"He's still lying," Octo-Cat revealed, but I could now see that for myself, too. "Definitely lying."

"Oh…kay," I said slowly, breaking the small word into two distinct sounds. "Then why don't you tell me about the last few days. Did anything unusual happen? Did anyone seem extra interested in Marco at this time?"

As I listened to the mayor prattle on about his busy life, I couldn't help wondering why he'd hire me and then withhold at least part of the truth.

A dishonest client, no doubt, would make solving the case much more difficult. Still, I couldn't allow Marco to suffer for his owner's crimes—whatever they were.

I guess we'd be finding out soon enough.

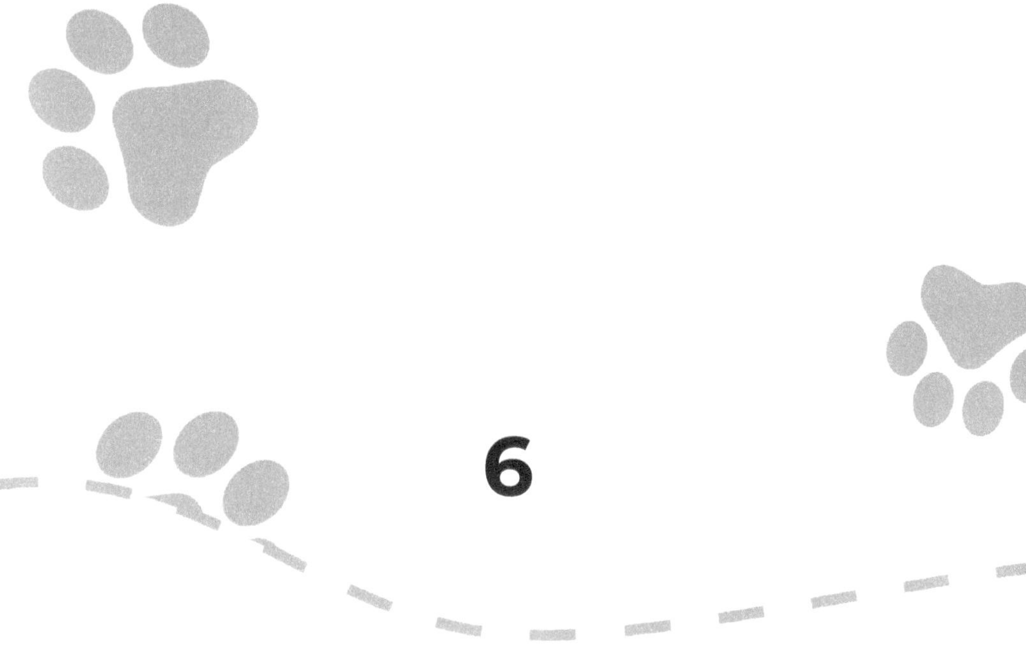

6

After Mayor Dennison left, Nan, the animals, and I huddled together at the large dining room table to recap.

"So we have another kidnapping," Nan said thoughtfully. "We've dealt with those before. Recently at that."

She was right. I'd already been thinking about our past abduction cases myself. They had both proven to be the most nerve-wracking investigations I'd ever faced. Both had hit incredibly close to home, too.

First, Octo-Cat disappeared at the exact same time the other beneficiaries of Ethel Fulton's will had called for an arbitration in an attempt to relieve him of his inheritance. The culprit in that case had been exceedingly angry when we'd found Octo-Cat and taken him back—she'd even wound up with a nasty cat-inflicted wound that would probably scar. We'd seen neither hide nor hair of the folks involved in that kidnapping in the time since.

Then the second one happened. On Christmas Eve, my cousin Mags had been taken right off the street at the annual Holiday Spectacular fair. She'd been kept blindfolded and was ultimately let go when the crooks—a man and a woman—got spooked and ran.

They'd meant to take me but had mistakenly abducted my eerily similar looking cousin instead. They called her "Russo"—my last name—and warned her to keep her nose out of places where it didn't belong.

Well, Mags had returned to her home in Larkhaven, Georgia, no worse for the wear, and we hadn't heard from her mysterious kidnappers since.

I doubted the ransomed retriever had anything to do with either of those cases, but reviewing our history at least gave us a place to start with this new investigation.

"Are you thinking about when Mags and Octo-Cat were taken?" Nan asked, steepling her fingers and tapping them against her chin.

I nodded, then sighed. "Both were so horrible."

"Mark is probably going out of his mind with worry for his poor dog," she said with a wrinkled frown.

"Actually, I'm not so sure." I shot a glance toward Octo-Cat, who'd seated himself on the opposite side of the table and taken up a vigorous grooming session focused primarily on his forehead and ears.

He paused and nodded his approval.

"Per Octo-Cat, the mayor was lying to us. Or at least hiding something important," I revealed as I played the conversation back through my head.

"About which part?" Nan wondered aloud.

I shook my head, yet again wishing I knew the answer.

She snorted. "Well, that's helpful."

"Still, at least we know to take what little he told us with a giant grain of salt."

Nan considered this, then stood suddenly, flinging her chair backward with such force it startled me and both animals.

"Where are you going?" I asked as she scurried toward the coat closet off the foyer.

She didn't look back as she explained, "If the mayor isn't going to tell us the truth, then we'll have to go find it for ourselves."

"Online?" I asked meekly even as she'd already begun to pull on her hot-pink snow boots.

"No," she said, shaking her head. "Outside."

Ugh. That was the exact place I wanted to avoid, given our current polar vortex situation.

"I'm not going," Octo-Cat said from his place a few stairs up from the ground floor.

I paused between shoving my mitten on one hand and readying it for the other. "Why not? You always come. You're my partner, after all."

He turned his nose up at me. "Yeah, well, this partner doesn't do subzero temperatures."

"It's still at least five degrees out there. And this isn't some stupid jog, it's part of our investigation. C'mon."

"Let me rephrase that." He paused and took several deep breaths before continuing. "I don't do cold and wet. It's like the whole world decided to take a bath and then let the water grow frigid. I don't do baths. And if my fur coat isn't enough to keep warm, then I'm not going."

"Fine. Then you're not going. But you also better not complain about being left out." I turned away from him and began to dress for the impromptu outing.

"Please. I have better things to do with myself than follow you around on your wild goose chase." He yawned to emphasize his point.

Paisley ran up beside Octo-Cat, wagging her tail so vigorously she stumbled and fell down one of the steps. "Mommy, I'm coming, right?"

"Of course you are!" I assured her.

"Just one last thing and we can go," Nan said, reaching for a plastic shopping bag on the top shelf of the closet and pulling out a baby pink sack. "It's the wrong shade of pink, but it will have to do."

I eyed the cloth accessory warily. "What is it?"

"I'll show you! C'mere, my sweet girl." Nan smacked her lips and bent down to pick up the Chihuahua who came running straight into her arms. She then worked the straps of the sack over her arms so that it rested against her chest.

Paisley realized what was going on about the same time I did and began to wiggle in desperate fright. "No, no, no! I don't want to go in the bag!" she yelped.

"Just hold still for a second, my dear," Nan instructed, wrestling with the Chihuahua to wedge her into the baby carrier.

Paisley continued to whine and squirm.

"Angie, can you please tell her this will be a lot easier if she cooperates?" Nan grunted.

"Sweetie, you need to—" I began, but Nan interrupted with a triumphant "Ah-ha!"

The poor little Chihuahua had been tucked into the carrier and strapped in securely. Only her tiny face and giant ears peeked out from the top.

Nan spun and posed. "What do you think?"

Octo-Cat laughed heartily. "Ha, ha, you look ridiculous!" he crowed.

Paisley whimpered and sighed.

"I'm not so sure she likes it," I offered.

"Well, she just has to get used to it is all. It will help keep her warm while we're out and about. It's made especially for little dogs like her, you know. By the way, you'll have to drive. We can take my car, though."

"Okay," I said and followed my grandmother outside to her car. It was easier to just go along with what she said. At least this wouldn't require any grueling exercise.

Or so I sincerely hoped…

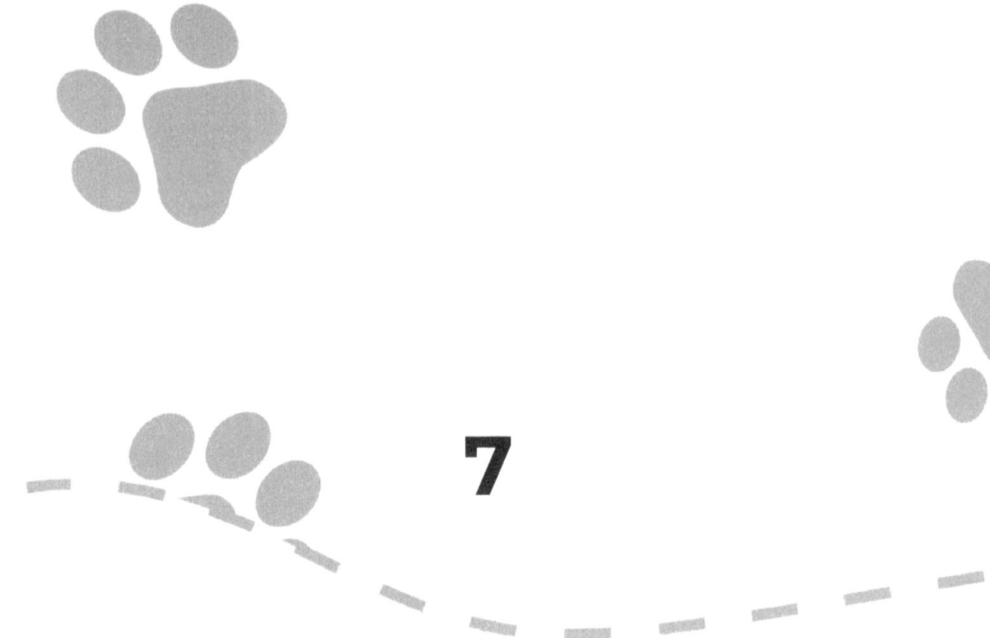

7

Mayor Dennison live in a surprisingly modest house on the far edge of town. Part of me had hoped we'd have housekeepers, cooks, butlers, and a full garrulous staff to question, but just like crime—small-town politics didn't pay.

It was clear Mayor Mark lived alone. It was also clear that nobody was at home. What wasn't clear was how Nan knew where to find him.

"Think we can break in?" she asked now, rifling through her pockets for who knew what.

Paisley heaved a giant sigh from her place affixed to the front of Nan's chest. I had to admit, she looked absolutely adorable in that Puppy Bjorn.

"I'd rather not start our investigation by committing a B&E," I said. My breath rose above us in icy puffs.

"Look at you with the lingo," Nan crooned, clutching a hand to her chest, or rather to Paisley on her chest. "You don't have to help, but—yeah—I'm breaking in."

I groaned. Of course she was.

Paisley whined and shivered so violently I was surprised that Nan didn't seem to notice.

"Are you okay?" I asked the dogcicle.

"S-S-S-S-So c-c-c-cold," she answered weakly.

"Nan," I called as she moved toward the porch with a sure stride. "Nan, we need to put Paisley back in the car with the heat running."

"N-N-N-N-No," Paisley cried, her eyes practically sealed shut with quick freezing tears. "I w-w-want to h-h-help."

"I'm not letting you catch your death," I promised whether or not she wanted to hear it. "C'mon, I'll take you back to the car."

"Hang on a minute there," Nan muttered. "We'll be inside the house in just a..." She bit her tongue as she maneuvered something in the lock.

"Second," she finished triumphantly and pushed the door open, motioning for me to lead us inside.

Oh, I didn't like this at all. As bad as it was to take part in this unlawful entry, it would have been even worse to send Nan inside unsupervised.

"Five minutes," I hissed between clenched teeth. "Then we go, no matter what."

"Well, you're no fun."

I ignored that last barb and searched the tidy open floor plan for something that might prove useful in our investigation.

"Look for a home office," Nan suggested, already sneaking deeper into the house.

"Hello?" A deep voice called from the top of the staircase, turning my blood cold despite the warm air inside.

My eyes zoomed toward the mayor, who stood in a matching flannel pajama set staring at us with huge, unblinking eyes. "Oh, Mark, hi," I sputtered, unable to rip my eyes away. How were we going to explain this one?

Even though I had no answers, Nan was quick to save the day.

"Didn't you hear us knock?" she asked, bringing both hands to her hips.

The mayor looked back behind him for a second. "No, I was—"

"Well, then you should at least lock your door. Really, anyone could wander in off the streets."

He ran a hand through his hair and then shook his head with a sigh. "You're right. Of course you're right."

We all stood staring at each other for a few silent moments.

Finally Mark spoke up, putting the uncomfortable moment to rest. "Can I, uh, help you with something?"

"We wanted to talk with you a bit more about the... the-the... the case," I explained quickly, stumbling over a few choice words. "We don't have much to go on and thought—"

"I told you everything I know," the mayor interrupted with a scowl. "It's all I have. That's why I hired you to find and put together the rest of the pieces. Are you suggesting you're not up for the task?"

Nan laughed at this. "Oh, we'll handle it. Don't you worry. Your case is as good as solved with Pet Whisperer, P.I."

I still hated that name, but Nan and Mom had both made sure I'd be stuck with it going forward.

Mark straightened to his full height and finally descended the stairs. "Well, good. That's just what I needed to hear."

"Since we're here," I jumped in smoothly before the mayor could push us out the door. "Would you mind giving us a quick tour as it relates to Marco and his daily schedule? It always helps to get into the victim's head when we can."

"Yes, a tour would be most helpful," Nan agreed, nodding vigorously.

Paisley barked her agreement. The way the carrier shook suggested that she had tried rather unsuccessfully to wag her tail.

"Sure. Okay." Mark shook his head, ran another hand through his hair, then waved for us to follow. What followed was a lengthy description of the missing golden retriever's daily comings and goings, including when and what he ate, where he liked to sleep, his favorite spots to pee in the yard, and more.

"So as I'm sure you can see," the mayor said when the tour concluded, "despite my own busy schedule, Marco was well taken care of and very much loved. Please bring him home safely. And soon."

"We will. We will," Nan assured him.

Personally, I would rather under promise and overdeliver. "We'll do everything we can," I said as we shook hands goodbye.

Paisley, however, had other, more important things on her mind.

"Marco has good instincts," she whispered in admiration on our way out. "If I lived here, I would choose to pee there, too."

I glanced toward the area on the side of the house the mayor had pointed out mid-way through our tour. The snow was too fresh and too deep to give anything away.

But, well, at least our abducted dog had good taste in pee spots. As for our case, we still had absolutely nothing to go on.

Yet.

8

"Wow, that human really loves his dog," Paisley observed on the drive home. I'd taken her out of the pet carrier as soon as Nan had handed her over to me and settled herself behind the wheel. She'd since repaid me with no less than a few dozen enthusiastic doggie kisses.

Her debt paid, Paisley had now turned her mind back to the investigation. "I feel so sad that they have been separated. We're going to get his dog back soon. Right, Mommy?"

I kissed the small white spot on the Chihuahua's forehead. "Yes, we will."

The little dog wagged her tail and opened her mouth in a panting grin.

Later, Nan sighed as she made the turn into our driveaway. "Well, that accomplished exactly nothing."

"I don't know what you expected. He's our client, not the suspect.

Even though I agree with Octo-Cat that he's hiding something. I also agree with Paisley that he really loves that dog."

"So much that he won't give us all the information that we need to get him back?" Nan chuckled and shook her head. "I don't think so."

"Whatever he's hiding, we don't know whether it's related to the ransom," I pointed out as the car bumped along the icy drive.

Finally, Nan parked and the three of us raced inside as fast as our feet would carry us. Octo-Cat sat waiting for us in the center of the coffee table.

"Well?" he asked with one raised eyebrow. "How did the break-in go?"

I stared at him in disbelief. "Who says we broke in?"

"Please. Nan went, so you were bound to break in. It's what she does." He chuckled merrily to himself.

Touché.

"So?" He raised the other eyebrow. "How'd it go?"

"Oh, right. Unfortunately, there's not much to tell. We got caught and then got a very detailed tour and description of Marco's day-to-day routine."

"Yuck. I'm glad I missed that." My cat shuddered, shaking off several loose hairs in the process.

I watched them dance through a nearby sunbeam, entranced.

"We're still at square one," Nan muttered, "but I refuse to stay there."

I watched her shrug out of her winter gear and then reach back into the closet. Sometimes I suspected our foyer closet wasn't unlike

Mary Poppins's magical bag. It seemed she never ran out of space and always had exactly what she needed waiting. This time, Nan pulled out poster board, Sharpies, sticky notes, and a pack of little magnifying glass stickers, then dumped them all onto the living room coffee table.

Octo-Cat had to leap out of the way to avoid being buried under the falling heap of craft supplies. "Watch it, old lady!"

I shot him a withering look, then returned my focus to Nan. Unlike my snarky tabby, she at least had a plan—one with flair at that.

She arranged all her supplies just so and then set to work, using a dark green marker to divide the neon green poster board into three evenly spaced sections. Next, she selected the black marker and scrawled People at the top of one column, then Places and Events on the others.

Out came the stickers, which she used to create bullet points, three down each column.

"We'll start with three each, but don't worry, I have enough stickers to match however many ideas we come up with. So what's the first one? How about a person?" Nan stared at me expectantly, a blue marker uncapped and at the ready.

She'd created a similar setup when Octo-Cat had gone missing, so I knew exactly what she expected during today's shared brainstorm.

"Start with his opponent," I directed. "The one he very narrowly beat in the election. He definitely has a grudge."

Nan nodded and wrote the name down. "I'll add Brenda Eaves. She was one of the folks protesting at the inauguration, and if we play our cards right, I bet we can get her to tell us the names of the others, too."

Octo-Cat watched in silence while Paisley snoozed on my lap. Tiny whimpering sighs escaped her muzzle as she dreamed.

"How about—?" I was just about to suggest a third suspect when a sudden, persistent tapping drew my attention to the window.

Octo-Cat spotted the source before I could and startled me by rearing up to hiss. He hissed often, but very rarely went full into Halloween kitty mode.

I followed his line of sight and found our favorite backyard roommate staring straight back at me with a cheesy smile. "Pringle! What are you doing here?"

He motioned toward his ear and shook his head. The raccoon's mannerisms seemed so human at times and were only becoming more so, given his insane addiction to reality TV.

"I know you can hear me!" I shouted louder.

He shook his head harder.

"Fine!" I threw my hands up and stomped toward the door. The very moment I flung it open, the plump gray ball of fur scuttled inside.

Our primary rule with Pringle was that he was not allowed in the house. He'd committed too much blatant destruction and secret thieving to keep that particular privilege.

"You invited me!" he shouted back over his shoulder without so much as a glance my way. "No takesy-backsies!"

"Noooooo!" Octo-Cat screamed in utter agony. "He's eating my Delectable Delights!"

I sprinted into the kitchen, but the raccoon had already gulped down the whole bowl of crunchies. Normally, Octo-Cat didn't do dry food, but ever since his beloved long-distance girlfriend Grizabella had become the spokesmodel for the new brand, he'd made the difficult choice to switch his loyalty away from Fancy Feast and toward Delectable Delights.

He stumbled into the kitchen and mock-fainted, falling to his side dramatically. The fact that his tail still flicked in irritation was proof enough he hadn't lost consciousness.

Still, I had to agree with him here. Pringle was way out of line.

"I didn't invite you inside," I hissed in the thieving critter's direction.

"You opened the door. Same difference, yeah?" He jumped onto the counter and helped himself to a freshly baked muffin, then stood on his hindlegs and simpered at me with narcissistic joy.

"So what did I miss?" he asked, taking a huge bite and chewing with his mouth open. "Did we have a new case come in?"

"It's not your case!" Paisley barked as she scampered across the tile floor to join us. Then, bless her, she began to jump in a desperate attempt to join the raccoon on the counter. There was no way the diminutive pup would ever reach, but I appreciated her moxie all the same.

So now there we stood in our private domestic calamity.

Paisley barked.

Octo-Cat swooned again, lifting himself slightly from the floor and falling down in a dramatic heap.

Pringle watched both and laughed as he feasted on baked goods.

“Stop dawdling and get back in here!” Nan shouted.

I downed a pair of painkillers for my quickly growing headache and marched back into brainstorm headquarters, AKA my former living room.

All the animals followed, and Nan jumped straight back into business.

“Now we obviously need to return to the mayor’s house when we can.” She paused and wrote that down. “What other places should we make sure to check as part of our investigation?”

“Ooh! Ooh!” Pringle’s hand shot high into the air. “I know! I know! Pick me! Pick me!”

I could scarcely hold back my irritated groan. Something told me this was going to be a very long and painful afternoon.

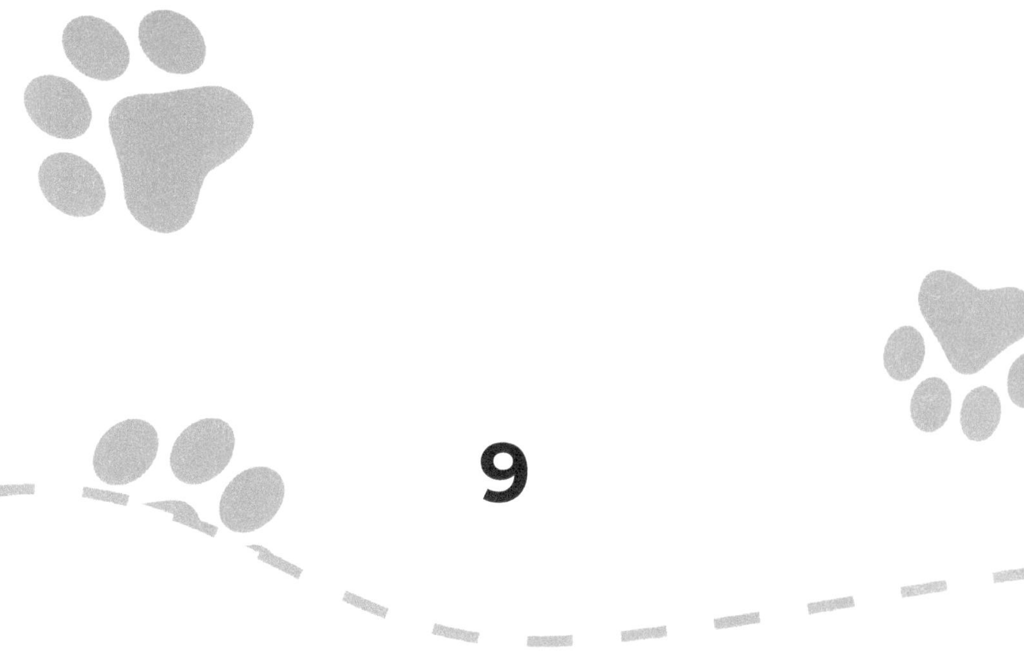

9

I had to work hard to hold back my laughter when Pringle marched across the room and ripped the marker right out of Nan's hand.

"I'll take that," he said as he began to scribble at the bottom of the last column, completely ruining Nan's perfectly organized mind map.

He scrawled furiously for close to a minute, then drew away from the board and recapped the marker with a self-satisfied smirk. "There. You're welcome."

I studied the writing closely but couldn't figure out what it was meant to say. We'd famously discovered that Pringle could read when he stole an important letter that revealed long-kept family secrets and turned our world upside-down.

Apparently, though, he didn't possess even minor writing skills. It wasn't just poor penmanship, either. The markings looked more like hieroglyphics than actual letters of the alphabet.

"Um, what's it supposed to say?" I asked at last.

He snorted, then crossed the whole thing out. "If you're going to act like that, you don't deserve my help."

Octo-Cat growled and pounced at the rude raccoon. "Nobody talks to my human like that—nobody except for me!"

"I'm the new and improved you, baby. Deal with it," Pringle spat back, placing a hand on each hip and laughing at the irate feline.

Paisley barked and ran large, looping circles around the other two animals as they prepared to fight.

"Stop! Stop!" I cried, but my pleas fell on deaf ears.

My cat pulled his front paws up and set his ears back flat against his head.

The raccoon drew nearer, stalking on all fours until he was mere inches away, then he rose upright as well.

I held my breath and the moment seemed to freeze in time.

Both combatants stared at each other, unblinking. Each waiting for the other to strike first.

Octo-Cat raised a paw slowly, slowly… and then like lightning he batted Pringle right in the face.

"Oh, no you didn't!" the raccoon shouted and began slapping Octo-Cat in the chest with both hands at rapid speed.

My cat swiped back, landing one strong blow for every ten mini slaps that came from Pringle.

I didn't know what to do.

Part of me wanted to grab a video camera and put this on YouTube to see if we could reach viral fame, but a much larger part was afraid that Octo-Cat would take a solid beating. I couldn't let that happen, especially since this had all started over him coming to my defense.

And then Paisley redirected the path of her latest circle and took a running leap, which landed her right on top of the battling mammals.

"Mommy said stop it!" she barked.

"Really? You sent in the pipsqueak dog?" Pringle shot me a venomous look. "I've never been so insulted in my entire life. I'm outta here."

He marched into the foyer with his nose held so high in the air that he nearly collided with the wall for lack of visibility. The shock of it stopped him dead in his tracks.

I watched dumbfounded as Pringle heaved a few giant breaths, then turned back toward us and came running on all fours. "I'm taking these," he announced before unceremoniously gathering up a handful of markers and the poster board we'd been using to chronicle the case facts and making his final exit—one made far less dramatic by the fact he had to push, pull, yank, and maneuver the poster board in several different directions before finally getting it out through the pet door with him.

"Great. That's just great," Nan groused. "Now we'll have to start all over."

"Let's take a snack break first," I suggested, still unable to believe how far off the rails this activity had already gone.

"I'm okay by the way," Octo-Cat informed me with a sniff. "You could at least show a little concern for your night of shining stars."

I shook my head; unsure I'd heard correctly. "My what?"

The tabby sighed and cast me a disapproving look. "Night of shining stars. You know, your rescuer?"

"My knight in shining armor," I suggested.

"Yeah, whatever. You humans have the weirdest expressions. I see a night of shining stars every day, but I've never seen a knight in shining armor. Have you?"

Well, he had me there.

A change of topic was needed, and fast. "I'm making sandwiches," I announced, heading for the kitchen.

"Turkey for me, please," Nan called after me.

"Me, too!" Octo-Cat added as he trotted after me.

"Me, three!" Paisley cried but remained with Nan.

When I returned with our tray of sandwiches, I found Nan engrossed in some story playing on the local news station.

A vision of my mother, the long-time anchor, filled the screen. She looked lovely today in a lavender blouse and dark pencil skirt. Mayor Mark Dennison sat opposite her in their in-studio interview room.

The ticker at the bottom of the screen revealed: Dognapped! The new mayor's golden retriever is threatened!

"I just can't believe anyone would take out their political frustrations on Marco. He's a great dog and doesn't deserve any of this." He turned toward the camera, eyes full of unshed tears. "Please, if you took my Marco, please bring him back. I'll do anything."

Nan scoffed. "Yeah, anything but resign apparently."

She said it. Pretty much the only thing I knew about our case so far is that I didn't much care for our client.

Why was he doing a publicity interview when he should be out searching for his missing dog?

It just didn't make any sense.

10

After the discomfiting news interview concluded, Nan switched off the TV and sashayed into the foyer. Apparently we were going out—again. Yes, for the third time that day. This wouldn't bother me so much if the temperature hadn't now dipped south of zero. Brrr.

Paisley pranced after me as I joined Nan at the coat closet. "Where to now?" I groaned.

"To the library!" Nan declared, raising a finger in the air and pointing dramatically toward the ceiling.

I glanced up with a curious expression.

"No, not that library. The public one." Nan looped a brightly colored, hand-knit scarf around her neck, then buttoned up her coat.

"Sorry, girl," I told the eager Chihuahua at my feet. "You're going to have to sit this one out."

"What? Why?" she whined, tucking her tail to cover her privates. "I want to come, too, Mommy."

"No pets at the library," I said with an apologetic shrug. "Besides, it'll be boring."

"Says you," Nan muttered, but luckily Paisley was far too focused on me to notice anything else.

"I'm staying here," Octo-Cat announced a moment later.

"Good, because you're not invited."

"What? No. I want to come," he protested.

Hmm. I'd have to try that reverse psychology trick on him later. For now, though, he honestly couldn't accompany us.

"Sorry," I said even though I didn't really feel it. "Library rules."

Turning to Nan, I mouthed, "go now." We rushed out the door and into the car before either pet could join us.

"What are you hoping to find at GPL?" That's Glendale Public Library, by the way. I'd always been a huge fan, which was why the library and I were on an acronym basis.

Nan shook her head. "Not me, you."

"Okay." I swallowed down my argument. "What am I hoping to find at GPL?"

"You're going to search back issues of all the area papers to see what you can learn about the mayor's past." She checked her hair in the rear-view mirror, then applied a coat of light pink lipstick.

I resisted the urge to check my appearance, mostly because it didn't much matter. "And what are you going to do?"

"I'm going to dig around on those social media sites to see what I can learn about his private life in recent years," my grandmother explained with a grin. Of course, she'd keep the more interesting task for herself.

"Remember," she said after parking outside the squat brick building. We were one of only a handful of cars that had braved the elements to visit the library today. One of them—an old van—looked familiar but I couldn't quite place it.

"Hmm?" I asked, drawing my eyes back toward Nan.

"Remember," she repeated with a sigh. "Same three columns. People, places, events. Jot down anything that sticks out, and we'll reassemble our brainstorm board once we're back home."

"Got it," I said with a quick nod of affirmation.

None of our cases had ever brought us here before, but then again none of our other victims had such a public record as Mayor Mark Dennison.

Even though we'd once investigated the murder of a senator, the circumstances had been totally different. Clues had thrown themselves at us left and right then; we'd never really had the chance to step back and research the history.

Today, Nan made a beeline for the computer bank as soon as we passed through the double glass doors. Since I didn't know quite where to begin with my task, I approached the librarian scanning in books at the main desk. She was young, probably new, given the fact I'd never come across her before—at the library or otherwise.

"Hi there. How can I help you?" she asked with a tight nod.

"I'm looking for back issues of the Blueberry Bay newspapers. Do you have, um, microfiche, I guess?"

Her eyes widened as she took me in a bit more fully. “How far back are you looking to go?”

That was a good question. How far back did I need to go to uncover the mayor’s political skeletons? Probably not too far, given his relatively young age.

“How about five years?” I decided at last.

The librarian chuckled as she stepped around the desk and motioned for me to follow her. “You don’t need microfiche for that. Everything’s digitized these days. C’mon, I’ll introduce you to the archives.”

She delivered me to the same bank of computers where Nan already sat deep in her research and clicked on an unfamiliar looking icon at the bottom of the screen.

“There,” she declared. “This is the homepage for our digital collections. We don’t have a lot compared to the fancy big city libraries like Portland or Bangor, but for such a small town, we have a rather impressive collection.”

“Thank you,” I said, scanning the list of periodicals on the site while the librarian hovered over my shoulder. I’d done some archival research during my college days, but on far broader topics. I’d never looked for something so specific or for something I wasn’t even sure I’d be able to find.

The young librarian patted my shoulder and smiled again. “I’ll just be at the desk. Give me a whisper if you need anything.” With that, she walked away, chuckling to herself.

I scanned headlines starting with this week’s and slowly working back through time. Like the mayor had said, most people who opposed him did so because of his relative lack of experience coupled with his status as a proud bachelor and his narrow win in the election.

I found several letters to the editor that complained about precisely these facts. By noting the names of the letter writers when available and the dates on which the letters were published, I was able to compile quite the list to share during our next group brainstorm.

"Find anything juicy?" Nan asked from across the way using a hushed tone.

I glanced up to find her peering between two of the computers to watch me. "Not much," I admitted.

"Well, then hurry. Come over here. You'll never believe what I just found."

11

I turned off the monitor on my computer and walked the long way around the computer bank, bringing myself to hover over Nan's seated form.

She had several different browser windows open; the topmost was Mark Dennison's personal Facebook profile.

"How long have you two been friends?" I asked in surprise.

"Since about twenty minutes ago," she replied with a distracted smile as she pointed to a status toward the bottom of the feed.

I had to hand it to her, she worked fast and effectively.

"Look right here," Nan continued. "This post is from several years back and about six months before the mayor adopted Marco."

I read over her shoulder:

Should we really elect this candidate just because his wife came down with cancer? Sure, it's sad, but it doesn't change his politics. Vote with logic. Not sympathy.

"What a charmer," I remarked.

"You said it." Nan scrolled back up toward the top of the page. "There are a few other posts commenting on current events in a similar manner, and then—boom!—puppy Marco shows up and takes over his feed."

I blinked hard. "So what do you think that means for our current case?" I asked, not wanting to connect the dots even as they were laid right out before me.

"Well, if you were really unpopular, what would you do to try to boost your own support?" Nan asked with a soft chuckle. "I, of course, can't answer that question, having always been well liked in my day."

I rolled my eyes. Sometimes Nan sounded too much like Octo-Cat for my liking. "Anything else?"

"You can see right here in plain writing that he believes these tactics work whether or not he likes them. And, look, he keeps referring to the new puppy as his family. The lack of a family has been the public's number-one criticism of him ever since he first decided to run for public office. He started with the local school board, I believe. It's the easiest in since there are so many spots."

I hated this. If Nan was right… That poor dog had never been anything more than an extra ballot.

"So you don't think he loves Marco? You think it is some kind of maneuver?"

"If you consider the timing of it all, things certainly look suspicious."

"Suspicious. Right," I said with a sigh. "Everything about this is suspicious. Maybe Octo-Cat is right. Murders are easier than kidnappings."

"For someone who didn't want him to come with us, you're sure talking about that cat a lot." Nan smiled to herself. "Now tell me what you were able to find in the papers."

I swallowed down a lump in my throat. "Nothing. We've only been here a few minutes."

"And yet that was enough time for me to find this golden nugget. Get it? Golden? As in retriever?"

I shook my head, refusing to laugh at such an obvious pun. "Does that mean we're done here?" I asked instead.

"Not quite." Nan closed all the Internet windows and brought up the library's internal search engine. "While we're here I think I'm going to check out a couple of books that have knitting patterns."

Nan never failed to surprise me, and this latest revelation was no exception. "Knitting? I thought you gave that up. You said it was for old ladies, remember?"

"I did, but it's been cold. And I thought EB could use a sweater to help keep her warm."

Ah, EB. Nan's new kind of, sort of boyfriend's pet rabbit. EB was short for Easter Bunny, and that nervous little rabbit had helped us solve our last case—two homicides and a kidnapping, all solved in record time.

Somehow, I didn't think EB would like being restricted by a knit straightjacket, but at least it would keep Nan happy and busy.

"Okay. While you do that, I'll keep searching the newspapers. Surely, there must be something helpful there."

Nan powered down her computer and shuffled into the back of the library.

I closed my eyes, willing something to appear on my screen, something that could help. While I appreciated Nan's theory, I couldn't believe someone would commit to a pet for such a superficial reason as a few extra votes.

I thought back to our conversations with the mayor earlier that day.

Whatever his motivations before, Mark Dennison clearly loved Marco now and wanted nothing more than his safe return… Right?

I flipped through the digital archives for another hour or so. The most interesting thing I found was an old editorial discussing bachelors in politics and how they really weren't suited to the job at hand.

Poor Mark. It seemed the whole world was against him. Part of me felt bad for questioning him about anything. Keeping the truth at least partially concealed came with the job; it was the politician's way. Obviously, the public would use whatever it could take to rake him through the coals, burning or not.

When I'd finished my uneventful research, I found Nan sitting in the Young Adult section chatting with a red-headed girl in braided pigtails. All she needed was a sock monkey and she'd be the perfect likeness of Pippi Longstocking.

While Nan was arguably too old for the literature at hand, Pippi here wasn't quite mature enough. She appeared to be nine years old at the absolute most. Her freckles covered her skin so completely it almost changed the color of her complexion.

"Are you ready to go home?" I asked, feeling like I was my grandmother's mother in this situation.

"Not just yet," Nan said with a higher pitched voice than usual. "Betsy and I here were just discussing the circumstances surrounding Lord Voldemort's second rise to power. Now Betsy, you were saying that Nagini was more than just a snake. Care to extrapolate on that?"

I groaned and turned away. As much as I loved Harry Potter myself, I suspected having a deep discussion with Nan about the lore would take some of the fun out of it for me.

Then again, I did love to read, and I was at a library. Maybe I could have a quick nose around, pick something fun to read for once this case was put to bed.

Although I normally favored novels, I found myself wandering toward the section on unusual pets. I'd been lucky so far with the animals who had inadvertently joined our P.I. Practice, but what would I do if I found an armadillo or a chinchilla or even a ball python wanting to join in and help solve mysteries?

Yes, it was definitely best to be prepared for anything.

Nan came and found me a short while later. "There you are. I've been searching for at least a half an hour."

Funny, because I had left her no more than ten minutes ago. I put the book I'd been thumbing through back on the shelf with its companions and zipped up my coat. "Let's get home then."

There wasn't much to say on the drive back. Nan kept trying to bring things around to her scholarly discussion of Lord Voldemort from the Harry Potter series and even attempted to parallel his rule with that of Mayor Mark Dennison.

Strange, considering how she'd been quick to defend him from the protestors at his inauguration.

Back at home, we found Octo-Cat lying in his usual sunbeam with Paisley nestled up at his side licking the fur on his neck.

Octo-Cat purred loudly and slowly blinked his eyes in contentment. When he noticed us standing there watching them, he jumped up in horror with the same level of absolute shock and disgust he displayed whenever he accidentally found a cucumber laying near him.

What? Sometimes I just couldn't resist.

"So, you and Paisley, huh?" I asked, making a kissy face and widening my eyes dramatically.

"It's not what it looks like, Angela, and you know it. The little dog just needed… Oh why do I bother to explain things to you feeble humans? Get out of here, dog!"

Paisley whimpered and scampered away.

"Do you want to hear about our trip to the library?" I asked, tilting my head to the side.

He stretched his front paws and then stretched his back legs one at a time. Finally Octo-Cat turned to me. "If you must."

I quickly caught him up on what little we'd discovered. I hadn't expected his response to be laughter.

"Oh, you humans, so needy. We cats don't need anybody telling us what to do. We can figure that out for ourselves, thank you very much. In fact, my fourth cousin twenty-three times removed, Stubbs, actually ruled over humans. They elected him to be mayor of their town for twenty years! He served his first term as a kitten, even. And he did a wonderful job. More cats should be mayors, if you ask me. I mean, you see how much better your life is since I've come around to teach you how to live it properly."

"I'm going upstairs," I announced, marching away before Octo-Cat could bore me with any more of his strange family connections or Nan with her far-reaching conspiracy theories.

"Dinner will be ready in an hour," Nan called up after me. "I don't know why, but for some reason I really find myself craving a nice Scotch egg. To the kitchen!"

We both disappeared in opposite directions. It wasn't until I reached my tower bedroom that I realized Paisley had trailed me there.

"Mommy," she said sweetly, wagging her tail and blinking up at me with eyes that always seemed to have tears in them even when she was happy. "I missed you today, Mommy."

"I missed you, too, sweetie. But it was very nice coming home to see you and Octo-Cat getting along so nicely."

"Yeah, but then he hurt my feelings," she whined. "Why does he do that?"

"Oh, sweetie." If only I knew the answer to that question, I could set up a second business as a cat behaviorist and make millions.

12

I spent much of that night tossing and turning as I replayed my conversations with the mayor and Nan's suspicions regarding his motives as a pet owner. Clearly I was missing something big... But what?

That question kept me from entering the deep sleep I so desperately needed.

Octo-Cat quickly grew frustrated with me and went to sleep somewhere else in the house. I missed his warm presence in bed, but it beat listening to him complain about my anxious insomnia.

I'd hoped to sleep in a little the next morning, but Nan would hear of no such thing. As soon as light began peeking from beneath the curtain, she burst in with Paisley yapping at her heels. "Good morning! It's a great day for a run! Our second run! You're going to feel terrible," she said with a sinister smile, "but we have to keep going and then you'll feel great. No time to waste. Chop, chop!"

I pulled the pillow over my head, not caring if it smothered me. Nothing could be worse than running with Nan on almost no shut-eye.

Then Octo-Cat, proving things could always get worse, appeared with a dead rat in his mouth and dropped it directly on me.

I shrieked and pushed the covers, and the rat, to the ground. Paisley quickly zoomed in and took possession of the deceased rodent.

"This is yummy! What a big fat rat." Her voice came out muffled, but undeniably glad.

"Why would you do that to me first thing in the morning? Why would you do that at all?" I asked Octo-Cat, still shivering with disgust.

"Consider it payment. Not a gift. I need something."

"I don't want it as a gift or a payment! I don't want it at all!" I shuddered again. These little gifts—or payments—of his were made that much worse by the fact I could talk to rats, too.

Octo-Cat never minded making me uncomfortable, though. All that mattered was his own needs.

"You really made me uncomfortable last night, Angela," he began with a sigh. See?

"With all that tossing and turning and mumbling in your sleep, I could scarcely catch any winks myself. That just won't do. I need my own bedroom. My own bed."

"You've got to be kidding me. I can't handle this right now. Nan, I don't feel well. I can't go for the run. I need to save all my energy for the case."

She waved away my concern. "Nothing like getting your blood pumping first thing in the morning to wake up that tired brain."

I groaned. Why couldn't they leave me alone for just five minutes? Was that so much to ask? Five minutes would help so much.

"I'm guessing there's no way out of this?"

"Nope," Nan answered pertly and then tossed a water bottle my way. I didn't catch it. Instead, it bounced back to the floor.

Paisley had already left the room, rat in mouth, which I desperately hoped I wouldn't be seeing again. I also would not be letting Paisley lick me until she had a good solid teeth-brushing.

"Let's go. Hurry up," Nan said, taking her role as my personal trainer far too seriously.

Octo-Cat jumped on the bed and stared daggers at me through his amber eyes. "Seeing as you accepted my payment, I'll expect services to be rendered by nightfall. Don't forget. When you get home, I get my own bedroom and it better be a nice one. This is my house, after all."

I ignored him as I got ready for what I already knew would be a terribly exhausting day.

Paisley was still off somewhere with my rat payment, making it easy to sneak away without her. Unfortunately, we still had far too much snow for her to be safe and warm outside.

For both of our sakes, I hoped the weather improved soon, but I knew better than to expect that of Blueberry Bay in early February.

Nan drove us to Cujo's house, then grabbed him from the side yard and clipped on his leash.

"I expect you to do better today." The disapproving muttsky

narrowed his eerie eyes at me. "Yesterday's performance was unacceptable, but I'm glad you're here to try again. We'll make a runner of you yet."

"I don't know why it's so important to you," I mumbled. "You don't even know me."

"Oh, but I know running," Cujo answered with a chuckle as he kicked his legs back in the snow.

And just like that, we were off.

"So," Nan said as we rounded the first block. "I still think there's something fishy going on about that missing golden retriever."

I knew I wouldn't be able to run in peace. Even small miracles were denied me as of late, it seemed.

"What's this now? A missing retriever?" Cujo asked, still running at breakneck speed.

I, for one, felt as though my shoulder might pop clear out of the socket as I tried to maintain my grip on Cujo's leash and keep pace with both him and Nan.

"Yes," I panted, already overexerted. "It's our case."

"Case?" He asked, his ears twitching and turning with interest.

"I'm a private investigator."

Gasp.

"Me and my..."

Gasp.

"Cat."

He snorted. "You can't give a cat a job. Cat doesn't care about getting it done. You need a dog. Luckily, I volunteer. You give me a job, and I'll get it done. That's what we working breeds do best. So tell me, how can I find this missing golden retriever?"

"What's he saying?" Nan asked and I remembered that while she couldn't make out the words, she could hear the barking and guttural noises uttered by Cujo and other animals as we conversed.

"He wants to help find Marco," I explained, taking several deep gasps for air yet again.

"Perfect!" Nan replied in her normal, unfatigued voice. Here I was about to drop dead and she hadn't even worked up a sweat.

"We'll head straight to the mayor's after we finish our run," she decided aloud.

"No. Please no. I need to rest," I begged. "It's too much all at once. "

"There you go. Disappointing me again," Cujo remarked with a soft growl. "Yes. You definitely need me on this case. I'm part husky, you know. And part Akita and even part Great Pyrenees. All the great strong breeds combined in one. That makes me the greatest."

Wow, this dog had quite the ego. As much as he didn't like cats, he actually reminded me of one.

I hesitated. "I didn't say you were hired."

It seemed to me having to look after Cujo would make the investigation more difficult.

"Of course he's hired!" Nan cried merrily. "Good boy. You tell us how you want your payment, and we'll make sure to get it to you. Do you like rawhides or bully sticks? What can we give you?"

I translated this to Cujo who sighed and said, "A job well done is payment enough, but it's nice to be appreciated."

He glanced over his shoulder and gave me a disapproving look before continuing. "Catch me up on the case so that I'm ready. I'll solve this in record time. You'll see."

I found it quite difficult to relay the facts while continuing our horrible run—but somehow, just barely, I managed. When we finished forty minutes later, rather than yesterday's thirty, I crumpled into the snow, content to die right there so I could finally get some rest.

"What are you doing?" Nan asked with a laugh.

Cujo was far less amused. "Get up! Now is not the time to be lazy. We can't rest until the job is done."

I made a snow angel, ignoring them both until my heart finally slowed to a steadier beat. Moderately refreshed, I got up and dutifully headed to the car

"Now that wasn't so bad. Was it?" Nan asked as she ushered Cujo into the tiny back seat. It barely contained his one hundred pounds of fluffy bulk, but he didn't seem to mind.

I laughed a bitter laugh and closed my eyes, leaning back on the headrest.

The sooner we solved this case, the sooner I could return to trying to get some shut-eye. Hopefully by the time we returned home, Octo-Cat would have forgotten all about his demand for a new bedroom.

Then again, when had he ever forgotten about anything? Or at least anything that concerned him?

13

Nan, Cujo, and I arrived at the mayor's house for the second time in two days. I had an uneasy feeling about snooping around, sorely hoping Nan didn't plan on breaking and entering today as well.

We'd been lucky enough to explain our unexpected presence yesterday, but if Mark caught us today, he would surely figure out that we were investigating him just as much as the disappearance of his dog.

"Is that the mark?" Cujo asked, panting heavily beside me. He'd stuffed his giant slobbery face between the two front seats and over the armrest. Funny that he didn't get winded at all during the run, but this new excitement of the investigation had his tongue lolling freely from his enormous maw.

I scanned the horizon just in time to see the mayor pulling away in his luxury sedan.

"I'll tail him," Nan said, nudging me in the ribs. "Get out. You can look around here, and I'll follow him wherever he's going."

As tired as I was, I also knew better than to argue. At least I'd be able to move at my own pace now.

But no.

A moment later, I found myself standing in the fresh snowfall with Cujo at my side. "Why didn't you stay with Nan?" I asked him, not so secretly wishing he had.

"And miss all the action? No thank you. I hate that metal dogsled, anyway. I'm supposed to be pulling, not sitting." He chuffed and pawed at the snow impatiently.

"Well, c'mon then." I tromped up the unshoveled drive. I'd have thought the mayor would ensure his home was one of the first on the local snowplow's route. Then again, it was probably hard for the city to keep up, given the record-breaking snowfall Glendale had seen during the past week.

"What are we looking for?" Cujo asked. "I don't like standing here wasting time. Not when we have a job to do."

I'd only stopped for a few seconds, but apparently that was long enough for the hyperactive work hound. "I'm not sure," I answered, bracing myself for the insults I had no doubt would be coming.

Luckily, whatever he'd been about to say died on Cujo's lips as a frigid blast of wind crashed into us face-on.

"Ah, that feels good," he said with a happy sigh, then his entire body stiffened as he took a long, exaggerated whiff of the air.

"I smell something," he informed me.

"Smell something, like what?"

"Pee."

Oh, great. "Yeah, um, we were here yesterday for a tour, and the mayor pointed out that Marco always peed on that side of the yard."

"No, that's not right." Cujo barked and turned his head in the opposite direction. "It's coming from over there!"

He pointed toward the woods, one paw raised mid-step.

"Are you sure? Nothing's back there," I explained.

"So trusting, you humans. I'd wager a healthy bit of skepticism is just as important to a private investigator as a snow hook is to a musher. At least it should be."

"Oh…kay," I said slowly, neither wanting nor knowing how to argue this point with him.

Cujo whined against his leash. "We need to go to the pee. It will tell us everything we need to know."

Wonderful. Still, at least it was something.

We plodded along much slower than Cujo would have liked until we were deep into the woods. Even though the sun was still high, the tall, aged trees cast shadows over us.

"I'm not so sure about this," I told him, taking out my phone and noting that my reception was down to one bar. "Nobody knows we're back here. What if…?"

Cujo interrupted me with a low growl. "No time for what-ifs. We have a case to solve. Have you forgotten already?"

I had two choices.

I could disappoint the very large, very angry-looking dog beside me, or I could take the small risk of heading deeper into the woods.

This time, I chose to go into the unknown, following the tireless muttsky through the trees.

By the time we emerged on the other side, I realized that Cujo's keen sense of smell had, in fact, led us somewhere new. A small log cabin sat nestled among the trees on the outer edge of the woods. It probably wouldn't have been visible, if not for the stark white snow that surrounded it. Smoke rose up from the chimney, and a faded trail of footprints led straight to the front door.

It looked like the perfect place to escape the cold and rest for a moment. Oh, how nice that sounded.

"The trail stops here," Cujo informed me, bounding up to the cabin, then lifting a leg and relieving himself with great satisfaction. "There. No more strange dog's pee."

"Is it Marco's? Do you think?" I asked, unfamiliar with the intricacies of dog pee.

"I've never met him, so I can't say for sure." Cujo blinked slowly in the sunlight. "But let me see..."

He stuck his snout in the snow. "This dog is male, about five or six years old, slightly overweight and enjoys snap peas as a snack. Not my favorite but..."

"Interesting," I said, thinking back over the mayor's tour of his home and our discussion of Marco's day-to-day routine. "Oh, wait. I remember something. The mayor did say that he used snap peas as snacks for Marco to help get his weight down since the meat ones were making him too fat."

"Well, then it seems we've found our dog," Cujo answered with a gaping smile. “I told you it was easy when you focused on the task to be done.”

He was right. I wouldn't have found this place without him, but still we had to face whatever was inside.

I pushed my body flat against the wall and slowly snuck toward the window. A quick peek inside confirmed that the cabin wasn't sitting empty. A portly golden retriever sat gnawing on a rawhide bone in front of a blazing fire.

“That's got to be him!” I cried, then covered my mouth with my hands, realizing I may have spoken too loudly to avoid detection. The dog’s ears perked up, but he didn't move his eyes from the bone. When no one came out to investigate, I realized that Marco must be sitting alone.

“What should we do?” I asked Cujo.

“Go in and rescue him, obviously,” Cujo said with a chuff. “It’s the final part of our mission. You can't back off now.”

I tried the door, but it was locked. “Any other ideas?” I asked.

“Fall back!” The muttsky jumped to the side, urging me to follow.

Sure enough, in the distance I spotted an approaching figure wearing a Russian fur shapka and thick mittens.

I leapt behind the cabin with Cujo and watched in horror as Mayor Mark Dennison himself finished the trek to the cabin and let himself inside. Could it be?

I carefully, painfully duck-walked to the window and peeked over the ledge. The mayor had settled himself beside his dog and was discussing the case—the one he’d hired us to solve.

I could barely make out his words.

"Well," the mayor said with a chuckle, "the first few interviews went great. My public approval rating must be soaring now. Not only does everybody remember that I have a great dog."

He paused to scratch Marco between the ears. "But they also feel genuinely sorry for me. It's one thing to disagree with my politics, but to take such a nice dog... Who would do such a wicked thing?"

Marco cocked his head to the side and Mark laughed again.

"Yes, it would take someone truly awful." He continued to laugh as the answer to our predicament finally became crystal clear.

No one had ever threatened Marco. The mayor had taken the dog himself and hidden him back here just long enough to get the public sympathy working in his favor.

So what was I supposed to do now?

Barge in and tell him he'd been found out?

He was the client after all, and the one responsible for paying us when the job was done.

Did a little ill-gotten publicity really hurt anyone?

The dog was clearly fine and happy.

So...

Was it better to walk away or to force a confrontation? Before I could decide, Mark let himself back out through the door and clomped away.

I held my breath, praying hard that he wouldn't turn around and see me.

14

I waited crouched in the snow outside that cabin for at least ten minutes, needing to make sure the mayor had well and truly gone before I headed back through the woods with Cujo.

"What's next? What's next? I'm ready for the next part," he begged, panting happily as he led me across the frigid February landscape.

I had to admit that he made a far more motivational partner than the crabby tabby I usually worked beside.

"That's a good question," I told him. "I still haven't decided. What do you think?"

Honestly I was torn. Should we confront the mayor with what we know? Or would it be better for me to call my news anchor mom so she could break the story and expose this scandal to the public? She'd definitely be happy to have such a juicy story. The network execs would be, too. They might even extend her coverage region over something like this.

Cujo stopped walking and stared up at me with his light blue eyes. "I don't care what you do. We found the culprit. It's up to you to navigate the intricacies of human propriety. Not me."

"Uhh....sure," I said in defeat. "Thanks for the help."

"Don't mention it," he yipped.

We walked silently through the woods for a while, neither having anything to say to the other. When we'd almost reached the clearing on the other side, my phone let out a series of high-pitched chirps.

"What was that?" Cujo asked in a panic. "That didn't sound good."

"Relax. It's just my phone." I pulled it out from where it had been wedged in my pants pocket and saw a missed text and two missed voicemails from Nan.

I listened to the first message. "I don't know where you are, Angie dear, but take cover. Mark's headed back your way."

The next voicemail was much the same. Although it definitely would have been nice to have advance warning, it was probably a good thing my phone hadn't chimed and given me away while I was spying through the cabin window.

I tried returning Nan's call to let her know I was okay, but the phone just rang and rang without stop. Meanwhile Cujo and I crept closer to the edge of the forest. I was so ready to get back into the warmth of Nan's car and hoped she'd be nearby and waiting for us.

"What's that?" Cujo asked again.

I turned but saw nothing—nothing except a gloved fist flying straight toward my face. It made contact, crunching my nose and forcing me down into the soft snow below.

Cujo growled, sounding more like his namesake than ever.

"Who's there?" I called, rubbing stars from my eyes, only to be kicked in my side for my efforts. The fresh wave of searing hot pain distracted me from all else.

Cujo lashed out with a snarl, and my attacker screamed in pain. I assumed he had landed his bite. I definitely didn't envy whoever had been on the other end of those giant teeth.

A large thud sounded nearby, and Cujo yelped in response.

"Get out of here, you stupid dog!" I heard someone yell, still too delirious from pain to determine whether the voice had come from a man or a woman.

And then I was alone with my attacker.

Cujo's familiar pant receded, leaving me to handle the assailant all on my own.

"Get up, Russo," he commanded, yanking me to my feet by my hair. A man. Definitely a man, and a strong one, too.

Everything hurt so bad I couldn't help but cry out. "What do you want? Leave me alone!"

"We already told you what we want, but you couldn't keep your nose out of our business," the man told me, but I couldn't make any sense of it.

"Again," another voice added. This one seemed to belong to a woman.

"You're coming with us," the man said, yanking me again.

Everything looked as if it were under water or part of a mirage. I strained to make out the features of either thug, but one them pushed a soft knit skullcap onto my head and yanked it down over my eyes.

"You move that, you're dead," the woman said, and I knew better than to test her on that.

"March," the man said, pushing me from behind. The woman walked just before me.

We turned around and headed back through the woods toward that lonesome cabin. Was this how I died?

Marching blindly through the cold at the hands of an unknown pair who hated me enough to kidnap me? Not just once, but twice now?

I had no doubt in my mind that this was the same duo that had abducted Mags just a month earlier at the Holiday Spectacular downtown. She said they called her Russo and warned her to keep her nose out of their business, just like these two were doing with me now.

What did they have to do with the mayor and his missing golden retriever, though? I'd already seen that he'd taken the dog himself. That neither of them had ever been in any real danger.

Yet here I was, blindfolded and being marched to an unknown end. My bones rattled from the icy cold. My heart hammered with fear—too bad it wasn't quite enough to get me warm.

If I ran, I wouldn't get far—not with these two around and with my vision already so disoriented, whether or not I was blindfolded.

And if I stopped moving, who knew what they would do to punish me?

This left no option but to comply, so back to the cabin we went.

Sometime later they shattered the window, then unlocked the door and shoved me inside. The warmth of the fire immediately put me at ease despite the ongoing danger.

My kidnappers whispered hurriedly between themselves before finally tugging off the cap that had blinded me.

Marco the golden retriever stood nearby, his tail covering his privates as he whined questioningly. "Who are you?" he asked in a friendly yet fearful voice. "Why have you come to my playhouse?"

I wished I could answer him, but I still didn't know who my attackers were or what they wanted. I had to play it safe. So I addressed them instead, hoping Marco would understand.

"Why are you here? Why am I here? What do you want?" I asked the questions in rapid fire, my jaw throbbing from where I'd been hit, blood gushing from my nose into my mouth. It was probably broken for all I knew. Maybe Mags could teach me a makeup trick or two if I even managed to get out of this alive.

But now I saw clearly that the first of my captors was a woman in her mid-fifties with elegantly coiffed hair and an expensive looking jacket. She seemed familiar, though I couldn't exactly place her.

The man stood in front of the fire with his back to us, saying nothing as he let his partner make an attempt to answer my questions.

"You already know who we are. Why you're here has yet to be determined. What we'll do with you... Huh." She laughed but didn't bother finishing her answer.

I swallowed down a nervous lump that had formed in my throat. Were they really crazy enough to kill me? For what? Sure I'd put a few bad guys behind bars in my time as a PI, but—

"What are you thinking, Russo?" the man said, turning toward me suddenly.

Oh. This face I knew very well. His wrinkled skin had been pulled taut from an apparent cosmetic surgery. The white hair and strong jaw, though, looked the same as ever.

"Mr. Thompson?" I asked as all the pieces began clicking into place. Could it really be my former boss, the partner at the law firm now headed by my boyfriend, Charles Longfellow, III?

"The very same," he said with a hideous smile.

"Why would you do this?" I squinted my eyes and willed myself to see anything but the horrible scene unfolding right before me. “And shouldn't you be in jail?"

He chuckled again, this time bitterly. "You don't do a very good job following up on your cases. Do you think they were going to hold me because some lady got hurt by her cats? No. My lawyer got me out of that one with a slap on the wrist and an accidental death decision. Minimal time served. Now I'm back, and I'm not leaving again. “

It still didn’t make sense. “But what do you want? Why come back here? Why follow me?"

"You think we followed you?" the woman asked, shaking her head. "Think again. You just happened to show up."

"I don't understand."

"What's new," Thompson sneered. "You were a lousy paralegal, so it makes sense that now you're a lousy P.I."

I wouldn't just sit here and take this abuse, both physical and mental. My time with Thompson had been served. That wasn’t my job anymore. Now I was my own boss.

As far as I was concerned, he could spend the rest of his life behind bars. It's what he deserved, and it's what I would make sure happened.

Just as soon as I figured out how to get away.

15

Thompson forced me down into a wheeled desk chair and used a coarse stretch of rope to tie my hands behind me.

Ouch. That hurts," I complained, which only made Thompson pull harder.

Satisfied with his work, he turned to me again. "Finally you get what's coming to you," he hissed.

"I don't understand," I muttered, trying hard not to sound as desperate as I felt. "I get why you don't like me, but what does that have to do with the mayor or his dog?"

Thompson chuckled and shook his head. "Denise," he addressed the woman who I now assumed to be his wife. "Go find that camera we stashed in the pack, just in case. Looks like it will come in handy, after all."

"On it," she replied and shuffled to the other side of the small cabin, passing the golden retriever as she did.

Marco glanced at up at her briefly, then returned immediately to his rawhide. Some help he was going to be.

"We had no idea we'd find you on our way here," my former boss said. "That was definitely a lucky break. As for the mayor, we didn't kidnap his stupid dog. But from watching his interviews on the local news, it was very obvious that he'd staged the whole thing himself."

I sucked in a sharp breath. How had Thompson figured this out before me? And why did it even matter to him?

His eyes bore into me as he studied my expression. "You always did wear your heart right on your sleeve. You know that? I can see those wheels turning from all the way over here. Yes, anyone with half a brain should have been able to figure out what Mark did. He never did do a good job hiding his... shall we say... loose ethics."

I still didn't get what he was playing at. "But what does that have to do with you? Why intervene at all?"

"Oh, that's easy," Denise answered for him, returning with the plastic camera in her hands. "Mark Dennison is a terrible mayor, and he never should have been voted in at all."

"And let me guess, you should have," I spat at Thompson.

He sighed. "No. Unfortunately even with my minor record, I'd never be able to hold office now. Denise on the other hand..."

He glanced over my shoulder and smiled as his wife closed the distance between them. They shared a sickeningly sweet victory kiss. Something much too maudlin for kidnapping thieves, if you asked me.

"I'm going to tell everyone what happened when I get out of here,"

I promised them both, wishing I could shake my fist to emphasize the point. My hands, however, were still tied uselessly behind my back.

"That's where you're wrong," Thompson informed me. He held the camera up and clicked a button. The flash glared bright in my eyes, and a second later, a Polaroid image popped out.

The picture slowly beginning to emerge from the milky film, and just as I had suspected, my nose had definitely been broken. Blood covered the lower half of my face and I looked as if I'd already lost, but I hadn't given up hope yet.

Somehow I would get out of this.

I had to.

After all, what kind of world did we live in if the good guys didn't win in the end? And make no bones about it, I was definitely the good guy in this situation.

"Nice photo." I forced a smirk, hoping to come across as confident. "Got a frame?"

"Quiet," Denise shouted as she slapped me across the back of the head. "We're in charge here, not you," she reminded me.

As if I'd forgotten.

When I turned in search of Thompson, I found him standing by the door, shrugging back into his winter wear. I didn't know where he was going, but I certainly liked my odds better having only Denise to contend with.

No one said anything as he finished getting ready and then departed with the photo in hand.

Denise came around and hopped onto the desk, crossing her legs at the knee as she eyed me.

"I bet you're wondering where he went." She smiled at me, taking her time with this revelation. "Well, that's the exciting part. The dog may not have been enough to make Dennison resign, but you certainly will be. So thank you for stumbling into our perfect little crime scene here."

"What are you going to do?" I asked through gritted teeth. "Threaten to kill me if he doesn't resign?"

"Oh no, that would still leave too many loose ends." Denise took a deep breath, then lowered her gaze to meet mine. "We are going to threaten to kill you if he doesn't resign, and then once he resigns, we'll kill you anyway."

She paused to let that sink in, and a shiver tore through my body. I could tell she meant business. "So either way I don't get out of this alive," I summarized for us both.

"Precisely," came her unfeeling response. She lowered herself back to the floor and winced in pain.

My eyes traveled down the length of her pants, where I found that the hem on one leg was torn and bloodied.

She caught me looking and raised the pant leg to show me the nasty wound that had marred her milky skin. "That stupid dog of yours. He didn't have to bite me."

I was glad he had as I watched her hobble through the cabin in search of something. Maybe it would be enough to give me a fighting chance, if only I could escape my bonds before Mr. Thompson returned.

"This will do nicely," Denise said with a satisfied huff. I twisted myself around in the wheeled chair to watch as she pulled a bottle of Glenlivet from a glass cabinet. "Very nicely, indeed."

She brought the bottle and a large shot glass back to the armchair by the fire and took a seat with them clutched in either hand.

"Want some?" she asked with a cruel laugh as she filled her glass and downed the first shot. "Now there's a painkiller I can get behind," she said with a happy sigh.

I could use a painkiller too, but more than anything I could use this as an opportunity. If Denise drank enough of her self-professed medicine to hamper her senses, then I would have her injured and drunk while my mind remained sharp ready to fight for my life.

She poured herself another shot, savoring this one with tiny, discerning sips.

"I never hated you that much," she revealed. "Sure, my husband had always insisted that you were useless even before the senator's unfortunate end, but I saw you more as clueless rather than incompetent. Not that there's much difference in the end, I guess." She shrugged and finished the liquor in her glass.

If I could keep her talking then I could probably keep her drinking. And the surest way to keep any conversation going was to get the other person to talk about herself, of course.

"Must be hard having your husband be tried and convicted of accidental death."

She shrugged again. "It's a small charge. But yes, it wasn't easy to undergo all that public scrutiny while the case was on."

I nodded. "So that's why you have to make sure to tie up all your loose ends. So that no one has any reason to question you ever again, especially once you yourself step in to run for office."

She pointed at me and made a clicking sound. "You're definitely smarter than my husband claims. I'll give you that."

I watched as she poured a third shot, smiling to myself without saying anything in response.

Yes, I was definitely smarter.

But was I smart enough to wiggle my way out of this one alive?

16

Denise downed another shot, and then considered her bottle of Scotch with a frown. "Not much left. I guess I should've paced myself," she remarked with a snort.

"How is your pain?" I asked kindly, hoping she wouldn't question my motives.

My inebriated captor pulled up her pant leg and moved her ankle from side to side. "Can't even feel it now," she chuffed. "A good liquor is better than any pill, I'm telling you."

I decided to take a chance knowing there wasn't much hope of it paying off. But if it did...

"Now that you're feeling a bit better, I don't suppose you'd untie me?" I asked with an innocent smile.

Denise shook her head and slammed the shot glass onto a side table "Untie you? What do you think? I'm stupid? He said to leave you exactly as you are until he comes back."

"Who's in charge here?" I pressed. "I don't see him anywhere. Do you?"

She sucked air in through her teeth. "No can do, and stop trying to trick me. You think that just because I have a couple drinks in me that suddenly..." Her words fell away as a scratching sound by the door caught both of our attention.

There Marco stood, whimpering and dragging his claws along the wooden door frame.

"What is it, boy?" I asked, hope sparking in me anew. "Do you need to go outside?"

Turning back to Denise, I said, "If you just untie me, I can—"

"No way!" she shouted. "I'll take the stupid dog myself."

She turned behind her and glanced to either side. "I don't suppose you saw a leash somewhere around here, did you?"

I shook my head and watched as Denise grew increasingly frustrated with what was quickly proving to be a fruitless search. "You know," I offered slyly. "The rope on my hands would make a mighty good leash. If you just untie me, I could—"

"No." She kicked at my chair. "Stop asking to be untied. It's not going to happen."

"What if I have to go to the bathroom?" I questioned in my last-ditch effort to gain freedom.

"If you have to go to the bathroom," Denise told me with a cruel chuckle. "You can go right were you're seated."

"Gross," I muttered. I'd already heard enough about pee to last a lifetime, thanks to Cujo's preferred method of tracking Marco earlier.

The last thing I wanted was to sit in a puddle of my own making while waiting to die.

Marco whined again, twirling in a frantic circle as he begged to be let out. "I have to go! I have to go number two!" he barked. "I can't hold it inside, and I'll be in such trouble if I go on the carpet here. Please! You've got to let me out!"

I glanced toward Denise, knowing she had understood enough to make out the dog's desperation.

"Fine, you stupid mutt," she said to the purebred retriever as she grabbed his collar and led him outside sans leash.

I watched through the broken window as Marco sniffed around the yard with Denise following closely behind. It didn't take long for him to find a place and squat down, forming an inelegant arc with his back.

Denise let go and took a giant step back. This was my chance.

"Marco!" I yelled. "Go get help!"

She didn't have to know that I could talk to animals to get upset by my latest attempt at escape.

The golden retriever kept his eyes glued on me as he finished going potty. Once finished, he finally spoke his answer. "Why do we need help? We have everything we need at the cabin. It's a nice place for a little break."

Denise grabbed him by the collar and pulled him back through the door.

"That was stupid," she hissed at me. "Try something like that again and I'll move up your date with destiny."

"What? Kill me now instead of later?" I shot back with a scoff.

"That's exactly what I mean," she spat. "Anyway, this stupid dog's not going to help you, so give up on that now."

"What makes you so sure?" I challenged her, raising one eyebrow.

Denise paced over to the mantle and grabbed a bag of Pupperoni. I clearly remembered the Mayor saying that Marco only ate snap peas as a snack, so the Thompsons must've brought this along with them.

Marco immediately sat at attention, thumping his tail against the floor. "Ohhh! Meat treat! Meat treats are the best! I haven't had one for years. Maybe even one-hundred years! Can I have that one? Oh, please, please, please.

He licked his chops as Denise pulled a treat from the bag.

"Do a trick or something," she told him, clearly not an experienced dog owner.

Still, Marco whined, turned in a circle, waved, sat, laid down, crawled, and then rolled over.

Denise laughed and tossed the treat to him.

He caught it easily and finished the entire thing in one big gulp "Another one?" he asked, repeating the lineup of tricks a second time.

Denise gave him a second treat, then put the bag back on the mantle.

"See?" she told me with a smug expression. "She who controls the treats controls the dog, especially with a fat one like this."

I was happy for Marco's sake that he couldn't understand. Things were bad enough without her insulting his weight.

Denise returned to the overstuffed armchair with Marco following closely at her heels. He panted while staring at her lovingly as she poured another shot from the green bottle, emptying it completely now.

"Shame," she remarked, swirling the last of the liquid gently in her glass.

Marco gave up waiting and flopped down at her feet with a sigh. I was running out of ideas on what to do here. Unfortunately, if I waited much longer she would start to regain her sobriety, and that would make my escape efforts significantly more difficult.

It was at that moment, I found myself wondering what Octo-Cat would do.

Yes, just like those WWJD bracelets that had been so popular in my childhood. What would Jesus do?

Finding myself faced with death, I chose instead to question the wisdom of my talking cat partner. He wouldn't take this kind of disrespect lying down.

That was for sure.

What wasn't for sure is how he would escape the situation if he found himself in my place. My odds of survival would have been much better if he'd accompanied me today instead of Cujo.

And thinking of the Muttsky raised even more questions.

Where had he gone after the attack?

And for that matter, where was Nan? Did she know I was in danger or how to find me?

Cujo was the only one who knew I'd been taken. Would he come back to save the day? Or did he prefer other more running-based jobs instead?

Unfortunately, there wasn't much I could do to save myself here. I'd try my best, but...

After I'd been stuck in my thoughts for quite some time, a grunting snore from Denise startled me from my frantic internal monologue.

Nice. While I was literally contemplating my death, she was sleeping like a happy, drunken baby.

And did she always snore like a steam engine rushing down the tracks or was her drunkenness to blame?

I watched in silence for a couple minutes just to make sure her sleep was deep, then began fiddling with the rope around my hands. It was tight and even twisting my wrist the smallest degree caused enormous pain.

Still, if it was the only way to escape, I'd need to be brave and weather whatever injuries came from wrestling these ropes. I continued to twist and turn, biting my lip to prevent myself from crying out.

I could do this.

I had to.

And I almost had it, too, when the abrupt sound of the phone ringing brought me to a dead stop.

I thought I'd lost service back in the woods... But no. Thank goodness for small miracles!

Who could be calling now, and would that person prove to be my salvation?

17

Unfortunately I'd had it right the first time. My phone was still out of service range. It was Denise's that had just rung. If I got out of this alive, I'd definitely need to switch carriers.

Denise awakened with a start and fumbled to answer. "Hello?"

She listened for a moment, then said, "Hang on, I can barely hear you. I'm putting you on speaker."

I thanked my lucky stars for stupid criminals.

"Can you hear me now?" Mr. Thompson's voice rang out loud and clear.

"Yes, that's better," Denise answered with a relieved sigh. "Now what were you saying?"

I pretended that I wasn't paying attention by focusing my gazing toward the window. Really though, I sat taking in every single word.

"We really got lucky running into Russo like we did," Thompson said on the other end of the call. “Dennison’s already agreed to resign as long as we let the girl go."

"We agreed to that?" Denise questioned; her words slurred from drink.

"I made sure not to state those exact terms," Thompson added with a cruel laugh.

Denise laughed, too, but it didn't seem to reach her eyes. Was it possible she could be undergoing a change of heart?

I could only hope.

Thompson continued. "He'll be going on the five o'clock news to tender his resignation live. One last publicity stunt before he goes out with a bang,” he added, placing eerie emphasis on that final word.

Denise squirmed uncomfortably.

"You have the gun, right?" Thompson asked after a brief pause.

"Yes," she said, quietly pushing herself to her feet. "It's been right here beside me the whole time." She began to search the cabin for what I assumed was the weapon in question.

"Good. Keep it on you in case she gets feisty. You never know with that one.” Thompson paused, but his wife didn't say anything in response as she continued her search.

"I'm going to stay nearby to keep watch,” he informed his partner in crime. “Just in case that fool Dennison tries to contact someone for help. I've already threatened to expose his false kidnapping, but he might still be stupid enough to try and double-cross us. Speaking of, keep a close eye on that door. He may try sneaking back to the cabin to grab the dog, and if he does..."

His words trailed away, and Denise picked up where he'd left off. "If he does, then I'll welcome him with my gun."

"Good girl," Thompson said, irritating me with the way he addressed his wife. They exchanged a quick I love you before saying goodbye.

Once Thompson was off the other end of the line, Denise finished her search at last, extracting the gun from where it had been hiding.

She picked the semi-automatic up and studied it in her hands. "I was hoping things wouldn't get violent," she said, not realizing the irony of her words.

Not only had they attacked and physically dragged me here, but they also planned to kill me before the day was through. Not violent, indeed. "

You don't have to do what he says, you know," I whispered quietly, hoping to fill this woman with a sense of sisterhood. "Just because he's the man, that doesn't make him in charge."

"Of course he's in charge," Denise replied with a firm shake of her head. "It's always been that way, but I don't mind."

"All right," I acquiesced.

And then a short while later started in on a different tact. "Tell me about your kids," I suggested.

They had to be around my age. Maybe if I could get her to make that connection, it would warm her to me. Maybe it would save my life.

I'd already decided it was worthless trying to appeal to her husband's sense of humanity. He'd made it clear that when he came back, I'd be taking the long goodbye.

But Denise...

With Denise, I had hope yet.

She rambled on about her two sons and their many, many great accomplishments.

“The boys are both lawyers, like their dad, although they’d both moved out of state after college,” Denise explained as her eyelids began to lower.

Yes, this was good. If I could just make her a little sleepier, then maybe I’d have a fighting chance.

"Now that you told me about your sons," I said, keeping my voice at dull and even cadence, “let me tell you about my family. First, there's Nan..." I went into great detail describing every memory I could think of that concerned my grandmother, listing out every single hobby she'd ever expressed even a passing interest in. I hadn't even reached my teen years by the time Denise had nodded off again.

Thank you, Nan. It seemed she was with me in spirit even if she wasn't here physically.

With Denise back asleep, I returned to tugging at my bonds once more. A part of me wished in vain that Denise had left a bit of "painkiller" for me.

As I worked on the rope, I surveyed my surroundings.

Marco dozed happily by the fire. Would waking him up also awaken Denise? Could I convince him to help me even though I didn't have any reason to trust him the way I trusted my own animals?

I just didn't know what to expect from the food-motivated pup, especially since he'd been raised by an owner with exceedingly questionable morals.

That left me to my own devices.

Denise had a gun.

There was also an empty bottle, which could be smashed open and used as a weapon. The dog treats on the mantle may be able to help me control the golden retriever.

And then there were the jagged window shards that still lay scattered along the floor.

Could I lean back far enough in my chair to grab one without tipping over and use that to cut the rope that bound me? Yes, that was my best shot. I just had to take it really slow and hope for the best.

Using the tips of my boots, I pushed my way across the cabin floor, struggling on the carpeted parts, until at last I reached the wall. I used one hand to hold tight to the windowsill, praying it would be enough. If I lost my balance and went crashing to the floor in this chair, that would surely wake Denise—and when she realized what I was doing, I'd be done for.

Maybe she'd even call Thompson who would move up their murderous plans. Not good for me at all. Leaning back, I pushed with my toes and strained with my fingers while leaning back as far as I could. I'd have to let go of the windowsill if I wanted to grab a piece of glass. But would I be able to make it?

First, I had to test everything carefully. Could I take it far enough without toppling over?

Oh, I hoped so.

After what felt like an eternity of maneuvering, testing, and trying, I finally decided to make the grab. I took several deep breaths and forced myself to focus on the task at hand.

This was life and death—and I definitely knew which one I preferred.

I closed my eyes and leaned back toward the floor, only opening them again when I felt the tips of my fingers brush the ground. That was when a heavy figure flew through the window and landed right on my chest, pushing me to the floor amidst the broken shards of glass. Fresh cuts opened on my hands and arms, while the sound of the crash sent Denise jumping to her feet.

What had just attacked me?

Had Thompson come back already?

Was this really the end?

Only one way to find out...

18

Denise screamed, her face turning white with fear. "Get out! Get out of here!" she cried, running to the edge of the cabin and pressing herself flat against the wall.

"Yeesh. What's wrong with her?"

I knew that voice. Pringle!

I watched as he hopped down from my chest and onto the floor below. Oh, I'd never been so happy to see that pesky raccoon in all my life.

"What are you doing here?" I sobbed, tears of relief flowing freely down my cheeks. "How did you know where to find me?"

"Enough with the questions," the raccoon said, tapping his thumb and forefinger together as he thought.

I sat quietly, waiting for him to reveal his master plan, praying desperately that he even had one.

Denise continued to shake and cry, realizing too late that she'd left the gun behind in her desperate need to escape the raccoon.

We both glanced down at the weapon, then our eyes met.

Pringle stood beside me, pushing the shards of glass away with his feet as he slowly cleared a path. He didn't appear to be in much of a hurry.

"Not to pressure you," I said softly, "but I kind of need to know what I'm supposed to do here."

Yes, I was speaking with Pringle right in front of Denise, but right now the only options seemed to be exposing my strange secret or dying an assuredly painful death.

Today, I chose to let my freak flag fly.

"Why are you talking to it?" my captor asked with a ragged shriek. "Get it out of here!"

Pringle drew in a deep breath, his furry shoulders shaking as he attempted to remain calm. "You might want to tell that lady to stop calling me 'it'," he warned. "I ain't no nightmare clown."

I would've laughed, had I not been so terrified. Instead, I simply relayed his message to Denise. "He doesn't like you calling him it. His name is Pringle and he's a boy."

He chittered in annoyance, then corrected me. "I am a man, thank you very much."

"He's a man," I translated, keeping my affect flat.

Denise gawked at the two of us with wide, unblinking eyes. It looked as though she wanted to say something, but only a raspy croak escaped her throat.

"So anyway," the master bandit continued. "Some giant, hairy dog showed up at the house, all panting and excited and saying you'd been carried off. I knew right then and there that it would be up to me to save the day."

I nodded my appreciation and would've hugged him if I hadn't still been tied to my seat.

"He led me back through the woods and now here I am. You miss me?" He smiled, showing off his pointy canines.

"More than you'll ever know," I told him, not caring if I was gushing. I would never punish him for stepping foot in the house again. Not only that, but I would keep him well fed with Fancy Feast, or Delectable Delights, or whatever he wanted. I wasn't above groveling, and I would also make sure to pay my debts, no matter how Pringle wanted them paid.

"I'm so glad you came," I told him. "They're planning to kill me."

"Well, that's a bit extreme," the raccoon observed, then turned toward Denise, taking several quick steps forward.

She pushed herself against the wall, still immobilized from fear.

"Were you really going to kill my neighbor?" he asked, squinting his eyes at her. "That's not very nice!"

Not vcry nicc? Sincc when had Pringle begun to sound like Paisley? Personally, I had lots of words to describe the Thompsons' plan for me and none of them were anywhere near that mild.

"You think you can untie me?" I couldn't take the chance that Denise would gather her bearings and make a run for the gun. No, I needed to be able to fight for myself when the time came.

And, already, I knew that it would.

"You're really impatient, you know that?" Pringle remarked with a nasally twang as he returned to my side, grabbed one of the larger shards of glass, and began to saw at my binds.

"Don't even give a guy a minute to relax. Do you know how far I had to run to get here? Ungrateful humans..." He let out a huff of air, and as he continued his work, he chattered along, whether to himself or to me, I wasn't quite sure.

"Anyway, I ran, and I ran. Do you know how deep the snow is out there? And that dog kept talking about pee. Dogs, I tell you. What weird creatures."

Just then, Marco got up from his napping spot by the armchair. I was surprised the ruckus hadn't roused him before.

"Oh, great. Here's another one," Pringle spat. "I'm up to my elbows in canines!”

“Speaking of, where's Cujo?" I asked, feeling one of the threads of twine holding me snap.

"Heck if I know," Pringle answered, continuing his work. "We got close enough for me to smell you for myself. Then the two of us parted ways. He said his job was done, informed me that he's a good boy and that he was going now. But me? I figured I might as well come and see. So what's going on, by the way?"

I swallowed back a sigh. I couldn't appear ungrateful. Not now.

"They kidnapped me and are threatening the mayor so that he'll resign. Then they're going to kill me," I summarized, hating the fact that these words were even coming out of my mouth—let alone that they were true.

"So if the mayor doesn't give in, they're gonna off ya?" Pringle asked, tugging on the rope and then resuming his work with the glass shard.

"Actually they plan to kill me either way."

"Wow. I really do not like this lady. Is it okay if I bite her? Give her a little rabies maybe?"

"Pringle, you do not have rabies," I chastised him. Talk about spreading negative stereotypes. "But yes, you can bite her."

"Lovely," he said, at last delivering the finishing slash to the ropes.

I yanked my hands in front of me and rubbed at my wrists where they'd gone raw.

Free! This felt so good.

Now I just had to... Oh no.

Denise had finally begun to move again, and she was rushing right to the gun. I moved as quick as I could, throwing myself halfway across the room, but I already knew I'd lost.

19

I didn't reach the gun first, but neither did Denise.

Pringle stood on the side table, clutching the gun to his chest as if it were a precious child. Given his size, the simple handgun looked more like a powerful rifle.

"Wheee, look at me! I'm the terminator!" He flipped the semi-automatic around and pointed it toward the fireplace. "I'll be back, baby! Hasta la pasta!"

My heart thudded behind my ribcage. I didn't want Denise to have a gun, but it was every bit as dangerous in Pringle's paws. "Put the gun down," I pleaded, too afraid to ask him to hand it to me directly.

"What do you mean *put it down?* I just got it! This is awesome! Seriously, how cool do I look right now?" He squinted one eye shut and brought his furry fingers to the trigger and—

The bullet flew right for the stone fireplace, tore through the flames, and then ricocheted back into the cabin.

"Duck!" I shouted, throwing myself to the floor as the bullet shattered another of the windows and disappeared into the snowy wilderness outside.

Denise gasped for air loudly and repeatedly. If I hadn't heard the bullet exit through the window, I'd have worried she'd been hit. Instead, she seemed to be having a panic attack.

Unlike my captor, I'd been in dangerous scrapes plenty of times before—never with an armed rodent, but still.

I pushed myself to my feet, ignoring the pain in my hands and wrists.

Pringle was staring down the barrel of his gun as if a peek inside would explain how the firing mechanism had just been triggered. If I tried to take it from him, it would probably go off again. I had to talk us out of this one, but first there was something else I needed.

In the rush for the handgun, Denise had forgotten her other asset —a working cell phone. I yanked it off the table and punched in a call to emergency services.

"What arc you doing?" Dcnisc cried. "No!"

"What's your emergency?" the operator on the other end of the line asked, but before I could answer, the gun fired a second time.

Denise screamed, and I spun myself around, expecting to find a dead woman, a dead raccoon, or both.

What I found truly surprised me. The golden retriever had pounced on Pringle, knocking the gun from the raccoon's furry, little hands. "Guns are for hunting. Not for hurting," he warned with a growl that bared his teeth.

I'd never seen a retriever look quite so menacing. Apparently it took a lot to send him into attack dog mode—or more precisely a rogue raccoon with a gun.

Marco snarled, the long sandy hair on his back rising at the hackles.

Denise continued to hyperventilate and cry.

Pringle chittered from his place beneath the much larger dog's paws. "You're not going to kill me. Are you? Look, I'm one of the good guys. You can tell by my charming smile. See." He raised his gums and showed his teeth, which the dog took as a threat.

Marco reared back, then lunged for Pringle's throat. *No!*

CRASH!

Another furry figure crashed through the window. This time it was Cujo, and he did not look happy.

"So it was your pee I smelled," he told the golden. "I should have known you were a no-good useless—"

"Quiet!" Marco snapped. "I'm the first dog of Glendale, and I will not be talked to that way!"

"Unhand that raccoon. He's not a villain. He's a hero!"

"Then why does he have a gun?"

"It's true. He was saving me! She's the one who was going to kill me!" I pointed at Denise, who sat rocking in the corner looking completely unthreatening.

"Her?" Marco whined. "But she gave me treats. Two treats! How can she be bad?"

"Oh, my fellow dog, you have much to learn about humans and their motives," Cujo said with a shake of his head. "Come. Let's share a pee outside, and I'll fill you in."

The dogs turned to leave, and I made a beeline for the gun. Yes, this time I reached it first. Mostly because no one else had attempted to collect it.

Pringle lay on the floor, too shocked to move. From what I could tell, Marco hadn't hurt him yet. Still, Pringle had never been outmaneuvered before. His pride was now hurt more than anything else.

I emptied the magazine, dropping the remaining bullets to the floor so no more dangerous mishaps could happen.

"Can I have that back?" Pringle asked, slowly bringing himself to a seated position.

"I'll buy you a Nerf gun when we get home. Much safer, and then you can use the soft ammo to play target practice with Octo-Cat." My cat was going to kill me, but at least the Thompsons hadn't managed to yet.

I ambled toward the door and opened it wide in case the dogs decided to come back inside. No need to force them through the broken glass when there was a perfectly good door on hand.

Although I'd complained about the bitter cold that same morning, now I sucked in the fresh air with a happy sigh. It felt good to be alive.

But we weren't out of the woods yet. Mr. Thompson could still come back at any time, and...

Speaking of woods, three people ran out from them and into the open field, Nan among them.

I ran outside, crying with relief.

When I flung my arms around her, Paisley yipped, “Mommy! I’m here, too!”

I laughed when I noticed her in the carrier on Nan’s chest and gave her a nice scratch between those giant ears of hers.

The other two people were Officer Bouchard and one of the newer cops I didn’t yet know by name.

Bouchard came over and placed a heavy hand on my shoulder. “We heard shots fired. Are you okay?”

I nodded so vigorously, my hair fell into my face. “Yes. Yes. I’m okay. But…” I let my words fall away as I motioned toward the cabin.

Both policemen drew their guns and headed inside.

Nan was quick to follow, dragging me along.

We were slowed by my injuries, but arrived just moments after the officers. Already, they had Denise Thompson in handcuffs and were pulling her onto her feet.

“Are you the one who took my granddaughter?” Nan asked, marching straight up to her.

“Yes, but I—“

Nan came in close, readying a punch, but before she could make contact, Denise cried out in pain.

“Ouch! It hurts so bad!”

Nan turned to me in confusion, which is when I noticed Paisley, a bit of blood lining her muzzle.

“That little rat bit me in the boob!” Denise screamed, motioning toward Paisley with her chin.

Nan and I turned toward one another and broke out laughing. "Good dog!" we both cried in unison.

"Yay, I helped!" Paisley sang as the officers escorted Denise away from the scene.

20

The doorbell rang, and I rushed to open it. My boyfriend, Charles, stood waiting on the other side.

"I keep telling you to just let yourself in," I teased him, looping my arms around his neck and accepting a kiss.

"No more almost dying at the hands of former partners at my law firm," he chastised me.

I stuck out my tongue playfully. "Fine, I'll stay away from the partners and stick to associates."

"Not funny."

Hmm, I thought it was.

The great cabin affair had started and finished just two days ago. Both Thompsons were in jail awaiting their bail hearing, while Mark Dennison had been forced to resign despite his best laid plans.

Me? I'd slept for a solid twenty-four hours straight despite Octo-

Cat's constant mewling outside my door. That guy had no patience. I'd almost died, and yet that wasn't a good enough excuse for him.

That brought us to today. Nan and I had invited Charles and my parents over for a special celebratory feast, and—boy—did we have a lot to celebrate.

Not only had I solved what would have been my first paying case, if the client hadn't been arrested as a result of my investigation, but we also had a room-warming for Octo-Cat and a hero's party for Pringle.

The tabby had claimed the room beside my library. Due to my "lengthy frolic through the woods" as he liked to call my near-death encounter, he'd had plenty of time to plan the decorations, based on a combination of old sitcoms he liked and a mobile game called Matchington Mansion.

"Make sure my three pillows don't match," he'd warned seriously. "Otherwise, they'll disappear, and we don't want that happening."

Even though I questioned his grip on reality, I did as he instructed, even though installing a one-hundred- and forty-gallon tropical fish tank in the upstairs bedroom had proven both exhausting and expensive.

It was now his prized possession, though, and he spent long-hours fantasizing about devouring his scaly new pets. He was definitely lucky that I was a better pet owner than him.

"Are we all here?" Nan asked, emerging from the kitchen in her favorite apron.

The doorbell rang again, and my parents pushed their way inside.

As soon as she saw me, my mom grabbed my head and peppered kisses all over my face.

"Oh, my baby!" she exclaimed.

"I'm not a baby," I grumbled in a futile attempt to extricate myself from her embrace.

"Ahh, but you'll always be our baby," Dad said with a chuckle.

Charles placed a protective arm around me, knowing I'd blow a gasket if my parents didn't cool it on the smothering and give me some space.

"To the table!" my grandmother shouted. She'd already laid out our best china, insisting that she preferred I rest rather than try to help.

Now she scuttled into the kitchen and returned with a tray of personal-sized potpies. My mouth watered in anticipation.

"No one takes a bite until our guest of honor arrives," she warned, shaking a finger at my father.

"Say no more, I have arrived," Octo-Cat declared, hopping onto the table beside me.

"She means Pringle," I whispered. Everyone here knew my secret, but it still felt a bit odd to converse so openly with the animals.

"Pringle? What's so special about that guy?"

"Um, he saved my life," I answered with a shrug.

My cat snorted and licked at the pie on my plate.

"Gross!" I cried.

"Don't worry, I've made pies for him and Paisley, too. We'll just swap yours for his. But it means he'll be getting the chicken, and you'll have the shrimp."

"Ha!" I cried in delight. Personally, I'd probably rather have the chicken, but knowing that Octo-Cat's bad attitude had cost him his favorite food gave me endless joy.

The electronic pet door zinged in the other room, and in walked Pringle, wearing his new chipped collar. Now he could come and go whenever he pleased; no invite required.

I knew I'd regret that soon enough, but—hey—I owed him my life.

Everyone cheered and clapped while the critter basked in the attention.

"This is all great. Very great," he informed me. "But can they maybe sing a song of my greatness?"

"Like 'For he's a jolly good fellow'?" I suggested.

He considered this for a moment. "That will do for now, but I'd really prefer a custom ballad."

We all sang as instructed, then enjoyed Nan's delicious meal. When we'd finished, I rushed to the coat closet and pulled out a present I'd wrapped carefully in custom wrapping paper pattered with the Pringles chips logo.

"Awww, you shouldn't have!" the raccoon guest of honor exclaimed. "But I'm so very glad you did!"

He tore through the wrapping paper in short order, then bit into the box, and...

"My very own gun! Yes!" he cried.

"Not so fast," I exclaimed. "Do you remember what we talked about?"

He cast his eyes down in shame. “Guns are dangerous, and I’m not the terminator.”

“Yes, and?”

“And?”

“Read the label on the box. This is a Nerf gun. Do you remember what I told you about Nerf guns?”

A smile crept across his face as realization dawned in his beady black eyes. “Roger that,” he said, loading a foam dart into the gun with far more skill than he’d handled the semi-automatic at the cabin.

Biting his tongue and squinting one eye, he aimed and—

“Ahh! I am wounded!” Octo-Cat cried as he fell from his spot on the table.

I gave Pringle a high five. I couldn’t wait to tell Cujo about this when I saw him on our next run.

Although it hadn’t quite gone as planned, I’d never forget our first paying case. Not in a million years.

LAWLESS LITTER

PET WHISPERER P.I.

It's kittens for Octo-Cat when an orphaned litter shows up at our doorstep. And although the needy litter may be cute, the deadly mystery they bring with them is anything but.

Charles has been hinting at a big surprise he's planned for our first Valentine's Day together, but the arrival of the kittens quickly changes everything. Now he's helping me figure out who put the babies on my porch and why their paws are covered in blood.

Meanwhile Octo-Cat is left to play babysitter to the unruly brood while we investigate, and he's none too happy about it.

Right, so all we have to do is keep the kittens safe, solve their mystery, find forever homes for them, and try to find a way to salvage Valentine's Day. That shouldn't be *too* impossible...

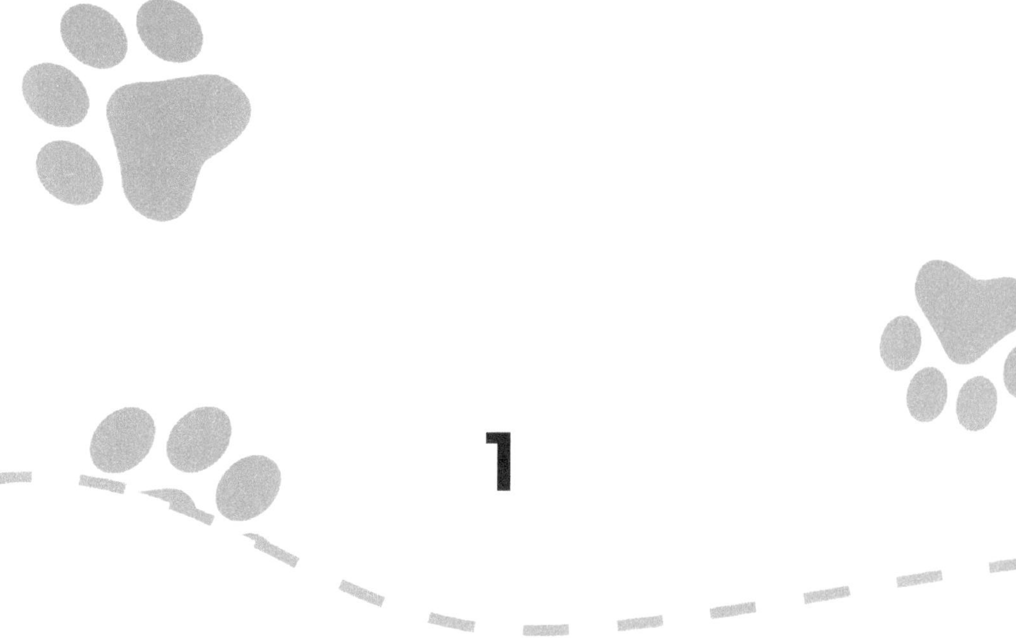

1

Hi, my name's Angie Russo. I used to be a paralegal, but now I'm a full-time private investigator... well, at least in theory.

We only get about one case per month, and they only sometimes pay. Luckily, my cat came with a very generous trust fund from his previous owner, which solves at least one major problem.

Oh, also, my cat talks.

Not to everyone, though.

Just me.

Considering his constant stream of criticism and unwanted life advice, I'm sure he wouldn't have the time to talk to anyone else even if he were able.

Did I mention he's my partner?

No, not like that. He's my *business* partner.

My romantic partner is a handsome, brainy, sweet, and considerate attorney by the name of Charles Longfellow, III. And while I may call him "Sweetie," my cat calls him "UpChuck."

I'll probably have to cave soon and make a deal with Mr. Kitty to get him to stop that. Valentine's Day is just around the corner, and I don't want anything to ruin it for us.

Besides, Octo-Cat should be busy with his own date that night. He and his long-distance girlfriend, former show cat Grizabella, are as in love as any two cats could be. I should know, because he's constantly lording it over in front of me, saying how much better his relationship is than mine.

Cats, am I right?

Well, I also have a dog—a little rescue Chihuahua named Paisley. She technically belongs to my nan, but we all live together.

Paisley is sweet like a double scoop of double fudge ice cream covered in sprinkles and chocolate sauce. Sometimes she's too optimistic about people's intentions, which means she's not exactly the best crime-solving partner.

Nan, on the other hand, uses all her varied life experience to solve our cases in the most unusual way possible. As a former Broadway actress, she's all about costumes, accents, and general over-the-topness.

Boy, do I love her for it.

Speaking of love, I have a bit of a love-hate relationship with the raccoon who lives in my back yard. His name is Pringle and he has zero boundaries. Not too long ago, he uncovered a long-buried family secret by snooping around the attic—we still haven't fully resolved that one—but he also kind of saved my life a couple weeks ago. I guess that makes us even.

As a thank-you, I now allow him to come into the house whenever he pleases. And he "pleases" quite often. Our grocery bill has risen precipitously. Meanwhile, Pringle is beginning to resemble a literal fuzz ball with all the junk food he puts away on a daily basis.

Sometimes I wish I'd never had that near-death experience that left me with my ability to talk to animals, but then I remember all the amazing things I've gained in life since then. Don't tell him, but the greatest of those things is my friendship with Octo-Cat.

Sure, he only sometimes shows me affection, but when he does it's enough to keep a smile on my face all day.

That brings us to today.

It's been T-minus six days since my cat deigned to let me pet him. My parents have been on a glamorous Alaskan cruise for the past three days, and I have had no cases since investigating the mayor's missing golden retriever last month.

All this downtime has got me wondering whether I should take up a hobby while I wait for the next big case to land in my lap. I have tried advertising, but that's mostly been a bust. So what else can I really do?

Ugh.

Maybe I should go back to school and finally work toward a bachelor's degree in Criminal Justice or something.

I have seven associate degrees, because I've always loved learning too much to commit to any one field for four whole years. But now that I'm a PI, I can't picture any other life for me. Would a degree help bolster the confidence of potential clients?

Or maybe someday I could officially join the police force and work as a salaried detective? Would they let me forgo a human partner in favor of my cat?

Hmm. If not, that might be a deal-breaker.

So many options, but none of them are just right.

I'm pretty sure I know what I need to do, and it's the one thing I've been trying so desperately to avoid ever since I got started.

My boyfriend Charles is the senior partner at his law firm and has offered on more than one occasion to hire me through the firm to help with cases. Sure, Charles was a good boss while I worked for him as a paralegal—in fact, that's how we first met and became friends.

But our relationship has evolved so much since then, and I'm worried it might hurt the good thing we have going together. Also, returning to the law firm feels like a giant step back even if my job title would change.

I guess what I'm trying to tell you is that I just don't know what to do.

Maybe the cat would be willing to decide for me...

* * *

Octo-Cat regarded me with a piteous look. He flicked his tail and knocked a bottle of painkillers from the nightstand on which he was perched. "See, this right here. *This* is why you need me."

I'd planned to do a little reading before tucking in for the night, but the two of us had gotten to talking about my conundrum and—as expected—the tabby had no shortage of opinions.

"Think about it," he continued, swinging the tip of his tail like a metronome. "Everything you have is because of me. House. Job. Boyfriend. Need I go on?"

I swallowed down my comeback. Sad to say, he was right. I hated that he was right.

"So what should I do?" I asked with wide eyes.

"Isn't it obvious?" He narrowed his eyes at me, then groaned. "Oh, right. Forgot who I was talking to for a moment there."

I resisted the urge to pick him up and carry him out into the hall so that I could shut the door between us and finally get some peace.

Octo-Cat, however, continued his lecture unaware of just how painfully it was being received. "You should take the work from UpChuck. *Duh.*"

"Don't call him that," I mumbled.

He rolled his large amber eyes. "You need more experience and references, and he's offering to help you get those. It's not just *you* you have to think about here."

I bit my thumbnail and sighed. "Okay," I said simply. "I'll talk to him tomorrow then."

My tabby seemed pleased with this conclusion. "Now are there any other parts of your life that you need me to fix for you tonight, or can I go about my nightly duties?"

"What nightly duties?" This was the first I'd heard of them, and while Octo-Cat *did* help solve cases, he did precious little else with his days. Could the nights really be all that different?

"Oh, you know. Keeping my favorite spot on the couch warm. Walking over all the counters and tables to make sure they're still sturdy. Protecting the house from ghosts. Watching the—"

"Wait. Go back a second there. Ghosts?"

He glared at me as if I should have known better than to interrupt his soliloquy. "Yes. Didn't you know? Only cats can see them."

I studied him for a second in an attempt to figure out whether he was being serious, but he just stared at me blankly, giving absolutely nothing away.

"Are ghosts really *real?*" I squeaked. I knew I had something of a magical ability, but I had a hard time believing that those fairytale supernatural creatures walked among us.

My cat yawned, and his smelly tuna breath hit me full-on in the face. "Guess you'll never know," he said flippantly before jumping off the side table and trotting out of the room.

Ghosts? *Huh.*

Something told me I might not sleep so well that night.

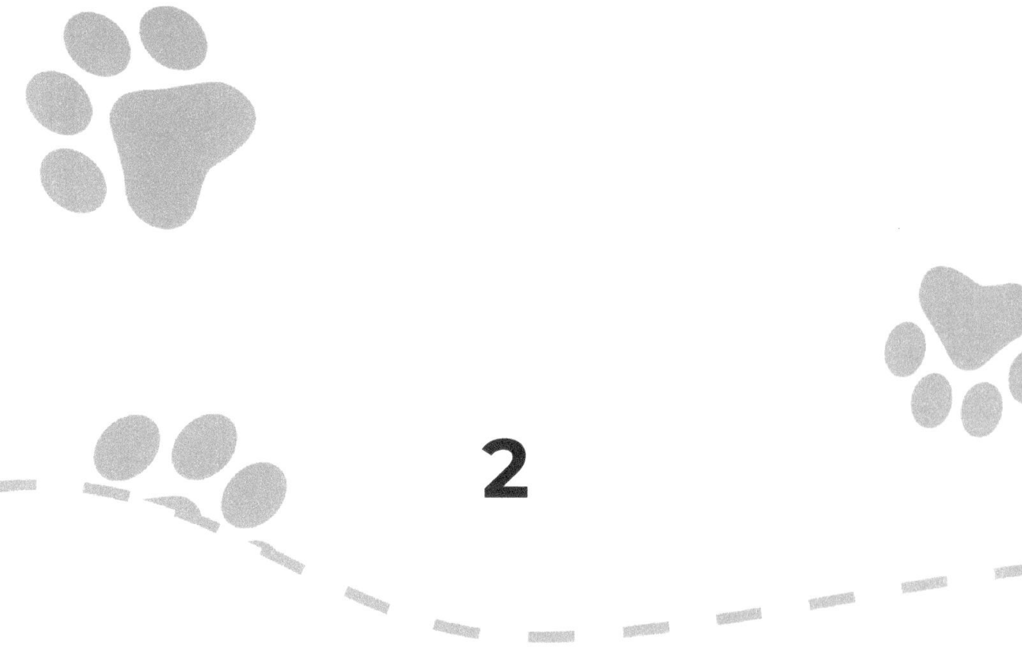

2

Saturday had arrived, and I was looking forward to sleeping in and waking up extra refreshed.

Nan, however, had other plans. She breezed into my room bright and early, carrying a coffee mug so full I had to wonder how she kept from spilling. “Rise and shine!” she sang, beaming at me from her spot next to my bed.

I wiped the sleep from my eyes and pulled myself into a sitting position. The wooden spindles of my old-fashioned headboard dug into my back, offering me a rather rude awakening, indeed.

Nan pressed the coffee mug into my hands. Some of the hot liquid escaped, sloshing over the side of the cup and onto my comforter.

That was when Paisley arrived. “Good morning, Mommy!” she barked before belting out a spirited rendition of some happy little nursery rhyme about a doggie in a window.

It was all way too much noise first thing in the morning, and I'd never been a morning person to begin with.

"What do you want?" I snapped, perhaps a bit too unkindly.

Nan narrowed her eyes at me. "Don't sass me, dear. I'm headed out for my new booty boot camp class in a few minutes."

"Thanks for asking, but I'm not interested," I groaned, attempting to take a sip of the coffee but spilling again.

My grandmother shook her head. "Good. Because I didn't invite you. I was lucky to get the one spot I did. This class usually has a six-month waitlist, but they somehow managed to squeeze me in at the last minute."

"Then what do you need?" I asked from behind the steaming mug.

She raised both arms and motioned toward me. "To give you that."

I eyed my coffee and nodded my thanks. Nan always brewed it for me, given my well-documented fear of coffee makers. It may seem silly, but I'd just never been able to look at them the same after my near-death experience last year. Of course I'd tried other forms of caffeine, but none sated my addiction quite like a good old-fashioned cup of joe.

"Have fun at class," I said sweetly, feeling guilty now for having snapped earlier.

Nan lifted her arms in front of her at shoulder height, then did a quick dip and squat. "I won't," she said with a grin. "That's the point. Beauty through pain."

"You're already beautiful, Nan," I muttered. Even though I'd taken up jogging with Nan a few days a week, she was still in far better shape than me—and, wrinkled or not, her body showed it.

She turned and shook her bottom, which was clad in pink velour sweatpants. “I’m looking to tighten and tone. If Grant ever gets around to officially asking me out, I want to be ready.”

I shuddered at the thought. While I was happy that my grandmother had found a close friend in Mr. Grant Gable, I definitely didn’t want to think about how said friendship might involve her needing a tight and toned bottom.

“Well, I’m off!” Nan trilled, heading back out my bedroom door with Paisley yapping at her heels.

I sat sipping my coffee and thinking about what I wanted to accomplish with my day. Saturdays used to be my favorite, but now that I was self-employed every day was both a work day and a vacation—not a good vacation, but rather the kind that happened when I didn’t have enough to keep me busy on the job.

Sigh.

“Morning, shrimpy.” Octo-Cat appeared in the doorway seeming rather pleased with himself.

I raised one quizzical brow. “Why shrimpy?”

“Why not? Humans call each other sweetie, sugar, and honey, so I figured I’d try calling you after a food *I* like.”

Given that my cat loved shrimp to an inhuman degree, I was very touched—and also glad that no one else could hear him calling me this strange new nickname.

A smile spread between his whiskers as Octo-Cat luxuriated in a long sunbeam that had stretched lazily across the bedroom floor. He looked really happy.

...too happy.

"May I help you with something?" I asked, suddenly very suspicious.

He did a crazy-looking cat yoga pose and then jumped up onto the bed beside me. "I thought you'd never ask."

Uh-oh.

"Since we don't have any active cases right now, I figured this would be a good time for you to drive me to Grizabella's for a visit."

I almost choked in shock. "But she lives in Colorado. That's a really long car ride. And besides, how would I explain such a trip to her owner?"

"Christine is *not* her owner," my cat said emphatically. "We both know the cat's always the one in charge."

"Fair point."

Octo-Cat shook his head in disappointment, then whipped his face back toward me. A sneaky smile stretched from furry cheek to furry cheek. "As for Christine, I'm sure you'll think of something during the long drive over."

His piece said, the tabby lifted his tail high, then turned to leave.

"Wait," I called before he'd made his exit.

Octo-Cat peeked back over his shoulder. "Yes?"

"I don't think we can manage a trip to see Grizabella right now."

"Why not? It's not like you have any work to do."

He had me there. "I just don't think—"

"No, it has nothing to do with thinking. The truth is *you don't want to,* but next Friday is Valentine's Day and I haven't seen my gorgeous Grizz since Thanksgiving week."

I sat higher in bed, hoping the change in posture might render me more convincing in my deceit. I supported Octo-Cat's relationship and wanted him to be happy, but this request was simply ridiculous.

"Yeah, it's Valentine's Day!" I practically shouted. "I already have plans with Charles."

"No, you don't."

"How do you know I don't?"

He heaved a giant breath. "When you're sleeping, Pringle goes through your phone and reads everything to me."

My heart dropped right into my stomach. "WHAT?! What's *everything?*"

He smirked. "You know, texts, emails, status updates, the works. And neither you nor UpChuck has mentioned any Valentine's Day plans."

I was stuck, stuck, so hopelessly stuck... but also very angry now. "You can't just look at my private stuff!"

Octo-Cat chuckled. "You're my human. There shouldn't be any secrets between us."

And with that he left.

I took another sip from my mug, but by now the coffee had grown cold. As much as I loved my bossy, overbearing feline, I just couldn't rationalize an impromptu cross-country trip, especially when his girlfriend's human had no idea I could talk to cats.

I needed to find a way out of this.

And I probably needed to change the passcode on my phone, too.

3

As much as I'd have liked to go back to sleep, the fresh coffee stains covering a good portion of my comforter made that inadvisable. Besides, I didn't need to lend any credence to Octo-Cat's argument that I should take him to see his Internet girlfriend all the way over in Colorado. He already claimed I did nothing with my days, and sleeping through this one would prove that theory of his.

Hmm.

Maybe I could trick him with a made-up case to keep us both busy until he found a new idea to obsess over. Then again, he wasn't the easiest cat in the world to fool. I could find a legitimate case before next Friday. Couldn't I?

Already at a loss, I padded my way down to the second floor. Once there, I found Octo-Cat in his new bedroom, sitting right on top of the giant 140-gallon aquarium I'd recently caved in and bought him.

Outfitted with richly colored silks and a baroque decorating scheme, my cat's room was nicer than mine. It also kind of resembled an eighteenth-century Parisian brothel—or at least what I assumed one might look like.

An accurate comparison or not, I felt immensely out of place whenever I entered, which meant I mostly gave Octo-Cat his privacy. Not that he ever returned the favor.

Still, someone needed to feed his fish—and it was better if that someone didn't find herself tempted to eat them every time the lid to their tank was opened.

"I've told you I can handle it," my cat groused when I grabbed the canister of food flakes and twisted off the top.

I shrugged off his argument. "Yeah. I'm not in the habit of inviting disaster into my home."

"My home," he corrected with an irritated sniff. "And what are you talking about? *Disaster* is basically your middle name."

"Maybe. But I doubt your fish would appreciate you sticking your paws into the tank and batting at them with those sharp little claws of yours."

Octo-Cat jumped off the tank and raised a paw to his chest. "Who are you calling *little?* I am deeply offended, and so are they. My fish have names, and I'll thank you to use them."

Even though I regularly talked to pets and forest animals, I'd never once heard Octo-Cat's fish utter anything other than "blub, blub." Was he simply pulling my leg about this? Then again, if other animals could talk, why wouldn't fish be able to as well?

Still pondering this, I sprinkled the food into their tank and quickly closed the lid to avoid any kitty shenanigans.

When Octo-Cat jumped back on top to watch them through the tiny opening for the water filter in the back, I decided to ask for a little clarification on the matter. "What are they?"

"They're fish, genius."

I met his eyeroll with one of my own. "Of course, they're fish. But you mentioned they have names. Right? So, tell me, what are they?"

He hopped back onto the floor and sat at my side, his eyes trailing the largest fish as it swam idly about the tank. "See, that big orange one? That's Tasty."

"Uh-huh. What about the striped one?"

He smiled and shifted his gaze to the aforementioned fish. "That's Delicious."

I was beginning to see a pattern here but continued to listen until all the fish had been named—among them were Yummy, Scrumptious, and Appi-teaser. My guess was he'd seen a few too many commercials for a certain restaurant chain leading to the made-up name of that last one.

I didn't point this out, though.

Instead I shook my head and said, "I'm not letting you eat your fish. They're supposed to be your pets."

"Angela," he said, aghast. "Who says I want to eat them?"

"You—" I began but was cut off by the merry chime of the doorbell. I didn't recognize the tune since Nan had recently changed it. It definitely had an upbeat doo-wop vibe about it, but I wasn't particularly fluent in that era of music.

"We'll finish this later," I promised the tabby before racing down the stairs.

Upon pulling the door open, I found my other half, Charles, waiting on the front porch with a giant grin on his face. He immediately wrapped his arms around my waist and pulled me in for a kiss.

"Gag. Get a room," Octo-Cat spat as he finished descending the stairs.

I chuckled as Charles and I finished our greeting.

"Great idea. We'll use yours," I told the mean kitty.

Charles bunched his eyebrows in confusion. "Use my *what?* Oh, right. You were talking to the cat, weren't you?"

"Sorry. He's just being bratty, but I'm focused on you now." I flushed and tucked a fallen strand of hair behind my ear. Sometimes I forgot that others could only hear one side of my animal conversations. "What's with the early-morning surprise?"

"I thought we could spend the day together, if that's all right with you."

"That's perfect with me." I gave him another long, lingering kiss.

Octo-Cat walked by, then stopped and pretended to retch—except that part-way through his performance, his faked motions led to a very real need to empty his stomach.

"Gross!" I cried when the puddle of puke landed just a few inches from my left foot.

"You're telling me," Octo-Cat responded before trotting into the kitchen and leaving me to clean his mess.

"Well, that's romantic," Charles quipped with a goofy laugh.

"Isn't it just?" I carefully turned away and grabbed the cleaning spray and a roll of paper towels from our coat closet.

"It's okay if today's not perfect," Charles assured me, accepting the dirty bunch of used paper towels from me. "Today's just Saturday. It's next Friday that's important."

"What do you—?" I stopped when I noticed Charles's face had crumpled into a frown. "Valentine's Day, yes. I'm really excited."

I wasn't a doting romantic, but I loved that Charles was.

"This will be our first one together, and I want to make sure it's special." He sprinted toward the kitchen to dump the soiled towels into the trash.

"Okay. What should we do?" I asked with an innocent smile as he jogged back.

"Don't worry. I've got it all planned out."

"Great. Tell me about it."

"Nope. It's a surprise." Something flashed in his eyes that made my stomach fill with butterflies, both because I loved Charles and because I had a tendency to fear the unknown.

"Just so long as you're not planning to propose," I joked before I could stop myself.

Charles's face fell again. This time my heart sped to a million beats per minute—or somewhere thereabouts.

"Oh," I said when nothing better came to mind.

My boyfriend reached his hand up to cup the back of his neck and averted his gaze toward the floor. "Um, I was going to wait until the big day, but…" His words trailed off as he sunk to the floor, took a knee, and then looked back up at me with bright, hopeful eyes.

"Charles, I..." I *what?* What could I possibly say to this?

I loved him. I'd committed to him. But I didn't want to get married just yet. Not until I had my life and business in better working order.

He licked his lips, took my hand in his, and then burst out laughing. "Just kidding!"

Octo-Cat guffawed with laughter as he passed by yet again. "Ha! Maybe UpChuck's not so bad, after all," he muttered to himself.

And as much as I hated that cat's snarky comments about my boyfriend, I hated the idea of them teaming up against me even more.

Luckily, Charles had no idea what Octo-Cat had just said.

I wouldn't be telling him, either.

4

Charles brewed a fresh pot of coffee for us while I warmed Nan's latest batch of homemade muffins in the microwave.

"Do you really have the full day free?" I asked again in disbelief.

"Not free," he corrected, pulling his favorite butterscotch-flavored creamer from the fridge and sending a wide grin my way. "I'm spending it with you."

"It's just you don't usually get a half day off, let alone a full one."

"Well, I'm making some changes at the firm to help me focus on what's most important."

"There's a lot to be said for work-life balance. I kind of have the opposite problem. Too much life and not enough work."

"Hmm. Then maybe we should meet in the middle." He winked suggestively, making me blush all over again.

"Excuse me," Octo-Cat bellowed as he joined us in the kitchen and stared down into his half-empty water dish.

I turned to face him. "Yes, your royal highness?"

"Oh, I like that," the tabby drawled as he twitched his tail in thought. "It's about time you referred to me properly."

"I didn't mean…" I began, then stopped myself. If I wanted to actually spend the day with Charles, I'd need to avoid unnecessary arguments with Octo-Cat in the meantime.

"What is it?" I asked amicably. The sooner I could satisfy his demands, the sooner I'd have some much-needed quality time with Charles—some much needed and *uninterrupted* quality time.

"I need you to bring my iPad into the mid-morning sunspot. I have a call planned with Grizabella, and I can't be late."

"Okay, give me a second," I said over the beeping of the microwave.

"I don't need it a second from now. I need it now." Octo-Cat stomped one of his front feet and glared at me with those strangely glowing eyes of his. "I'm going to tell her about our visit next week. I can't wait to see the look on that beautiful face of hers when she finds out—"

"No," I interrupted, perhaps a bit too emphatically.

My cat's head shot back as though he'd been slapped. "What do you mean *no?*"

Apparently I didn't say this word enough, given that Octo-Cat seemed to have forgotten what it meant or that it was ever a possible answer to something he wanted. *Uh-oh.* I needed to think fast before he could either outwit or guilt-trip me into doing his bidding.

"I, um… I was just talking with Charles, and you were right. He does have work for us at the firm. We can't leave town, because we need to get started bright and early Monday morning."

He lifted his tail and bent it to resemble a question mark. "Is that so?"

I jabbed Charles in the ribs, and he nodded despite not knowing what was going on.

"Hmm, I guess that's good," Octo-Cat conceded a moment later. "I've always thought St. Patrick's Day was far more romantic, anyway. Green is a much nicer color than pink or red, and who doesn't like pots of gold?"

I laughed nervously. "Yeah. Good point."

He nodded and glanced toward the living room. "You can have the inferior romantic holiday then. Now about that thing I needed."

Even if I hadn't claimed an outright victory, at least I'd managed to delay the problematic road trip for another month. That was pretty good for a morning's work. "Right. I'll go get your iPad for you."

"What was that all about?" Charles asked after I'd returned.

"Shhh," I hissed. "He can still hear you."

Charles leaned in close and pressed his lips to my ear. "You're cute when you're arguing with your cat. You know that?"

My knees turned to Jell-O as he traced kisses down my neck. "Stop that, you."

Charles chuckled as he pulled away.

While he finished fixing our coffee, I grabbed my phone from my pocket and typed out a text.

Charles's pocket buzzed a moment later. "What the—? It's from you?"

I widened my eyes and motioned toward his pocket. Yes, it was silly to text when we were standing in the same room, but I didn't want to risk Octo-Cat overhearing what I needed to say.

My boyfriend's eyes trailed down the screen and his lips moved as he read.

I need you to assign a case for us. Even if it's fake, just something to keep us busy. Otherwise he's going to force me to drive him out to Colorado.

He snorted and typed back, *What's wrong with Colorado?*

I'll miss V-Day.

Can't have that, he typed, then jammed his phone back into his back pocket and wrapped me in his arms.

"Thank you," I whispered against his shoulder.

That was when a projectile thumped into the back of my head.

I spun on my heels, not at all surprised to see Pringle the raccoon standing nearby, his Nerf gun still pointed straight at me.

"You're not supposed to use that on me," I reminded him with a groan.

"How else was I supposed to get your attention away from lover boy?" The masked nuisance crossed his arms but continued to shoot darts at me with those dark, beady eyes of his.

"What do you need?" And why were my animals constantly inserting themselves into my love life? I hardly got any time with Charles as it was. The last thing I needed was to play human servant to the furry creatures all day. Paisley, at least, was busy with Nan, but that didn't help me with the ones who were still here.

Pringle widened his eyes and tsked. "Watch the attitude, toots. I come in peace."

"That's a fine thing to say when you literally just shot me."

Pringle chittered happily. "Yeah, that was pretty good. Wasn't it?"

I tapped my foot, refusing to say anything more until he just came out with whatever it was he needed. The sooner he told me, the sooner he could be on his way.

The raccoon dropped to all fours and raced back through the living room. "I have something important to show you. C'mon!" he cried. "Follow me!"

"What does he want?" Charles asked with one suspicious eyebrow raised.

"No idea. Let's go up to my bedroom and lock the door."

He raised the other eyebrow. "Not that I don't like how you think, but we should probably find out what has him so worked up."

I grabbed the plate of muffins and one of the coffee mugs. "Not interested. Now let's go."

Unfortunately, Pringle intercepted me just as I reached the stairs. "And just where do you think you're going?" he demanded before shooting a foam dart into each of my kneecaps.

"Ouch! Stop it!"

He shot another dart at my face. "I'll stop when you come out to the porch with me."

"What's on the porch?" I asked with a sigh.

He landed a shot near my bellybutton.

I growled in frustration. "You want me to go the porch? Then give me that gun. You've lost Nerf privileges for the rest of the year as far as I'm concerned."

Pringle bared his teeth and hissed, reminding me that no matter how well he spoke, he was still very much a wild animal. "Touch Carla and you'll deserve what happens to you next."

"Enough with the theatrics." Charles pushed past us and flung open the door.

"See!" the raccoon shouted in indignation as our eyes fell upon the bloody scene waiting on the front porch. He bolted past us and leaped off the porch.

"It's your problem now!" he called as he disappeared around the side of the house.

And, yes, a problem it most definitely was.

5

"Mamamamamamamamama!" one of the babies cried when we stepped out onto the porch. Her feet were covered in blood, but she didn't seem to be in pain.

Her brothers and sisters clambered over her in an attempt to break free of the battered cardboard box they'd been crammed into.

"Are those...?" Charles let his voice trail off.

I nodded to confirm. "An abandoned litter of kittens."

Octo-Cat marched past us both. "What's all this noise? I'm trying to speak with Grizabella and—"

A chorus of excited mews rose up to interrupt him. "Daddy!"

I glanced toward Octo-Cat in just enough time to see his already large eyes grow wide in horror.

He coughed and took a fearful step back. "No, it can't be. The vet stole my cathood at least..."

He lifted a paw and extracted his claws, counting until he was satisfied with the conclusion. “At least four years ago. These… These *things* can’t be mine.”

“Daddy!” the kittens chorused again.

“It’s impossible,” Octo-Cat insisted, stepping forward to sniff at the box. “And besides, they look nothing like me.”

They, in fact, looked very much like him with the same golden eyes and the same brown tabby coats. The only difference was that their fur was already longer than his. Based on my limited experience as a crazy cat lady, I guessed that this was a litter of Maine Coons. Fitting, given that we lived in Maine and that Octo-Cat liked to claim this particular breed as part of his proud heritage.

The kittens rushed to one side of the box in an effort to get close to the grown-up feline, and in so doing, knocked the box over. Free at last, they rushed up to my cat and began to rub affectionately against him.

“Oh, great! Now they got this red sticky stuff all over me, too,” he moaned but surprisingly made no move to back away.

Pringle reappeared then. Once on the porch, he started scooping up kittens and tucking them into his armpits. “How much do you think these guys are worth on the web market?”

“No,” I shouted. “Both of you stop! Nobody’s accusing you of being their father,” I informed my tedious tabby. “And we are not selling them on the Internet,” I growled at the handsy raccoon.

Charles placed an arm around my waist and pulled me to his side. “What are we going to do?”

“Let’s start by bringing them inside and getting them cleaned up,” I decided aloud. At this point, I was feeling quite thankful that Nan was out and about. If she'd been here to discover the kittens with us, I had no doubt in my mind that all five would become permanent residents of our home—and that Octo-Cat would make me suffer for it.

Charles helped me wrestle the babies back into the box, then picked it up and carried them toward the biggest of our bathrooms, the one with the claw-footed tub.

Both Octo-Cat and Pringle followed along.

Pringle no longer had his Nerf gun, so that at least offered a small measure of relief. "I'm telling you," he said in a raspy whisper. "We should be able to get at least $100 each, and with there being five kittens in all, that's like a thousand dollars."

Apparently Pringle's math wasn't as good as his reading. Given a choice, I'd have gladly flipped that the other way around.

"Go on," Octo-Cat urged, dollar signs practically popping up in his eyes. "I'm listening."

I crossed my arms and glared at the naughty animals. "That's it! If I hear any more talk of selling the kittens, I'm demolishing your tree house."

Pringle crossed his arms and glared right back at me. "Which one?"

"Both."

"You wouldn't."

"Try me."

"If I had Carla, you wouldn't be so fast to make threats."

"Is that so? Go on. Go get her then."

When Pringle raced out of the bathroom, I slammed the door shut behind him. Locked it, too, for good measure.

"It never gets old watching you interact with them." Charles chuckled as he twisted the knobs on the tub.

"Shut those off, please."

"Why? I thought we were giving the kittens a bath."

"Not like that we aren't."

I grabbed a pair of wash cloths from the linen closet, wet them both, and handed one to Charles. "They've had enough trauma for the day. Let's do it this way."

Once the little bit of water had drained from the tub, we placed the kittens inside and worked on wiping the blood and grime from each of them in turn.

"There." Charles returned the last of the kittens to the floor with triumph. "All done."

"Not quite," I whispered. Unfortunately, my whisper wasn't quite quiet enough.

"What do you mean *not quite?*" Octo-Cat, who had been watching with great interest from his perch on top of the toilet tank, questioned.

Realization flashed in his eyes a moment later. When it did, he pressed his ears back against his head and hissed. "I can wassssh myssssself!"

"Grab him now!" I shouted to Charles.

And he made a good job of it despite the cat's violent flailing.

"This will only take a second," I promised.

"I'm not a baby," he grumped. "I don't need to be coddled by you."

"Maybe so, but you've got blood on you, too. And we need to get it off."

“I hate you,” Octo-Cat growled over and over until we’d finished.

If I hadn’t been every bit as miserable as him, I might have considered extending the impromptu bath just to punish him for his cruel words.

By the time Charles let him back onto the floor, he was covered in a flurry of little striped hairs that had resulted from Octo-Cat’s stress-shedding.

“That wasn’t so bad now. Was it, big guy?” Charles asked, attempting—and failing—to wipe some of it off.

“You better watch your back, UpChuck,” my cat moaned, knowing Charles couldn’t understand the threat. “Actually, *don’t.* It will make my revenge that much sweeter.”

I shot him a warning glance, then opened the door to let him run out.

WOMP!

No sooner had the door opened than something hit me square on the nose. And that something was one of Carla’s foam darts.

“Pringle!” I screamed in frustration.

Six distinct laughs rose in the bathroom—five from the kittens whose lives we’d just saved and the last of them from my sweet, loyal, loving boyfriend.

Maybe Octo-Cat was right.

Maybe he should watch his back.

Foam or not, those darts hurt, especially considering Pringle’s unforgiving aim. I needed to find a way to get that thing away from him once and for all… But first, kittens.

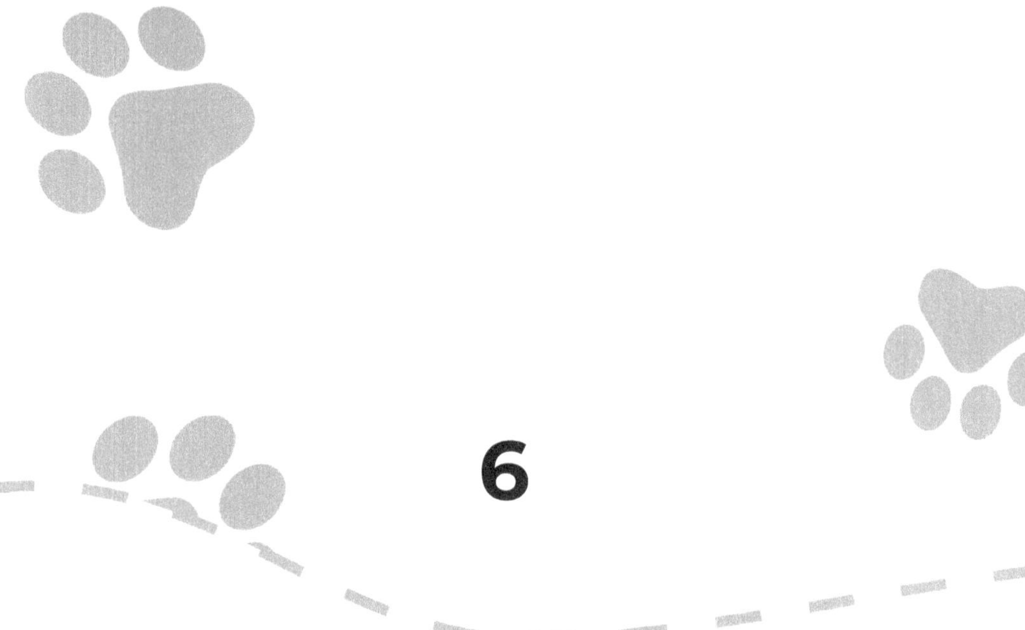

6

I couldn't get the Nerf gun away from the raccoon ranger, but I did manage to chase him outside and shut the pet door tight. Hopefully now there wouldn't be any more surprises this morning.

When I returned to the bathroom, I found Charles sitting on the edge of the bath tub and holding a swaddled kitten in each arm. As much as I wasn't ready yet for kids and marriage, the scene melted my heart into a pulsing puddle of goo.

He noticed me watching him and gave me a sweet smile—so sweet I forgave him for laughing at my unpleasant run-in with Pringle's dart. "C'mon, grab some purritos, and let's head some place more comfortable."

Oh, this man definitely knew my love language.

"Let's get them settled in Octo-Cat's bedroom," I suggested, knowing that there would be heck to pay but also knowing that it was our best option on such short notice.

Somehow, I managed to juggle three swaddled kitties as we crossed the short distance to Octo-Cat's bedroom.

My cat stood waiting at the threshold, flicking his tail so violently I worried it might snap off. "Don't even think about it," he grumbled.

But I refused to be scared off. His bedroom was the safest place for the squirmy kittens. After all, it had already been thoroughly cat-proofed and there were no large pieces of furniture for them to hide under. Octo-Cat would just have to suck it up for a change.

I set my jaw firm and my gaze straight ahead as I stepped past him into the room.

He trotted after me, screaming like a banshee. "I will throw up! I'll shred the curtains! I'll go on a hunger strike. I'll—"

"I'll tell Grizabella they're yours," I countered.

He sank back. "You wouldn't."

"I know this is mildly inconvenient for you, but they're babies and they need our help. Can you please try to be civil for once in your nine lives?"

He scoffed and turned tail. "You owe me. You owe me so big, Angela," he shouted as he ran fast and far from that room.

Whatever. I could worry about him later. For now Charles and I had kittens to attend to.

After shutting the door tight, we unwrapped each kitten and set them in the middle of the carpeted floor.

"Daddy?" one of the striped kidlets asked.

Then all the others joined. "Daddy! Daddy!" they whined, becoming increasingly agitated with each syllable.

"What got them so worked up all of a sudden?" Charles laughed, failing to realize that the cries were ones of anguish and not excitement.

"They want Octo-Cat back," I explained as Charles sat with the kittens on the floor and I stood awkwardly by the doorway. "They think he's their father."

Charles laughed. "Do they?"

"Either that, or they're just calling him *Daddy.* They don't seem to know many words."

"Well, they are babies." He picked up one of the kittens and set it on his lap. "Maybe they need to learn to talk the same way humans do. Then again, I haven't heard you talk *to* them yet. Just *about* them."

"You're right." I shook my head at this oversight, then lowered myself to the floor and sat cross-legged so the kittens could approach me. "Hi, guys. My name's Angie. What are your names?"

"Want Daddy!" one of them informed me. His whiskers brushing up against my bare foot as he sniffed me. Even though the mewling fuzzballs were adorable, they were already proving to be a ridiculous amount of work.

"I'll go get him in a second, but first I was hoping you could tell me how you wound up on my porch?"

No sooner had I asked this question than the entire litter broke into hysterics—even Charles could sense their distress. He reached out to pet the nearest kitty and received a clawed swipe for his efforts.

“That settles it.” I pushed myself back to my feet, careful not to make contact with any of the angry babies as I stood. “We need to get Octo-Cat.”

“Something tells me he’s not going to be happy about playing translator.”

I giggled. “And what *something* is that? Every single past experience to date?”

Now we both laughed. It was funny because it was true.

Charles followed me out of the room, carefully shutting the kittens inside before looping his arms around my waist. “This reminds me of the first time we really got to know each other. Remember the Hayes double homicide?”

“How could I forget? But it’s kind of weird that you seem to consider it a romantic memory.” I spun out of his arms and headed down the stairs.

“Hey, our relationship may be a little bit different, but it’s all ours,” he explained, trailing behind me. “Speaking of, I can’t wait for Friday. I am going to knock your socks off with my big Valentine’s Day surprise.”

At the bottom of the stairs, I surveyed the foyer and the living room but couldn’t see Octo-Cat anywhere. Turning back to Charles, I frowned. “Either tell me now or stop teasing. You know I hate surprises.”

As we headed toward the kitchen, Octo-Cat shot out from under the couch and raced away as fast as his little paws could carry him. “You hate surprises? Well, not as much as me!” he yelled while fleeing.

We gave chase. "I need your help," I called to the raging tabby. "Please. It's important."

"Not going to happen," he muttered from the safety of the litter box where he'd taken up refuge.

"Please?" I asked, sticking out my lower lip pathetically and attempting puppy eyes. I didn't expect either gesture to work, but I had nothing else at my disposal. Even when he was in a good mood, Octo-Cat made a stubborn opponent—and he was far from a good mood now.

"No," he spat.

I sighed and hung my head. "Just remember. You forced my hand."

"Where are you going?" Charles asked as I left Octo-Cat behind and headed toward the kitchen.

"Stay here and keep watch," I instructed. "I'll be right back."

After a minute or so rummaging through the junk drawer in the kitchen, I found what I needed and returned to the guys. "Last chance," I warned the cat.

"Still no. No, no, no, no, no," came my cat's reply.

That was my cue to activate the laser pointer and trace a small shaky pattern along the floor. Sure enough, Octo-Cat emerged from his safe haven to pounce at the captivating red dot. For whatever reason, it was the one thing he could never resist.

"Haha, gotcha." Charles grabbed Octo-Cat tight and held him against his chest.

Together, we headed back toward the grand staircase, ready to deliver our hissing cargo.

"I hate you," my cat told me for what must have been the hundredth time that day. And as much as I didn't like hearing that, I shook his words off.

He'd been mad at me before and he'd be mad at me again, but if we didn't help these kittens now, they may not get another chance.

7

We returned to the cat bedroom with a very unhappy Octo-Cat in tow.

The kittens, on the other hand, were ecstatic to see him again. Their once-anguished cries immediately turned to purring as they crowded around Octo-Cat and pressed their bodies to him.

"There's a reason I never had kids, you know," the poor guy wheezed, almost making me feel bad for him. Almost.

He extricated himself from the litter and went to wait by the door. "I like to be appreciated, but this is way too much for anyone."

Could have fooled me on that one. Until now, Octo-Cat had never indicated that he could receive too much love or praise—as long as each was given on *his* terms.

"They love you," I said gently.

He kept his pointed gaze on the door. "They don't even know me. Now let me out."

I had to stop myself from answering, “That’s probably why they love you.” Octo-Cat only enjoyed snark when he was the one giving it.

“Can I try something?” Charles asked.

I motioned for him to go ahead.

“Think back to when you were a kitten,” he addressed Octo-Cat with a placating expression. Of course, he had no idea how his words were being received by the subject. “Wouldn’t you have liked to have a bigger, cooler cat to help show you the way?”

Octo-Cat snorted. “And this guy is considered smart by your kind? Oh, brother.”

Well, I could have told Charles that appealing to the tabby’s sense of compassion would be a no-go. We needed take a harder tack. “You’re not getting out of this room until we help these kittens.”

“Fine. Let’s help them back where they came from. To the porch!” He shifted on his paws but remained glued to the spot.

I raised one eyebrow. “Still not convinced?”

“Not in the slightest.” Octo-Cat kept his nose high in the air, refusing to look at either me or the kittens despite their continued efforts to claim his attention. They’d scrambled their way over and were now sitting in a straight line behind him, also staring at the door.

“I’m not backing down on this. But since you seem to need an extra bit of convincing, I’m going to send a text to Nan right now to see if she can help.” I pulled out my phone and began typing away.

He scoffed. “Oooh, I’m shaking in my fur.”

“What’s Nan going to do?” Charles wondered aloud.

I smirked as I hit send. “She and Paisley are going to stop by the store on their way home from booty boot camp. I’ve asked her to pick up some generic brand *dry* cat food.

My cat seethed with rage. He obviously wanted to take a swipe at me, but still remained rooted to the spot in front of the door. “You wouldn’t.”

“Oh, but I would.” I cackled like a witch. Although I hated having to resort to such measures, I also somewhat enjoyed giving my cat what was coming to him. “I’ve asked Nan to get store-brand crunchies for you and a new bowl for Paisley.”

“Why would Paisley need a new bowl?” He cocked his head to the side and thought about this. Understanding dawned a brief moment later. “NO!”

“Yes!” I insisted. “You’ll be eating those new generic dry crunchies from Paisley’s used dog bowl. And guess what else?”

He took a couple steps back and pressed himself against the wall. “Not my Evian.”

“That’s right. It’s about time you developed a taste for tap water,” I said with a shrug.

“You are an evil woman, Angela. A very evil woman.”

I simply smiled and gave him a couple minutes to process everything.

Finally, he turned toward the line of kittens and lay down with his forelegs folded beneath him. “So if I agree to help, you’ll agree to cancel any changes to my menu or dining service?”

“Correct. Plus the sooner we figure out what’s going on with the kittens, the sooner we can find new homes for them—also the sooner we can get them out of your hair."

"I do like the sound of that," he conceded as one kitten yanked on his tail and another climbed onto his back. "But you should still know that I'm helping out of duress."

"Noted. Now let's get to work. I need your help talking to them."

He sighed, then yawned, then flopped onto his side.

The kittens pushed themselves against his belly and purred.

That was too much for Octo-Cat. He jumped back onto his feet and shouted, "Stop that! I am not your mama."

"Daddy," the kittens mewled merrily.

"I'm not that, either. I don't even know who you are. Maybe you can start by telling me that."

"Hungry," one of the other kittens said without properly pronouncing the *R,* so it came out more like *hungee.*

Octo-Cat looked to me. "Did you get that?"

I nodded, then translated for Charles, "They're hungry."

He pulled out his phone and began to browse the web in response.

"How old do you think they are?" I asked Octo-Cat.

"It's hard to say. A couple months, maybe."

Charles set his phone on top of the closed aquarium and lifted a kitten in one hand, then handed her to me. "That's about a pound, right?"

I nodded, unsure of it myself.

"Then we should be okay trying some soft cat food."

"Should I get some of Octo-Cat's?" I offered. It's not like we had anything else in the house that could work.

"Don't you dare!" he growled, startling the kittens.

"We need a special kind for kittens," Charles explained. "Could you text Nan back and ask her to get some from the store?"

"I could, but I didn't actually text her. That was a bluff."

Octo-Cat glowered at me, clearly not pleased with anything about our current situation.

"I'll head out then, if that's okay," Charles offered. "I'll be back as fast as I can." He placed a kiss on my forehead, then carefully let himself out of the room so that none of the felines could exit after him.

"Can I go now?" my cat asked me as the kittens continued to lick, nip, and bat at him.

"Sorry. I still need your help. Do you think the kittens will be willing to talk once they've been fed?"

"Maybe," he answered with an exhausted sigh. "But little ones this age don't know very many words. Much more advanced than humans at this age, but still with nowhere near the intellect of a full-grown cat."

This was turning out to be quite the challenge. "Then what do we do?"

"I say we revisit the raccoon's idea to—"

"Don't finish that sentence if you know what's good for you."

"You're no fun," he groaned. "If you want to figure out what happened to them, you're going to have to mount an investigation, AKA you're going to have to do your job for a change."

Ouch.

But also… *touché.*

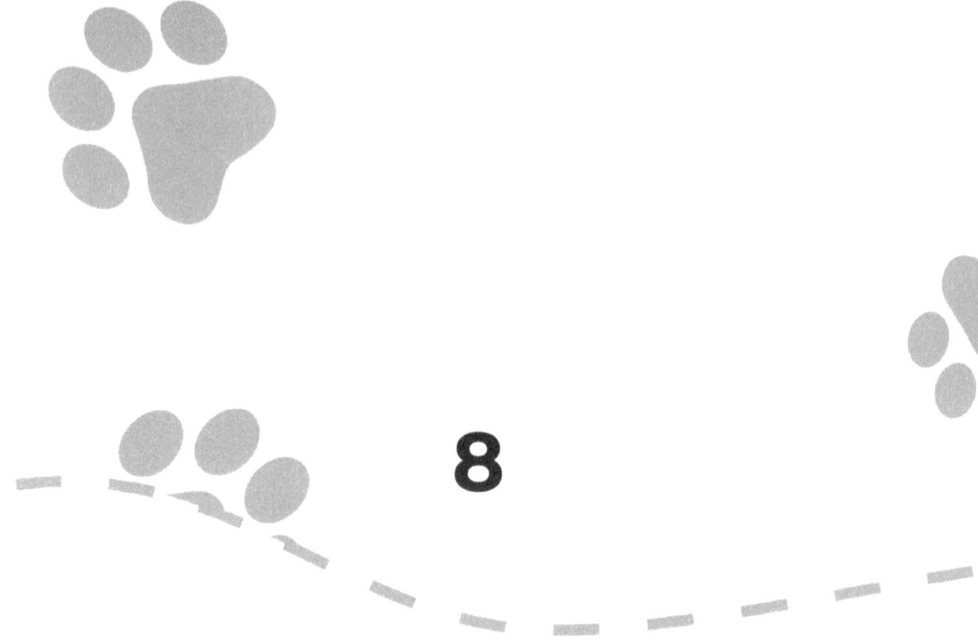

8

After Octo-Cat assured me he'd keep an eye on the little ones, I went to survey the scene of their abandonment. Other than a few bloody pawprints, the porch looked normal enough.

A faint pair of boot prints could just be made out under the fresh snowfall. I put my foot into one as a gauge for size. It was larger, but only just. Nothing about the style of the print gave away the wearer's gender, and I could find no other clues nearby.

Any tire tracks that may have been left behind had already mixed in with the ones Nan made when leaving for her fitness class. For all I knew the mysterious doorstep-dropper could have been on foot.

"I thought I smelled your unique aroma wafting through my treehouse." Pringle climbed up the porch railing and hopped down to stand beside me. I was pleased to see he'd left Carla at home. I was also quite offended by what he'd just said to me.

"How dare you say I stink!"

"I said you smelled," he corrected, wagging a finger at me. "Not *bad,* exactly. Not good, either, though."

I took a deep breath and forced myself to focus. If Pringle insisted on bothering me, maybe he could offer some assistance while he was here. "Did you see who brought the kittens?"

"Nope. I heard the car driving away but didn't get here in enough time to see anything."

Okay. So they were delivered by vehicle, which meant that someone had intentionally chosen my house for this very special delivery.

I could unpack that later. Right now I needed to use Pringle while I had him. "Usually you're so fast. How did you miss this?"

He sank to all fours and sighed. "I had to wait for a good place to pause my show."

"Survivor?"

"You know it. I'm on season twenty-seven, and it is definitely the most dramatic one yet."

Didn't he know they said that every season about every single reality show? Well, at least this addiction of his kept him from creating havoc for me 24/7.

"*Uh-huh.* Are you least learning valuable survival skills from all this binge-watching?"

He blew a raspberry. "Please. I watch it simply because it's so bad. I could teach these humans a thing or two or two hundred about wilderness survival. By the way, I sent in an application for next season, using your name and video."

It was already bad enough he snuck into my texts and social media. Now there was a video? Wait… what? "What video?" I boomed.

"Why, the one I took through your window when you weren't paying attention, of course." His answer came out flippantly, as if he saw nothing wrong with his actions at all. That made it worse, because it meant that things like this would happen again… and again.

And again.

I clenched my fists tight at my side but forced myself to keep calm. Recording private videos of me was definitely not okay. If he were a human, I would have called the police to come and get him.

Unfortunately, I still needed Pringle's help with the kittens. After that, I could rain down all kinds of punishment on him.

"Since you like spying and finding out secrets," I managed at last, still unable to look the raccoon in the eye, "maybe you can figure out where the kittens came from?"

"Where they came from?" he asked in that grating nasal voice of his, although perhaps I was coloring the situation red with the rage of his recent revelation. "Why does it matter?"

I balked. How could he not understand? "Because didn't you see all that blood?"

He shrugged off my concern. "So what? Blood happens. It's a fact of life."

"Not for humans, it doesn't. Blood usually means something has gone seriously wrong." How could he know so much about humans, yet still know so little? A lot of good all his reality TV viewing and covert spy operations were doing him.

"Yes, but you found *kittens,* didn't you? *Not humans,* so thus not a big deal."

"Still, it would really help put my mind at ease. Can you just... I don't know... follow their scent or something?"

"Ex-squeeze me? Follow their scent? What do you think I am? Some kind of dog?"

I stared at him with my mouth open for a moment before answering.

Over the last year or so, I'd found there were two effective ways to deal with Pringle when I needed him to do something. The first was to give him something he wanted—treehouses, an adventure, a Nerf gun named Carla. The second, although harder to pull off, was much easier on the wallet. It was time to pull out this strategy and hope it did the trick.

It was time to employ reverse psychology.

"Aren't raccoons part of the dog family?" I knew that they weren't, but that was beside the point.

"Yeah, maybe the disgruntled cousin. Either way, we're not having Thanksgiving dinner together. Capiche?"

I frowned, all part of the act. "So you're saying raccoons can't smell as well as dogs? That's okay. I understand. Paisley will be home soon, so I can just—"

"Wash your mouth out with soap right now! Raccoons are superior to dogs in every single way. I could sniff out the culprit if I wanted to."

"Yeah, but Paisley has a lot of experience. I bet she could trace the scent without even having to lower her nose to the ground."

The raccoon placed a hand on each hip. "I don't need experience to be the best. I was born that way. Now, you get out of my way!"

Satisfaction wrapped around me like a warm blanket as I watched Pringle scurry down the driveaway and out of sight. I hoped he'd be able to trace the source of the kittens, but even if he couldn't, at least he was out of the way for the next couple hours.

Meanwhile I had one more piece of evidence to process before calling in some outside help, and it was waiting for me in the upstairs bathroom.

To the box!

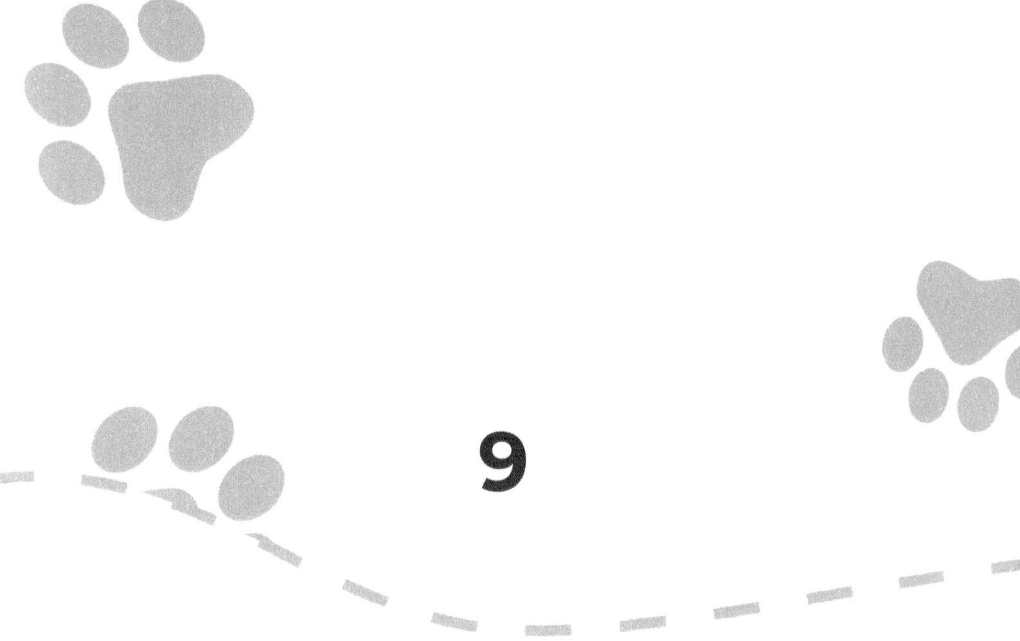

9

The box was not in good shape. Not only had it been soiled with bloody pawprints, but it had also been badly shredded around the top edges and the inside. Whoever had packed the kittens inside had decided to fold the top flaps inward rather than letting them hang down over the outside.

I pulled each of the flaps out to take a closer look. Sure enough, beneath all the stains and scratches, I spied a white shipping label. Would this give me the address of the person who'd dropped off the litter?

I grabbed a container of bleach wipes from under the bathroom sink and began to carefully dab at the label. By the time I was done, I had a partial address:

1 8 ir S

Gle le, E

Well, that was helpful.

I could tell that the second line should read Glendale, Maine, but the first was so scratched up I found it impossible to read more than two numbers and three letters. None of which helped my tired brain.

Maybe Charles or Nan would have some idea. I'd be sure to ask them when they returned home.

For now, I was all out of clues—and Octo-Cat was probably all out of patience. I took a snapshot of the address label for safekeeping and then returned to the cat room.

I'd left the cats alone for fifteen minutes at most, but the scene that greeted me upon my return felt lightyears apart from the one I'd left behind.

Octo-Cat had lined up the kittens in a straight row right in front of the fish tank. He now walked back and forth, holding his tail high and erect as he spoke. "To be a cat, you have to be strong, brave, and —above all—well-groomed. Do you understand me?"

"Daddy! Yes, Daddy!" the kittens shouted in unison. Their high-pitched baby voices made this scene even more absurd than the fact they were cats.

Octo-Cat did an about-face, unable to hide the smug grin on his face even as he caught sight of me.

"What are you doing?" I asked cautiously, curious but also not wanting an earful.

"Training up the new recruits," he barked—or at least made a canine-like noise, one I'd never heard him utter before.

"Daddy! Yes, Daddy!" the kittens responded in kind.

While I was glad he'd changed his stance on spending time with the youngsters, I was also now very worried. "Training them to do what exactly?"

"To be cats, of course. It's a very important and very demanding job." My cat grinned a jokeresque grin, which would have frightened me were it not so comical.

I choked down a laugh. "I'm sure it is. How much do they even understand?"

"While it's true their vocabulary is limited, it's never too early to begin training. Also I'm more than happy to lead by example. Watch and learn." He turned back to his recruits and plopped his rear down before them, then lifted one paw to his forehead in salute and waited for the kittens to respond in kind.

"Are you ready for your next lesson?" he shouted.

"Daddy! Yes, Daddy!" they shouted.

Well, it seemed Nan and Paisley weren't the only ones to go to boot camp today. There was entirely too much shouting going on.

"I call this one operative 037. Observe." Octo-Cat came flying in my direction, suddenly pulling to a stop just before smashing head-first into my legs.

I winced, expecting some kind of attack, but all he did was rub his head lovingly against me. A loud purr rumbled in his throat as he glanced back toward the line of kittens.

Aww, this was nice. He was teaching the babies how to be little love balls. I didn't know he had it in him.

"Now you give it a try, cadets!" he shouted again, jarring my nerves.

The kittens trotted over and rubbed their heads and bodies against my feet and ankles, just as their instructor had done.

"Well done. Well done, indeed." Octo-Cat took a brief moment to dote on them, then shifted back into business mode. "From here we'll move straight into operative 038."

Before I could ask what was next, Octo-Cat sank his front claws into my leg and climbed from the floor to my shoulder, using me as his ladder.

"Ahhhh!" I cried, but it did nothing to stop all five kittens from following suit. "I don't like this!"

Octo-Cat ignored me as he jumped down onto the floor. "All right. Now disengage."

"Daddy! Yes, Daddy!" One brave kitten leaped to the ground, but the others went back the way they'd come—down my poor, pained body.

"Why would you teach them that?" I moaned as I pushed myself flat against the closed door.

Octo-Cat studied his paw rather than looking at me. "We cats have to use any resources at our disposal."

Ouch. Way to add insult to injury. "Is that all I am to you? *A resource?"*

"It's not *all* you are, but it is part of it. Trust me, you'll be glad I've trained them up. Just wait and see."

"They aren't staying," I muttered as several pinpoints on my body pulsed with pain. Now I was even more determined to see the kittens safely off than Octo-Cat had been earlier that afternoon.

Had he planned it this way? The evil genius.

"Listen," I continued, still pressed firmly against the door and eyeing my cat warily. "You've done a great job looking after them. Why don't you take a little break?"

He scoffed and took a step closer. "And leave their education to you? I think not."

Crud. Well, it was worth a try. If he insisted on turning the kittens into some kind of deranged domestic soldiers, I could at least make sure I wasn't around for the next operative. The kittens had already lined back up and were awaiting further instruction when I crept out of the room and headed back downstairs.

I still couldn't believe how quickly Octo-Cat had changed his tune about our litter of foundlings. We needed to find them homes and fast, before my ever-scheming cat used them to execute total world domination.

What? I wouldn't put it past him.

Both Charles and Pringle would be back soon. Until then I would wait safely on the porch and scroll through my social media feeds to pass time.

It didn't take long for someone to return, and that someone was Nan. She and Paisley looked wicked worn out, which was rare for them.

"How was class?" I asked as the two of them crept slowly up the porch steps.

"Painful." Nan winced with each movement. "Now what are you doing out here?"

"Hiding from the cats," I explained, although it embarrassed me somewhat.

My grandmother paused and shot me a worried look. "*Cats?* As in plural? Am I going senile already? I could have sworn we just had the one."

I nodded. "It's a long story. Come upstairs, and I'll show you."

Nan shook her head slowly. "I'm not sure I'm ready to tackle the big stairs just yet. It may take me a few hours. At least until these pulsing fireworks stop going off in my quads."

"She did, like, a million squats," the equally exhausted Chihuahua informed me. "But not once did she go potty."

I chuckled at this. "Did you do squats, too?"

Paisley wagged her tail at my attention. "Nope. There was a big dog there, and we wrestled while the humans busted their booties."

"Did you at least win?"

"Oh, yeah," she barked happily. "That will teach that silly old Great Dane to underestimate me!"

Ha! Our sweet Paisley, always full of surprises.

10

Once inside, I helped Nan get settled on the couch. And with every gasp and groan that escaped her mouth, I thanked my lucky stars there hadn't been an open spot for me in her new fitness class.

"You wait here," I told her after fluffing a pillow behind her back. "I'll go get the kittens."

Paisley followed me up the stairs, whining slightly as she went.

I turned to look back at her, but she just kept climbing like a champ. "I thought you were tired, too?"

Her ears perked up. "I am, but I still want to go with you, Mommy. I missed you while Nan and I were away."

Why couldn't my cat ever be this nice?

Even though she was nice and even though she was tired, I still couldn't take any chances when it came to the kittens. I scooped Paisley into my arms and entered Octo-Cat's bedroom.

Paisley let out a sharp bark and squirmed furiously in my arms. "Oh, my! Puppies! Cat puppies!"

"Don't be so insulting." Octo-Cat sniffed derisively. "These are kittens. Not *cat puppies,* you simpleton."

Paisley didn't so much as whimper at the insult. She was far too excited to care. "Please set me down, Mommy!" she begged. "I want to go say hi!"

The moment I did, she bounded over to the line of kitty cadets and squealed happily as she licked the insides of each young feline's ears.

They giggled and fell to their sides.

"Can't you see I'm leading a class here?" Octo-Cat seethed, his tail twitching aggressively.

"Yes. And your class is about to take a field trip. Nan wants to meet them."

"Then have her come up here? It's best we don't disturb their environment. Otherwise it could undo all their training."

If only. With any luck they'd forget operative 038 forever.

I sucked air through my teeth and shook my head. "No can do, Mr. Kitty. Nan is stuck downstairs, so we're taking the babies to her."

"How many times have I told you not to call me that?" Octo-Cat sighed heavily as the two of us watched Paisley cuddle and lick the mass of kittens. It's official; they're ruined now.

"Mommy?" one of the kitties asked the others as she cuddled up to the doting Chihuahua.

"Mommy!" the rest cheered in response.

Octo-Cat gasped.

I chuckled.

Paisley trotted over to us with the kittens ambling behind. "Mommy," she addressed me, "the cat puppies are calling for you."

I bent down to scratch between her ears. "Actually, I think they're calling for *you*. They've decided you're their mommy."

"Me? A mommy? Oh my love!" Paisley's dark eyes welled with tears. In just a few more weeks, the kittens would probably all be larger than Paisley, but she would now forever be their mother—I had no doubt about that.

"Mommy," the kittens cooed, and then turning to Octo-Cat, "Daddy!"

"*Octavius,*" Paisley warbled, still crying tears of joy. "We have puppies together. Does that mean we should get married?"

"I'm ready to go now, Angela," Octo-Cat informed me, turning to face the door, his voice devoid of any emotion—the poor guy had clearly had his fill of insanity for one day.

"Paisley, can you watch them for a minute? I'll be right back."

"Yes, Mommy." She returned to her litter and started a game of chase. She'd gone from zero to sixty mighty fast upon meeting the kitties.

"Hey, now you're Grand-Mommy!" she pointed out just as I was shutting the door behind Octo-Cat.

Oh, great. I wasn't ready to marry and have my own kids, but somehow I'd become a grandma anyway. *Wonderful.*

Brushing that thought aside, I went to retrieve the cat carrier from storage. I needed some way to get the kittens downstairs, and it just didn't feel right putting them back in that bloody, battered box.

Paisley spoke calmly to her litter as I loaded them into the carrier, making the task a piece of cake.

Once downstairs, I set the carrier beside Nan on the couch and opened the wire mesh door.

"This is Nan. She's *Great Nan* to you," the proud doggie mother informed them. "Be careful not to fall or jump off the couch. We Chihuahuas are a fragile breed."

Just as I was wondering whether Paisley understood that these were not her actual babies, Nan caught sight of the kittens for the first time and gasped with delight.

"Where did you come from?" she squealed in the high-pitched voice she normally reserved only for Paisley.

I caught Nan up on the particulars while she petted and cuddled the babies.

"How horrible! What kind of monster would abandon such sweet babies?" she asked once I'd finished.

I shook my head, still at a loss. "I'm less concerned with why someone would leave them here than with where the blood came from."

"Blood?" Paisley barked. "Are my cat puppies hurt? We need to go to the vet right now!"

Not only was the little dog proving to be quite the helicopter parent, but she also had a really good idea. I would have chastised myself for not thinking of it earlier, but we'd only found them very recently and have been very busy trying to figure out where they came from, get them food, and make sure they stayed out of trouble.

"We should go to the vet," I agreed with a nod. "They don't seem hurt, but it's better to know for sure."

"Let's go now. I need to make sure my puppies are okay!" Paisley whined and gave out another round of licks. For whatever reason, the Chihuahua seemed to think that inner-ear kisses could solve anything. If I wasn't careful, she'd sneak up on me and push her warm, wet tongue into my ear, too.

Luckily, Charles pulled into the drive just then, causing Paisley to temporarily forget her panic and instead start barking in excitement.

The kittens mewled their best attempts at a bark, and I broke apart in laughter. It seemed Paisley wasn't the only one confused about what species our litter belonged to.

"I'm back," Charles sang as he passed through the foyer and joined us in the living room. "Did you miss me?"

I smiled in relief. "You have no idea how much." He really didn't. Even though less than an hour had passed, a record-breaking amount of activity had occurred.

Charles set the bag from the pet store on the table and pulled out a pair of stainless-steel bowls. Next he took out the canned cat food and pulled the tabs to open them.

The kittens definitely recognized the smell as being something to eat.

"Hungry!" they cried in their cutesy baby voices, stumbling toward the edge of the couch.

Paisley managed to catch one by the scruff of its neck before it toppled over the edge. "Careful, my darling dear."

Charles, Nan, and I placed the kittens on the floor with the two bowls of food and watched them gobble it down.

"Should I open up another can?" he asked me with a questioning glance.

"Better not. They still have tiny bellies, and I don't want them to get sick. Especially since we're going to the vet after this."

"I'm not going!" Octo-Cat called from the other room.

"You're not invited!" I shouted back. Now that Paisley had graciously taken responsibility for the litter, we didn't need drill instructor Octavius's help any longer.

Let's just hope the poor doggie foster mom didn't become too attached. I'd hate to see her heart break when we sent them off to their forever homes.

11

And off to the veterinarian's clinic we went.

Charles called ahead to let them know we were stopping by without an appointment, but that the adorable kittens would surely make it worth their while.

The three of us must have made quite the spectacle as we marched into the animal hospital, holding the mewing crate high as their Chihuahua mother ran at our sides yapping a constant stream of encouragement.

"Don't worry, my cat puppies. You're not sick. The doctor's just going to make sure you stay that way. It's all part of growing up. You will be brave for Mommy, won't you?"

"Mommy! Yes, Mommy!" Well, it seemed not all of Octo-Cat's training had been forgotten.

"Let me guess," the receptionist said as she rose to her feet and peeked into the cat carrier. "You must be the Russo party."

"That's us," I confirmed with a nod, even though I was the only one whose last name was actually Russo.

"Come with me. Dr. Lowe is just finishing up with another patient. She should be with you shortly." She smiled and motioned for us to follow, swinging her hips the whole way.

We obediently followed her into exam room two.

"Good luck!" the receptionist called, closing us inside.

Charles remained standing so that Nan and I could take the two chairs. "Did you see that her scrubs had pawprints and bones on them? That is so neat. I wish lawyers got more interesting clothing options, but everyone in the courtroom would look at me like I was crazy if I came wearing a suit with a gavel or the scales of justice patterned all over it."

"You should do it anyway," Nan offered with a wink. After all, she was the queen of outrageous costumes. She'd wear just about anything, just so long as it was the right shade of pink.

I laughed uncomfortably. At least Christmas had already passed, or else Nan might be gifting my boyfriend with a new hot pink lawyer suit. *Cringe.*

As promised, a few minutes later, Dr. Britt Lowe entered the room, clipboard in hand. She was the youngest of all the veterinarians in the office and the one who most regularly saw our pets. She widened her eyes and puckered her lips as she took us in. "I hear you have kittens."

"Not intentionally," I was quick to clarify, though I'm not sure why. "They were left on our doorstep this morning."

She glanced down at her chart. “I have a note here that they were covered in blood?”

“Well, not covered,” Charles explained. “But they had it on their paws and a little in their fur as well. We had to give them a bath.”

“That must have been fun,” the vet said with a chuckle. “Let’s take them out and have a look. One at a time, if you don’t mind.”

“Okay, children,” Paisley barked. “Be good for the doctor. No biting or growling.”

Dr. Lowe bent down and gave the dog a pat. “Oh, hello. I didn’t see you there, Paisley.”

“She’s become quite attached to the litter,” I said with a frown. Every single minute that passed before rehoming the kittens would only add to Paisley’s eventual heartbreak.

“I bet your cat is none too pleased,” Dr. Lowe said with another chuckle.

“You would definitely win that bet.” Yes, even among other cat lovers, my cat had a reputation for being a diva. He couldn’t help that he was raised in excessive luxury for his first several years, but still.

Charles handed our vet the first of the kittens.

“Hello, there, you cutie pie,” she cooed. “This is why I love my job.”

A huge grin stretched across her face as she examined the patient. “Girl. About seven or eight weeks. Most likely a Maine Coon or Maine Coon mix.”

She placed a stethoscope against the kitten’s tiny chest. “Heartbeat is good, and from what I can see, she has no injuries.”

"So the blood wasn't hers?" Nan asked, her hands clasped against her chest.

"No, but I still have four others to examine."

I took the first kitten back, and Charles handed Dr. Lowe the second. This one was also deemed fit as a fiddle.

One by one, the doctor declared each baby—three girls and two boys—healthy and without injury.

"So then where did the blood come from?" Charles wanted to know.

Dr. Lowe shook her head. "Sorry, but I couldn't say."

"Are there many litters abandoned on people's doorsteps around Glendale?" I pressed. I was glad the kittens passed their health check but felt uncomfortable leaving without any answers as to their origin.

"This would be the first I've come across it," she responded, which didn't mean much given how short a time she'd been working here. "Do you think it was a random drive-by or that someone meant to leave these kittens with you specifically?"

Charles answered for me. "That's what we're trying to figure out."

"And not having much luck, unfortunately," I added with a heavy sigh.

"Well, the important thing is that they're safe now that they're with you. If you need help finding them homes, we could put a flyer up in the office," she suggested while jotting a note on her chart. "No charge for today's visit. Good luck!"

Having been dismissed, we settled the kittens back in their carrier. I was still so confused by their sudden appearance. Could someone be sending me a threat? Is that why they'd been covered in blood? It may seem farfetched, but I'd had my life threatened before—so why not now? Why not with this?

"What should we do now?" I asked Charles.

But it was Nan who answered. "For whatever reason, these kittens found us. I say we provide them with a loving home and stop worrying about the rest."

"Yes! Yes! Let's do that!" Paisley yipped with excitement, then ran fast, tight circles around the office. Zoomies.

"Nan," I growled. "These are things we should discuss *in private.*"

She crimsoned under the scrutiny of my gaze but didn't apologize for making the suggestion.

"Do you want to keep one?" I asked Charles.

"Jacques and Jillianne would never forgive me if I brought another animal home. You know that." He was right. His two hairless cats weren't exactly hospitable. They also spoke only in rhymes and riddles, which would, no doubt, drive any kitty we sent to live with them batty.

Thankfully, Nan and Paisley both remained quiet as we made our way out of the clinic. Was I a bad person for not wanting to add an army of cats into my daily life? I mean, who knew what kind of damage Octo-Cat could do to their psyches with the opportunity to raise them up from this young age? My side still hurt from where Octavius and all five kitties had climbed up my leg and torso. No, I definitely couldn't handle this kind of havoc every single day.

Another thought popped into my mind and scared the living daylights out of me. *What if the kittens wanted to help with the P.I.*

business? Dealing with one cat already took a great deal of both patience and delicacy, but six?

No, thank you. I'd sooner work as an underappreciated paralegal for the rest of my days.

"We're not keeping them," I sputtered a couple minutes later, my mind more than made up. "But we will make sure each of them finds the perfect home."

Nan crossed her arms over her chest and pouted while Charles nodded his agreement. "We'll find them great homes," he said, lacing his fingers through mine.

I looked to Paisley who lay dejectedly on my lap. "I guess all puppies have to grow up some day. I just didn't know it would come this soon for mine."

I had to bite my tongue to keep from reminding her that she'd only known her "puppies" for less than an hour.

The clock was ticking fast. Now I needed to protect both the kittens and their dog mom. Nothing else mattered until we could find a way to give everyone a happy ending.

12

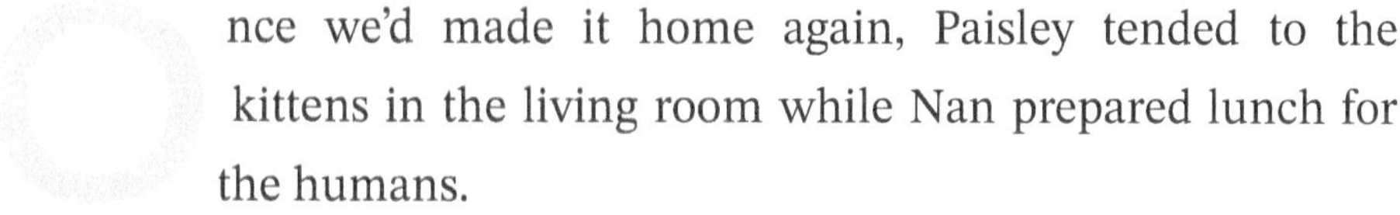

Once we'd made it home again, Paisley tended to the kittens in the living room while Nan prepared lunch for the humans.

Charles and I ventured up to my work library to work on posting an ad for the kittens online and to design a flyer for the vet's office. Despite Pringle's earnest advice, we were offering them free to a good home—provided the would-be owner could provide a great veterinarian reference.

"I'm sorry our big day together got ruined," I told Charles while navigating the same free graphics program I'd used to create a simplistic logo for the Pet Whisperer P.I. website.

Charles moved behind me and rubbed my shoulders while I worked and we chatted. "What are you talking about? This is great. A real memory in the making."

"I guess it's better than watching TV," I conceded, although I wouldn't pass up the opportunity to cuddle and relax with my dashing other half. In truth, we never took it easy, such was the nature of our crazy lives.

A rapping at the big bay window broke my concentration. Our not-so-friendly neighborhood raccoon stood on the ledge, waiting to be let in. This happened somewhat frequently these days and was why I no longer kept a screen in the window.

"What's up?" I asked after cranking it open.

"What's… up?" Pringle asked, gasping for breath between the two words. "That all… you got? After I… tracked those… annoying little… furballs for… you?"

Oh, yes! In all the fuss, I'd almost forgotten that I'd sent him on a fact-finding/ raccoon-distracting mission. "Welcome back. What have you got for me?"

He hopped down and pressed a hand against the wall for support. "First refreshments… Then I'll spill."

"Be right back," I told Charles.

"What?" he asked, taken aback. "Don't leave me alone with that thing!"

"With this *thing?*" Pringle raged. "With this thing? I'll have you know that I'm the most pedigreed—" Suddenly his words gave way and he moved one furry hand to clutch his chest. "I mean… Please… Need food."

"Nice try. I don't like lying," I scolded, returning to my desk chair and spinning in it to face him. "I'll feed you, but you'll talk first."

Knowing the act was up, Pringle straightened his posture and cracked his neck to either side. "Fine."

I waited for him to comb at his fur with his fingers as he gathered his bearings.

Finally he began. “I ran for miles but got nowhere with the case.”

“Did you even try?” I asked with indignation. He’d been gone for so long, I’d let myself hope he’d found something. *No dice.*

“You insult me,” he hissed and bared his teeth. “Of course I tried. I asked every animal I came across, but nobody knew nothing about no orphaned kittens.”

“When this is all over and done, we need to work on your grammar,” I muttered without thinking.

Pringle dropped to all fours and raised his back, making his body appear much larger than its usual size. “Really? I spend all morning doing your dirty work, and this is the thanks I get? I’m leaving.”

“Wait. I’m sorry. Let me get you some food first. Fancy Feast?” Even though Octo-Cat had switched to a new brand of cat food called Delectable Delights to support his girlfriend’s modeling career, I still had to buy Fancy Feast to satisfy the raccoon’s frequent cravings.

“Yes, and some steak, please,” he added while licking his chops.

“How much is *some* steak?”

“How much you got?”

“I’ll get it,” Charles offered. As he passed me, he leaned close and whispered, “That way you can’t be held accountable if I get it wrong.”

“I heard that,” Pringle complained to me once Charles had left the room. “And now you owe me double. Quality or quantity, it’s your choice, but I wouldn’t turn my nose up at some prime rib served medium rare. You never buy me the good cuts of steak.”

I never bought the good cuts for myself, either. And weren't raccoons supposed to feed themselves?

Nope. I wasn't falling for his sob story.

"Sorry. I don't think so. Not after you've invaded my privacy left and right."

"I don't get humans' obsession with *privacy.*" He made air quotes around this last word. "It's not like you give any to us."

I refused to let him get away with that one. "What are you talking about? I never bother you. It's always the other way around."

"So now I'm a bother?"

"That's not what I meant. It's just—"

"Just what?" He widened his eyes in challenge while awaiting my response.

Reasoning with him never got me very far, and I was too busy with everything else to bother trying now. "Forget it," I said with a deep sigh.

"Yeah, like I said, you owe me, but don't worry. I already know exactly what I want, and it won't cost you much at all."

Oh, joy. Maybe if I didn't respond, he would keep quiet until Charles returned with the raccoon's ill-gotten gains.

"I love my Carla, but I think I'm ready to handle two of her kind," he explained while he mimed taking aim at me with the gun. Thank goodness I knew Carla was what he had named his Nerf weapon, otherwise I'd be seriously offended for all womankind—human, raccoon, or otherwise.

"I'm not getting you another Nerf gun," I said firmly. If I showed any signs of weakness, he'd pounce.

"It's okay if it's not name brand. I ain't picky."

"Great."

"You can deliver it to my left treehouse by sundown." And didn't that say it all? The fact he had to specify *which* treehouse he wanted to receive the hypothetical delivery.

"I'm not doing anything until we figure out the deal with these kittens," I said, more than fed up with his demands. "And if you'll recall, you didn't actually even help."

"Hey, that's not my fault! I tried!" he squeaked. Finally he'd begun to lose his cool, which meant he was also losing his leverage.

"Okay, who's ready for some lunch?" Charles sang as he rejoined us. He'd brought up two plates with grilled gruyere and tomato sandwiches and a grocery bag stuffed full of assorted junk food.

"Nan wanted us to eat up here so she could have some alone time with the kittens," he said in response to my unspoken question.

"And this, my man, is for you." He handed the shopping bag to Pringle, who eagerly accepted it.

"Door, please," he told me without so much as a backward glance my way.

I had no desire to keep him around, so I opened the door and watched him clamber down the stairs. The pet door was still closed, so I had to follow him down to assist.

"I'm starved," I said upon returning.

Charles settled into the window seat and waited for me to join him.

I accepted the plate he handed to me and took a giant bite of my sandwich after mumbling a quick thanks—so warm, so gooey. I shrugged and took another bite.

We scarfed down our sandwiches in much the same way the kittens had inhaled their meal earlier.

"Any idea why Nan would need some alone time with the kittens?" Charles wiped at his mouth with a napkin. "You don't think she's going to pull something to try to make you keep them? Do you?"

I jumped to my feet and cried, "Well, I didn't before! C'mon, we've got to hurry!"

I tugged Charles's hand, pulling him into the hall and down the stairs. If we were fast, we could still stop her from whatever it was she planned to pull.

Oh, that nan of mine!

13

Sure enough, the only thing we found downstairs was a smug Octo-Cat sitting on the coffee table and quite obviously waiting for us.

"Missing something?" he asked with a cruel chuckle as a Cheshire grin swept across his face.

Well, that confirmed it. Nan had hit the road and taken the kittens along with her. "How long has she been gone?" I asked the still gloating cat.

"She left the very minute UpChuck headed upstairs with the food." He yawned and stretched before settling back into a seated position. "By the way, nobody offered to feed me."

Oh, boy. I could already tell this would take a while. Nan could make it all the way to Florida in the time it took me to convince my cat to help.

"You never have lunch," I reminded him gently, all the while praying my instincts about this encounter were dead wrong.

"You only eat in the morning and night," I added pathetically.

"It's still nice to be asked. Especially since I know you promised the raccoon steak."

"I definitely never promised anything."

"Well, it seems we've reached an impasse then." He turned around so that his back was to me. I could just imagine him laughing at my gullibility, but I didn't have any time to spare if I wanted to protect Paisley's feelings and discover where Nan had taken the kittens—and I definitely wanted to do both of those things ASAP.

"Do you know where she went?" I asked in a shaky whisper.

He flicked his tail twice and then slowly shifted back my way. "Maybe," came his curt reply.

Maybe wasn't yes, but it also wasn't no. I'd have to play his little game, whether I liked it or not. I couldn't hold back my sigh as I asked, "All right, what's it going to take? A can of food?"

"*Pfffshaw.* It'll take a lot more than that." Octo-Cat's eyes glowed as he licked at his chops. "Like steak, for starters."

"Do you actually like steak? You've never even tried it." Although I'd only just eaten, now my stomach rumbled, too.

"No, I haven't. And honestly that's the whole problem. You just don't consider me and my needs as much as you should."

I held my breath to keep from screaming. My whole life revolved around my crabby tabby and his wants and needs.

He sniffed and turned his nose up at me. "I will require at least nine steaks, one for each of the lives I was born with."

I sighed and nodded along with his lengthy list of demands. The sooner we got this over with, the sooner he might actually help me.

"I will also need a lobster roll from Little Dog Diner."

He paused to take a breath, and I jumped in with another objection. "But Little Dog Diner is all the way over in Misty Harbor."

"I know where it is. I also know they make the best lobster rolls in all of the bay, so you're going."

I gritted my teeth and clenched my fists. "Fine. Anything else?"

"Yes. I saved the best for last." His smile laced a knot of dread into my heart. Heaven help me.

"You see," he continued, unaware of how anxious I'd become during our very one-sided conversation. "As much as I enjoy spending time with Pringle *on occasion,* he's been rather insufferable lately."

"Let me guess. Carla." This, we actually agreed on. Maybe we could join forces to teach that raccoon a lesson.

Octo-Cat made a clicking noise and waved a paw my way. "Bingo."

"So what? You want a Nerf gun, too?" I asked with a chuckle.

"Oh, Angela. Haven't you noticed that I don't have any opposable thumbs? Really, I thought you were more observant than that. I need a specialized weapon that doesn't discriminate against those of us without thumbs."

I sighed. Maybe we weren't on the same side, after all. "Such as?" I asked politely.

My cat's eyes locked on mine, trapping me within his gaze. "I was thinking a battle axe."

"Are you kidding me?" I sputtered in disbelief. "There's no way I'm getting you a battle axe. You'd chop my foot off the first time I forgot to feed you."

"Maybe that's a sign you shouldn't forget to feed me."

He let out a sinister laugh as phantom pain smarted in my ankle. There would definitely be no battle axe.

"I do my best. You know that. I'm not getting you a battle axe, though. So try again."

He cleared his throat and tried again. "A sword."

I shook my head.

"Mace."

"Like pepper spray?" I asked. "I guess that's not so bad. I can—"

"No, Angela. Not like pepper spray. Like a big spiky ball on the end of a chain."

"Remind me again why you need all this heavy-duty medieval weaponry?" I managed to choke out. This wasn't the first time I'd been afraid of my cat, but it was the worst. Talk about an unstable genius.

"To defend myself," he answered as if this all made perfect sense to him.

"Against foam darts?"

Octo-Cat smiled and nodded. "Precisely."

"I could get you a foam sword," I offered with a sad shrug. "Or maybe a toy lightsaber. That would be fun. Um, wouldn't it?"

He rose to his feet and paced the length of the coffee table. "Angela, really! Real problems require real solutions, not a cheap childproof stand-in."

Rather than pointing out that Pringle's weapon was also a toy, I remained quiet. It seemed every time I spoke, the rabbit hole I'd fallen down grew deeper and deeper.

The wheels in Octo-Cat's brain, however, continued to crank. He started and stopped several times before finally saying something that made sense. "You seem to be biased against medieval weapons. How about we turn to the martial arts instead?"

Yes, martial arts. He'd only have as much power as he held within his own paws. That wasn't so scary. It could actually work.

I nodded vigorously to show him how much I liked that idea. "I'm sure we could sneak you into a dojo so you can learn some self-defense moves."

"That's not what I meant, and I'm guessing you know that. I don't want to dirty my paws on that feral beast. I need a weapon to do it for me, so how about nunchucks?"

"Nunchucks?" I squeaked.

"Yes, I can hold one end in my mouth and swing the other to hit Pringle with," he explained matter-of-factly.

"Do you promise not to use them on me?"

He glanced toward Charles.

"Or Charles!" I added.

My cat shook his head as if his answer pained him. "Sadly, I can't promise that, but I can promise I'll cancel my plans to ransack your bedroom if you agree."

Wonderful, another bribe.

"Okay, fine. I'll get you nunchucks if it's so important to you. Now, tell me, what do you know about Nan's whereabouts?"

Octo-Cat gave me a Cheshire grin and hopped down from the coffee table. "I don't know where she went, but I do know how you can find her. If you'll just follow me please."

I waved for Charles to come with us, too.

"Why were you and your cat just discussing all those weapons?" he wanted to know.

"Trust me, it's not that unusual for us." This was sad because it was true.

"Talking animals are weird." Charles laughed, but I couldn't bring myself to—the image of my crazy cat swinging a battle axe was still too fresh in my mind.

14

Octo-Cat led us to the backyard where Pringle sat holed up in one of his treehouses watching *Survivor* with the volume turned up to its max.

“Pringle. I brought you a client!” Octo-Cat shouted from the base of the tree.

“We are not clients,” I hissed at the tabby. “I’m more like his landlord.”

A few moments later, the TV clicked off and Pringle stuck his masked face out the window. “Have they brought payment?” he asked, ignoring me and Charles entirely.

“No, but they’re good for it.” Octo-Cat nudged me forward with his paw.

“Excellent,” the raccoon chittered and climbed down with surprising speed to join us on the lawn. He put on a phony grin and reached forward to offer his hand. "Pringle Whisperer, P.I., here. How can I help you today?"

I declined to shake it and instead nodded toward Octo-Cat. "I already paid him to help. I'm not paying you, too."

"That was my finder's fee," the cat corrected. "Pringle Whisperer, P.I., requires his payments to be arranged separately."

I threw my hands up in the air. How did we ever get anything done around here? "Can we stop wasting time, already? And can't either of you ever do anything just to be nice for a change?"

Octo-Cat and Pringle laughed for a solid five minutes at that one.

"What's going on?" Charles asked me, leaning close so I could hear him over the two guffawing animals.

"He wants another bribe, or he won't help us."

"Oh, no problem. I'll take care of it." Charles took out his wallet and began thumbing through a stack of folded dollar bills. "How much does he need?"

I knew my boyfriend made good money as the senior partner for the region's busiest law firm, but it surprised me when he didn't even hesitate to offer a giant wad of cash to our dear raccoon racketeer.

Pringle, however, refused to accept his generous payment. "Sorry, bro. Human money's no good here."

"But you can use it to buy things," I pointed out.

He made a face. "That's too hard. I'd rather not have to worry about the math. Besides, I've never once found a human shop owner willing to sell me what I needed. That's speciesism, I tell you, and I'm not okay with it."

"Okay, what do you want then?" And why had my entire day

turned into agreeing to give everyone whatever they asked for? With the likes of Pringle and Octo-Cat around, this was a very dangerous proposition, indeed.

"Besides the steak you've already promised me and the new friend for Carla, I'll need—"

"I'm getting nine steaks," Octo-Cat stopped grooming his coat to brag.

"Cool, cool. Make it nine for me, too," Pringle confirmed.

"And a lobster roll," my cat betrayed me once more.

"Sure. I'll also take that." The raccoon rubbed his hands together in anticipation of all the tasty things coming his way.

"Stop helping!" I shouted at my cat.

Pringle chittered blissfully. "This is awesome. We should work together more often, my fine feline friend." He stuck out his hand, and Octo-Cat gave him a high paw.

It was official. My life was over. Dealing with the two of them separately was already hard enough. Them joining forces fell into nightmare territory.

"I'll also require a new plasma TV," Pringle added as if it were one last small negotiation and not a gigantic expense.

"I'm out of here!" I stomped away, resigning myself to never finding Nan, Paisley, or the kittens again. There was negotiation and then there was extortion. I would have no part of that.

Pringle scurried in front of me and threw his hands up. "No, wait! It doesn't have to be plasma, but I do need a television. I really do."

"You already have one." I crossed my arms and gave him the stink eye. I may have been a softie, but I was no fool. I'd already bought him his own TV not too long ago.

"What's he asking for?" Charles wanted to know.

"A TV," I spat, still reeling from the audacious request.

"Doesn't he already have one?"

See, even Charles knew.

The raccoon put his hands together and begged. "Please. I wouldn't ask if I didn't desperately need it." He was an incredible actor, but he couldn't summon tears on demand.

I wasn't buying it. "Why the desperation?"

He hung his head and sniffed. "Because my TV-less treehouse is jealous of my TV-full treehouse."

I rolled my eyes at that. "Sorry, no. Treehouses don't have feelings."

"Fine, fine, fine, fine, fine! I'd like to use my houses more equally but don't want to spend time away from my show while I do it."

"That means you *don't* need two treehouses, not that you *do* need two TVs," I explained just as a headache swarmed by brain.

Charles placed a gentle hand on my shoulder. "I know you're worried about the kittens. Let's just get to them, okay? I'll pick up a TV for him later this week."

Pringle raised his index finger in objection. "Actually, I need it—"

"Later this week," I interrupted with the best scowl I could muster. "Take it or leave it."

The raccoon's whole demeanor softened. "You drive a tough bargain, Angie Russo, but sold! Now how can I help?"

"I need to know where Nan went with Paisley and the kittens."

"I don't know where they went, but I can find out."

"How long will that take?"

"I'll do it right now. Wait there." He climbed back into his tree-house and returned with iPad in hand. That was another excessive luxury we'd given him. True, it was Octo-Cat's old iPad, but why did either of them need their own personal tablet?

Sticking his tongue out while he worked, Pringle tapped the iPad several times, cycling through a number of apps until he found the one he wanted. He turned it toward me, revealing a flashing yellow dot moving along a map. "There. She's on the highway. Good?"

It was good, but it was also suspicious. "How did you do that?"

"I've got high-tech trackers on all of you. If one of you goes somewhere, I can trace your phones to see where it is." He puffed with obvious pride. "I actually have you to thank for giving me the idea and for letting me use your credit card to purchase the licensing I needed."

Once again, my privacy had been unforgivably violated by this rascally raccoon. I didn't know he'd used my credit card for this. Had he used it for other things, too? I clearly needed to keep a better eye on my expenses. I also needed to report my card stolen and to invest in a small safe. I could keep my wallet and electronics locked inside every night to curtail Pringle's all too pervasive snooping.

Ugh. This was seriously getting out of hand.

15

We took a few minutes to set up a family plan on our devices. Once we had it in place, I was able to use Pringle's sneaky app to track Nan's location while Charles and I drove after her in pursuit.

"Stay here and call me on FaceTime if she comes back before we do," I instructed Octo-Cat, who agreed without too much pressure. Hmm. Maybe he felt guilty about driving up Pringle's payment by sharing what I'd agreed to give him—or maybe he just wanted to avoid the car trip.

Charles placed my phone into the clip on his dashboard and studied the map for a moment before starting up his engine. "She's got close to a half-hour lead on us, and she's still driving. "Wherever she went, it's pretty far."

I leaned closer to the dash to study the map. "She's almost made it to Pineville. That's all the way at the other end of the bay. Maybe she really is running away in a desperate ploy to keep the kittens."

We turned onto the main road and began the trek toward Pineville.

Charles took a pack of gum from the cupholder and offered me a piece before taking one for himself. "Why would she run away? I mean she has to know she'd eventually need to come back. Right?"

"To bribe me, maybe?" I sat back in my seat and watched the trees pass by my window.

My mean old boyfriend laughed at me. "Man, you're just letting everyone manipulate you today."

"Don't get used to it, and don't try anything," I warned in a growl.

He laughed again and turned on the car's radio. An upbeat pop song danced forth from the speakers, and we sang along in a horrible, no-talent duet. It gave us a nice break from all the kitten, cat, raccoon drama back home.

"Look!" I cried, just as we'd finished our third sing-along. "She's stopping!" I unclipped the phone and zoomed in on the map. "A Donut A Day?" I read the address label aloud. "Why would she drive so far just for some donuts?"

"Maybe A Donut A Day is to donuts as the Little Dog Diner is to lobster rolls. Worth the long drive."

My stomach growled at the thought of fresh cinnamon donuts straight from the oven. But no, this still didn't make sense even if it seemed delicious.

I returned the app to navigation mode and clipped it back into the holder. “She prefers to bake her own desserts, though, and she’s never once mentioned this place to me.”

“I’m sure it was just an oversight. Your nan always has a million things going on. It can be hard to keep track.”

“Are you saying she told me and I forgot?” I grumped. “Oh, look! She’s moving again!”

Nan’s dot carried on for a few miles, then stopped again about five minutes later. I zoomed in but couldn’t see any nearby businesses. It seemed Nan had chosen a residential area as her destination.

This time she stayed put until Charles and I were able to catch up.

Charles parked beside the curb behind Nan’s gleaming red Audi. “I feel kind of out of place here,” he mumbled as we both surveyed the neighborhood. Everything was well-kept but tiny—a far cry from my palatial manor home back in Glendale.

We emerged from his luxury sedan while a rusted-up beater rumbled down the road ahead of us.

“Who does Nan know here?” he asked as we watched the other car disappear around the block.

“I have no idea.”

“Well, let’s go find out.”

We held hands as we walked up to the nearest house and pressed the doorbell. An exuberant cacophony of barks greeted us almost instantly—one clearly belonged to our Paisley, but the other was that of a much larger dog. Could this be the same Great Dane she’d bested in wrestling earlier that day?

It was Nan who opened the door. If she was surprised to see us there, she didn’t show it.

"You might as well c'mon in," she said while a massive furry dog strained to push past her.

"Jasper, get back!" another voice called from inside the house, a much younger voice.

A woman about my age appeared and put the dog in a sit-stay. "Sorry," she said with an apologetic grin. "We're still working on Jasper's doorbell manners. Anyway… You must be Angie."

Who was this girl? And how did she know me?

"Mommy!" Paisley ran over the moment I stepped through the door and danced on her hindlegs. "Pick me up! Pick me up!"

I did as instructed, still confused out of my mind.

"Sorry. My name's Sunny. I should have started with that," the young woman said, letting go of her dog then wiping her hand off on her pantleg before offering it to me in greeting.

I let go of Charles's hand to accept it.

"Your grandma is friends with my neighbor who's kind of like a grandma to me and—"

"Just call me Nan, dear," Nan interjected while fussing with her hair in the hallway mirror. "Everyone else does."

"This is Charles," I said, reclaiming Charles's hand, so thankful we were in this together. "And you're right, I am Angie. Angie Russo. Um, are the kittens here by any chance?"

"Oh, yes! I was just picking out which one I wanted. It's so hard. They're all adorable!" she gushed.

I glanced toward Nan for an explanation.

She just shrugged. "I called my old friend Tilly to see if she knew anyone in need of a kitten, and she put me on to Sunny here."

As the girl nodded, a strand of dark hair shook loose from her messy braid. "Jasper needs a friend, but I'm afraid our place isn't quite big enough for a second dog."

"So you'd like to adopt a kitten?" I asked. How could such a tiny creature be a match for the massive, slobbery guy standing before me?

Sunny's bright blue eyes flashed with worry. "That's okay. Isn't it?"

"Of course, it's okay! I just wish Nan had told me before disappearing on us."

"Sorry about that. I was really excited, which is why she offered to come over straight away."

"I didn't even wait for Tilly," Nan supplied with a wink. "Although I'm still hoping she'll adopt one of our babies, too."

Sunny laughed. "I'll be sure to pass that on. Hey, now that you guys are here, could you help me decide on a kitten?"

"We'd be honored," Charles answered.

"Do I smell donuts?" I asked Nan before joining Charles, Sunny, and the kittens in the living room. My rumbling stomach was more than ready for a treat.

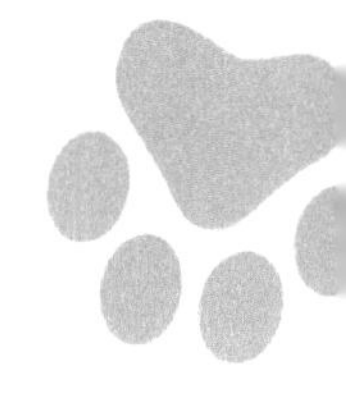

16

We spent the better part of the next hour at Sunny's. She ultimately chose the only gray kitten of the bunch and then immediately dubbed the little miss *Princess Muffin.*

While we were on the way out, Paisley confided in me, "I didn't want to say goodbye to any of my cat puppies."

I waited until Sunny had shut the door behind us to respond. "I know, sweetie. I am so sorry."

Much to my surprise, Paisley wagged her tail so hard her whole body shook. "That's okay, Mommy. I didn't want to say goodbye, but it made me feel good that Sunny and Jasper are so happy now. Do you think Princess Muffin will like living with them?"

I smiled and reached down to pat Paisley on the back. "I know she will."

"That's all any good Mommy can do. Prepare her cat puppies for the world and give them the best opportunities they can." The little dog's capacity to love never ceased to amaze me.

"You're a great mother, Paisley," I told her.

"You are, too, Mommy."

A wall of emotion crashed into me, and I couldn't help but tear up after receiving those tender words from Paisley. Luckily, I always kept a tissue stashed in my pocket during cold and flu season. I drew it out now and used it to wipe at my eyes.

"What's wrong?" Charles asked, concerned etched around the edges of his mouth.

"Nothing," I lied. How could I tell him that maybe I was readier for our future than I thought? Yes. Maybe I *could* be a wife and mother someday, because I already helped to raise one wonderful little doggie and one mostly okay cat.

"All right!" Nan waved to us from the driver's side of her little red sports coupe. "See you crazy kids back at home."

"Wait!" I trudged across the slushy road after my grandmother. "Why didn't you tell us where you were going before you left? And why didn't you answer your phone when we tried calling you?"

"Oh, sorry about that. I silenced it after the bootcamp instructor yelled at another gal for receiving a text alert. Seems I forgot to turn it back on after."

"But you called Sunny," I argued.

"No, I called *Tilly*, then she put me on to Sunny. And I used our landline, dear. Sometimes the simplest option is best." She rummaged around in her giant handbag until she found her phone and waved it in front me. "See. It's right here."

Unsurprisingly, her phone had accumulated so many unread notifications the list of them fell off the screen.

"Give me that." I grabbed the poor, neglected device from her hands and entered her highly secure passcode, *1-2-3-4*.

"It looks like you have several texts and missed calls from... um, *Diamond Guy?"* That was definitely a new one.

Nan blushed and took the phone back. "That's private."

"Who's Diamond Guy?" I teased, unable to suppress the giant smile that spread across my face.

She fluffed her hair, but it did little to distract from the deep blush that had taken over both cheeks. "It's just a new nickname we're trying out. After all, he does sell diamonds for a living."

"Oh my gosh. Is this how you and Mr. Gable flirt?" I broke apart laughing. Nan was usually so brazen with her friendships but acted completely different in her recent flirtations with the local jewelry shop owner.

"Hush up, you," she clucked. "You and Charles were no better in the start."

My smile had become stuck on my face. "Aren't you going to see what he wants?"

She jammed her phone back in her purse while shaking her head. "You know I'm a very private person."

I laughed right in her face. "Really? Since when?"

"Fine. I'll call him back now. Happy?" She grabbed her phone again and pressed the CALL button.

"Why not just check your messages?" I suggested as the line continued to ring.

"I don't have my voicemail set up. Don't need it, because I have an answering machine—"

"On the land line," I finished for her. "What about the texts?"

She ended the attempted call. Apparently Mr. Gable didn't have his voicemail set up, either. Old people are so funny sometimes.

Nan showed me her phone again. She did, indeed, have six new texts from Diamond Guy, but every single one said the same thing: *Hello, Dorothy. Please call me when you get the chance.*

Jeez. Diamond Guy needed some serious advice on flirting for the modern age. For starters, didn't he know that my grandmother preferred everyone call her Nan rather than her given name of Dorothy?

"There. That's done. Now can we please go home?" Nan turned her key over in the ignition to punctuate her request.

"I think Charles and I will just stop by Diamond Guy's on the way home." I snickered. "You're welcome to come with us."

"Goodbye, dear." Nan slammed the car door and sped off.

I returned to Charles with that same huge smile on my face.

"What's got you so smiley?" he asked, before giving me a quick peck on the cheek.

"Nan and her boyfriend. They're just so adorable."

"I didn't realize she was seeing anyone."

"She's not exactly, but remember all the flirting happening between her and Mr. Gable over New Year's Eve?"

He chuckled at the memory. "Do I ever."

"Good, because we need to stop by his store and see him, and I might need your help playing Cupid."

"Aren't we supposed to be focusing on the kittens today?"

I shrugged. "We've run out of clues as to where they and the blood came from, the vet declared them healthy, and both Nan and Paisley have agreed to find new homes for them. What more can we do at this point?"

He nodded. "But are you sure it's right to push them? Shouldn't we let those two get together in their own time?"

I scoffed at this. "Don't you remember how she was to me before we got together?"

"Oh, right." He winced, likely recalling how Nan had forced an awkward confrontation between him and my other potential suitor.

"With that in mind, then yes. We should definitely meddle," he agreed. "Turnabout is fair play and all that. Um, could you give me the address to his shop? I've never headed that way from so far out and I'd hate to waste time taking the scenic route."

"It's downtown," I reminded him. I knew he was still relatively new to town, but surely he couldn't have forgotten that.

"I know, but the GPS likes it better when I give her an exact address."

I raised an eyebrow in question. *"Her?"*

"Yeah. Her name is Carla," he said as if naming his GPS was the most normal thing in the world.

"Hey, that's the same name as..." As my raccoon's Nerf gun. Awkward. "Never mind."

"What?"

"Seriously never mind. Anyway, I have the address for you. Are you ready?"

"Shoot."

"It's 1385 Third Street. Oh my gosh!" I shouted, practically dropping my phone in my lap from the shock.

Charles glanced about in panic. "What? What?"

"Look at this," I said thrusting my phone in his face. I'd pulled up the picture of the partially obscured address label and sure enough… we had a match.

Charles got it right away. "That looks an awful lot like the address you just gave me."

My smile was back and wider than ever. "It does. Doesn't it?"

"Let's go."

17

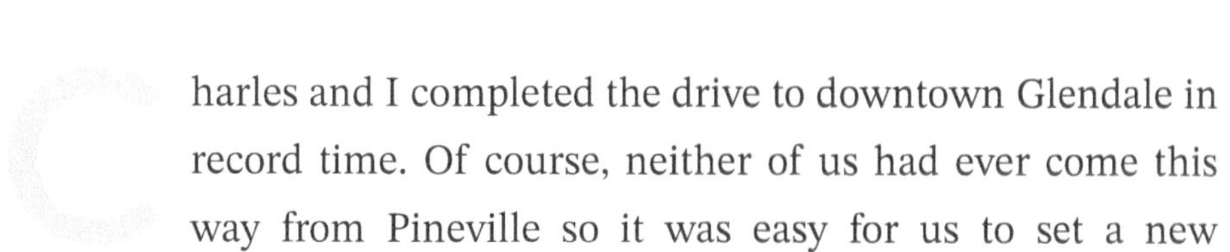

Charles and I completed the drive to downtown Glendale in record time. Of course, neither of us had ever come this way from Pineville so it was easy for us to set a new record.

No sooner had we parked than Nan pulled her little red sports car into the space beside us.

"I hoped you were only kidding about interfering in my love life," she grumbled, getting out of her car and slamming the door behind her. "Luckily, I decided to come by just in case. You'll have to make whatever you plan on doing quick, because I'm not leaving those kittens for more than a few minutes."

I peered in the car window and saw the kittens waiting in the carrier on the passenger side seat. Nan had even left the car running, presumably to keep the heat going for them.

“Let’s go see what Diamond Guy is up to.” Charles offered Nan his arm, but she refused to take it.

“You should have chosen the other guy,” she mumbled in my direction as she stormed off across the parking lot.

Charles and I caught up with her in front of Mr. Gable’s jewelry store, and the three of us entered together with Paisley following close at our heels.

“Hello, Dorothy!” Mr. Gable waved from behind the counter. “Hi, Angie. Charles.”

We all said our hellos, and then the shopkeeper returned to his customers.

A mother-son pair stood before him examining engagement rings and occasionally asking to see one closer up.

“Congrats,” Charles told the son who had rusty red hair and appeared to be somewhere in his mid-thirties.

The other man’s skin turned a ruddy shade of red. “Not me.” He jammed a finger his mother’s direction. “Her.”

His mother beamed at me and Charles. “Isn’t it so great to finally find the one?” she asked us.

Charles pulled me to his side and gave me a kiss on the cheek, which made the newly engaged woman swoon with delight.

“We’re just finishing up here, if you could give me a few more minutes,” Mr. Gable said, his eyes focused only on Nan as they blinked an apology.

“I like it here,” Paisley barked, drawing the engaged woman’s attention.

"Oh my goodness. What an angel!" She dropped to her haunches and accepted excited kisses from the hyper Chihuahua.

"Mom," the woman's son nudged her impatiently. "That's not what we're here for."

"Oh, stop. The ring will wait. Give me a minute to say hello."

He sighed, but his mother didn't seem too bothered by it.

Mr. Gable used this opportunity to extricate himself from behind the counter. "Hello," he said to both me and Charles before saddling Nan with a giant hug. "What brings all three of you in? Is this about the kittens I left on your porch this morning?"

Ah-ha! I knew it!

Nan blinked in confusion. We hadn't yet gotten the chance to catch her up on the address label match-up. "*You* left them?"

"Of course. I'm sorry I didn't have the chance to clean them up. When I called, you didn't answer. I was in a hurry to get back for a customer appointment. I figured if anyone would know what to do with them, it would be you two."

"Wait." The female customer stopped petting Paisley and rose back to a standing position. "There are kittens?" she whispered reverently.

"Mom, we need to focus on—"

"Oh, shush. You're not the one who gets to make the rules." She waved him off, then approached us with wide, shining eyes. "So about those kittens?"

"Would you like to meet them?" Nan asked with a chuckle. "I left them in the car for a minute. Didn't expect to be here long."

"It sounds like the perfect wedding gift. My fiancé John is quite the animal lover but hasn't been able to keep any pets in his apartment."

Her son tugged at her sleeve in a gesture reminiscent of a much younger child. "But, Mom, I'm allergic to cats."

"Then I guess it's finally time for you to move out and establish your own home," she told him with a pointed glare.

"I'll just go get them," Nan said before sweeping back into the cold outside.

The woman followed after Nan and her son followed after her.

"Where did the kittens come from?" I asked Mr. Gable, eager to finally get the answers I'd craved all day. "And why were they covered in blood?

"A frightening sight. Wasn't it?" He shook his head and spoke in the direction of his feet. "I found them in the alley when I was walking in to work."

"The one just outside?" Charles asked, picking up Paisley and allowing her to lick his face.

"Not this one, no. I like to park in the far lot to get a bit of exercise. Plus the fresh air helps wake me up in the mornings. When I spotted the kittens, I picked up the pace, grabbed a box and left a note on the door to let my customers know I'd be a few minutes late opening today, then I went back to get the kittens and drove them straight over to your place. I tried calling Dorothy, but…" He shrugged again.

"I know. She's had her phone off all day."

"Speaking of Nan," Charles edged in. "I've heard she's looking for a plus-one on Valentine's Day."

The old jeweler's breathing suddenly became labored. I half-expected him to a pull an inhaler from his pocket and take a hit. "Is that so? A plus-one for what?"

"Well, actually she doesn't," I began to explain.

Charles squeezed my hand to get me to stop.

He cleared his throat. "It's a beautiful evening she has planned. It starts with an intimate hike along the coastline. After about half an hour, you'll find yourselves at a secluded ice castle built especially just for the two of you. You'll have just enough time for a quick snowball fight before a private chef will treat you to a freshly prepared meal suited perfectly to your individual tastes. Finally, the night will end with dancing under the stars to a string quartet playing only the greatest '80s hits."

Mr. Gable looked like he might be moved to cry. "That sounds wonderful. She did all that for me?"

Charles squeezed my hand again. "She did, but I think she's nervous to make things official by asking you to accompany her. You should do the honors."

I gave an encouraging nod. "Yeah, I bet she'd say yes."

"Okay, I'll do that," Mr. Gable promised.

We made small talk with Mr. Gable as we waited for Nan, Paisley, and the customers to return. I knew Charles had planned that date for me, and as amazing as that special evening sounded, it meant even more to me that he'd given it all up to help two elderly people start their own love story.

Boy, did I have a keeper or what?

18

The woman in the jewelry store ended up adopting two of the kittens, a boy and a girl. She and Nan exchanged phone numbers, and she also promised to text updates and pictures every single day.

That meant we only had two of the original five kittens left with us now, one boy and one girl. At the rate things were going, we'd probably have homes for them by nightfall.

"You wouldn't happen to know anyone in need of their own personal feline overlord. Would you?" I asked Mr. Gable once mother, son, and kittens had departed.

He sighed. "I wish I could take them off your hands, but I fear E.B. would never forgive me."

I'd met his pet rabbit, E.B., and knew Mr. Gable was definitely correct in his assessment. The poor little mite was afraid of any and everything, especially predators like cats.

"Well..." Nan shifted her weight from one foot to the other. "We should probably be off," she told the ground.

Charles exchanged a meaningful glance with Mr. Gable, while I clasped my hands and waited for the magic to happen.

"Dorothy?" Mr. Gable said, causing her to look up.

She lifted Paisley from the floor and nuzzled the little dog to her chest, using Paisley as her own personal security blanket. All this shyness was so unlike my grandmother!

"Yes, Grant?" she mumbled into Paisley's fur after taking one slow, steady breath.

His voice quavered as he asked, "Would you like to spend Valentine's Day together?"

Nan jerked her head a little. "Sure. You mean, as friends?"

No, Nan! No! I wanted to shout but didn't.

Mr. Gable shot an anxious glance Charles's way, who nodded his encouragement.

"No," the nervous shopkeeper said at last. "I meant as in a date. Our first date."

Nan blushed as she continued to stroke Paisley for a couple silent moments. At last, a smile blossomed on her face. "I'd like that," she declared just like the heroine always did in old-timey movies.

"Me, too," Mr. Gable said. He looked as if he'd just won first prize in life. In a way, he had. As trying as my nan could sometimes be, she was still my very favorite person in the entire world. I couldn't blame the besotted jeweler for feeling the same way.

"I should be going now, though." Nan backed away, accidentally bumping into one of the jewelry counters in the process.

"See you soon, Mr. Gable!" I called while pushing my clumsy nan toward the exit. "Bye!"

Once outside, Nan straightened her back and ran her fingers through her hair. "Well, that was rather unexpected."

"Was it, though?" I teased, making my voice high and sarcastic. "You were just telling me this morning that you enrolled in booty boot camp precisely because Mr. Gable—"

"Angie!" Nan shouted and gave me a light slap on the arm. "That's private! Besides I don't want Grant to overhear that."

"What does booty boot camp have to do with Mr. Gable?" Paisley asked, tilting her head to the side.

"I'll tell you when you're older," I whispered while scratching her head.

"Are we going home now?" the Chihuahua asked as we all moved toward the parking lot.

"You, Nan, and the kittens are," I answered. "Charles and I still have a bit of work left to do here."

"Okay, byeeeee!" she sang as Nan practically floated away.

Charles turned to me once we'd seen Nan and the animals off and asked, "The blood?"

I nodded. "Mr. Gable told us where he found it and the kittens. Now all we have to do is go take a look for ourselves."

He motioned for me to go ahead. "Lead the way," he said, placing his hand at the small of my back.

Downtown Glendale wasn't very large, which meant it took us less than ten minutes to reach the other end. From the far parking lot, we headed toward the nearest alley.

"We probably should have kept Paisley with us," I admitted, kicking myself for not realizing that earlier. "She'd have been able to sniff this out for us in a heartbeat."

Charles paused midstep. "Should we go get her?"

"*Nah.* We just have to trace and retrace our steps until something turns up."

"What are we looking for exactly? Bloody pawprints?"

I kept my eyes on the ground before me, studying it closely so I wouldn't miss anything. "Yeah, that's probably our best bet."

"Look there." He pointed toward a big green dumpster that hadn't been properly sealed to keep animals out. Not only were there little red pawprints at the base, but something inside created an ominous rustling sound as soon as I locked eyes on the dumpster.

"Stay back," Charles warned me, putting his arm out to stop me before continuing forward. It was nice he wanted to protect me, but Charles was forgetting one very important piece of information here —*I* was the one who could talk to animals.

"Who's in there?" I called. It had already been a very long winter, and the local wildlife often got desperate as the cold months continued to bear down on the region.

For all I knew, there could be a fox, coyote, lynx, or some other kind of potentially dangerous predator in there. I'd never spoken to any members of those species, so didn't know how easy—*or how difficult*—they might be to negotiate with. And that worried me.

"Hellooooo!" I called again. "You in the dumpster. Come out and nobody gets hurt."

Of course, I would never hurt an animal, but I needed some kind of leverage if I were to protect Charles.

A large raggedy looking dog popped his head out of the dumpster. His wiry coat was also matted with blood around the muzzle. "Don't hurt me," he whined. "I was only trying to grab a quick bite."

Relieved, I closed the distance between myself and the dumpster. "My name's Angie. What's yours?"

When the dog whimpered, his half-cocked ears went back against his head. "I don't have a name. You need a home to have a name, and I've never had one of those."

"I could give you one if you'd like," I offered with a gentle voice. The poor thing.

"A home?" he squeaked in surprise. "I would love nothing more."

"I meant a name, but I suppose I can find you a home, too. First can you help me with something?"

"Anything," he barked excitedly, his tongue now lolling from the side of his mouth.

"What are you eating in there?" I asked, craning my neck but failing to see into the dumpster.

"I'll show you!" he shouted, then dived back into the dumpster and tossed a bloody carcass in my direction. Luckily, it missed hitting me.

"Ewww. What is that?"

"Not ewww. *Yum.*" The stray dog licked his chops. "I hardly ever find something this good to eat."

"What is it?" I asked in disgust. As much as I liked to be polite, it was hard to ignore the churning in my stomach at the smell and sight of his half-eaten meal.

"Looks like some kind of roadkill," Charles said.

"Why is it in the dumpster?"

"Good question. Do you think this is what the kittens got into before Mr. Gable found them?"

"Kittens? You mean cat puppies?" the dog asked, tilting his head to one side and studying us with teary, dark brown eyes.

"Yes, cat puppies," I confirmed with a smile.

"They were the ones who first found this delicious feast, but then some man took them away before they could finish, and I took over."

There.

That was the last piece we'd needed to piece together the entire story of the mysterious doorstep kittens. No wonder they had been so hungry. Their first meal in who-knows-how-long had been interrupted.

"Thanks for your help," I told the dog and then added, "By the way, how do you like the name Digger? You know, because when I first met you, you were digging in the trash?"

"It's perfect!" he barked enthusiastically. "I'm part Airedale terrier on my mother's side, and—boy—do our kind love to dig."

A nameless stray no more, he jumped out of the dumpster and trotted to my side, his tail wagging mightily with each step.

"Then it's definitely perfect." I patted him between the ears as they appeared to be the cleanest part of him. "Hi, Digger. It's nice to meet you. Now come with us, and we'll see what we can do about finding you a home."

19

Luckily, Mr. Gable had a tarp leftover from when he'd painted his shop that summer. He was also more than happy to lend it to us so that we could take Digger back to my house while avoiding the spread of blood, dirt, and trash all over the back seat of my car.

Paisley immediately took the new, much larger dog under her wing. She came running straight up to him and stood on her hindlegs to complete the requisite butt sniff.

"Hi. My name's Paisley!" she shouted while allowing him to bend down and sniff hers.

"My name's Digger," the other dog answered proudly, finally having a name to share.

"I will teach you everything about being a pet!" Paisley promised, then she and Digger disappeared outside. Digger didn't fit through our pet door, so I had to open the human door to let him out.

“Where are the kittens?” I asked Nan, surprised they weren’t in the living room with her.

“Upstairs with Octavius in the fish room,” she answered casually between sips of tea.

“Don’t let him hear you call it that,” I warned with a quick eyeroll. “Have you found any of the other kittens homes yet?”

“Not yet, but I may have a couple leads.” She smiled over the rim of her teacup before taking another slow sip.

“Think you could find one for Digger, too?”

“I’ll see what I can do,” she promised, setting her cup back on the table. “Would you like some tea, too, dear?”

I shook my head. “No, thanks.”

“Not you.” She turned to my boyfriend. “You. How about it?”

“I’m not really—”

“Oh, come now. You and I need to have a little chat,” she pressed, already up and heading toward the kitchen.

Understanding that I’d been dismissed, I headed up the stairs and let myself into Octo-Cat’s room. I needed to check on the kittens, anyway.

The vision that greeted me practically took my breath away. Our two remaining kittens lay snuggled up against Octo-Cat as all three cats napped.

I was just about to turn around and head out, when Octo-Cat’s wide amber eyes blinked open and he whispered, “Wait.”

He carefully extricated himself from his slumber companions without waking either. “I wanted to talk to you about something,” he told me once he’d successfully come to stand by my side. “Let’s go out into the hall."

"What's up?" I asked curiously

"Those little guys aren't so bad, you know. It was hard when they first got here and were pouncing everywhere, but truth be told I've liked having them around," he revealed with a wistful sigh.

"Are you saying you want to keep them?"

He hissed at this. "Eeeesh, no! Nothing so extreme. But having them here reminded me of my own kittenhood. Have I told you that I was one of seven?"

"You may have mentioned it a time or two." *Or twenty.*

"Today has got me thinking about my own brothers and sisters. I haven't seen them since Ethel adopted me all those years ago."

"You must miss them." I ran my hand along his back, hoping he'd appreciate the comfort of the gesture rather than attacking me for it.

He leaned into my hand and purred. "Yes and no. I'm definitely happier being an only cat, but I do wonder if they turned out as awesome as I have."

"So you want to track them down?"

My cat nodded. "I think I do."

"I guess it makes sense to use our P.I. skills to help ourselves every once in a while."

He smiled and gave me a paws up. "Exactly."

"Are you sure you don't want to keep one of the kittens?" I tried again. I liked seeing this softer side of him. Maybe having a long-term kitty companion would help him mellow out.

He shuddered and turned his backside to me. "Completely."

"Okay. Well, I'll let you get back to your cat nap, then."

"Thank you, Angela," he said before running back through the door I'd just opened. I couldn't blame him for wanting to find his long-lost family. After all, I was still trying to do the same thing for myself—and finally meeting my cousin Mags had definitely changed my life for the better.

Knowing now that the kittens were in good paws with Octo-Cat, I headed back downstairs to ask Charles for a quick favor.

"Would you mind heading to the store for me? I need large dog breed food and some steak."

He took one last slurp from his tea, then asked, "How much steak?"

I made a tally in my head. "Um, twenty-two should do it."

Charles laughed. "Time to pay your debts, I see."

"Yes, and if you happen to find a TV, Nerf gun, or nunchucks while you're there, you know what to do."

"What about the lobster rolls?" he asked with one eyebrow raised.

"Those can wait for a few days. We're having steak for dinner tonight."

While Charles was at the store, I planned to give Digger a bath, but first I needed a short break so that I could catch my breath. I took a seat by Nan, who was busy typing into her phone and smiling like a fool in love.

"Let me guess. *Diamond Guy?*" I teased.

Nan clucked her tongue. "I have much more going on in my life than that," she chided.

"Still it must be pretty exciting to have your first date on the calendar at last?"

Nan frowned for a few seconds before transitioning back into a smile. "I only wish I would have had a few more sessions of booty boot camp first, but—yes—I am very excited."

"If you're not talking to Mr. Gable, then who are you texting?" I said, trying to catch a glimpse of her screen. "You're not cheating on him already?"

She looked sad rather than angry. "Oh, dear. I am many things, but a cheater, I am not. You should know me better than that."

"Well?" I prompted when she still hadn't answered my first question. "Who are you chatting with, then?"

She rolled her eyes. "You're so nosey sometimes. You know that?"

"I learned it from the best." I winked, and she winked back.

"That was my good friend, Gertie."

Ahh, Gertie. I'd never actually met her, but I'd taken several jogs with her muttsky Cujo. Cujo had also helped to save my life last month, so he rated very high in my books and so did his owner, Gertie.

Nan continued along. "Remember how she was having trouble exercising Cujo since her grandkids went off to college?"

I nodded.

"I've just suggested she adopt a playmate for him. You and I will keep exercising Cujo as we do, but a second dog could give him some nice company during the day. Wouldn't you say?"

I gasped with excitement. "Digger?"

"Digger," she confirmed.

"That's great," I cried and gave her a tight hug.

"I also have a lead on a home for the last two kittens," Nan revealed. Man, she was good at this. Perhaps she should volunteer at the local animal shelter for more than just fundraising events.

"Really? Who?" I asked, so happy for all the animals who'd found new homes that day.

She shook her head and wagged a finger at me. "I don't want to say until it's a sure thing, but I promise to tell you as soon as I can."

I stretched my arms overhead, then forced myself to my feet. "I better get Digger in the bath."

"Before you go, I take back what I said."

I stared at her blankly. "Take back what?"

"I'm really glad you chose Charles. He's a good man."

"You know," I stated, referring to the fact that Charles had so willingly given up his special Valentine's surprise in order to offer it to Nan and Mr. Gable.

She nodded. "Thank you both for that. Although if it's not too late, I might ask the string quartet to play something other than '80s covers."

20

After our twenty-two-steak dinner, Charles said goodbye and headed back to his house. I felt bad that our "relaxing" day together had become so hectic and that he'd also sacrificed his big Valentine's surprise, but I vowed to make up for it by planning a few special surprises of my own.

By the time Friday rolled around, I had my work cut out for me.

I started with a quick good morning call to Charles, who would be working until early evening. I spent the morning with Nan and Paisley until they departed for one of her community art classes.

The last two kittens had gone to their new homes the night before, which meant Octo-Cat and I had the house to ourselves for the next few hours.

"Happy Valentine's Day," I crooned as I placed a giant box onto the floor in front of him.

His eyes lit up as he beheld the cardboard behemoth. "For me?" he gasped with obvious delight.

"Yup. And there's even a surprise *inside* the box."

He raised a paw to his chest. "Double presents? I'm touched."

It had been so hard to keep this surprise from him for the last few days, and I couldn't wait another minute for the big reveal. "Well, go on and open it up," I urged.

Octo-Cat jumped into the box, then popped his head back out with a satin blue swatch of fabric clenched between his jaws. "What is it?" he mumbled, unsure.

"It's a bowtie," I explained. "I figured you could wear it on your video date with Grizabella this afternoon."

"It matches her beautiful sapphire eyes," he said after setting it carefully on the floor.

"Yes, it does. And if you take another look inside, you'll find a green bowtie as well."

He narrowed his eyes at me, then cocked his head slightly to the side—a sure sign that Paisley was beginning to rub off on him just a little bit.

"Why green?" he asked.

I put a hand over my smiling mouth and waited for it to sink in.

Octo-Cat swooned with delight less than a minute later. "Green. Glorious green! Does this mean…?"

I picked up where he left off. "Yes, I'm taking you to visit Grizabella for St. Patrick's Day. That is, if you still want to go."

He zipped up and down the stairs in a rare show of kitty zoomies, then came back to rest at my feet. I reached out to pet him, but before

I could, he licked my fingertips. "You are a very good human, and I love you, Angela."

I stroked his soft back. "Awww, I love you, too. Now are you ready to FaceTime with Grizabella?"

"Yes! Yes! Yes!"

I fastened the blue bowtie to his collar and showed him what he looked like in the selfie mode of my phone. "I am a very handsome cat. Aren't I?"

I nodded my endorsement. "Grizabella is very lucky to have you."

"And I'm lucky to have you," he said sweetly before zooming away to call his girlfriend.

My heart melted a little at that. Getting love from any cat—but especially Octo-Cat—was a rare treat, and I planned to savor every single second.

At five o'clock on the dot, I pulled into the parking lot outside Charles's law firm. He wasn't expecting me, but that was part of the surprise.

It felt strange being back in the location where our love story had first begun—and also where I'd almost died and then woke up with the strange ability to talk to Octo-Cat. Yes, Longfellow & Associates had given me so much during my brief tenure there—love, friendship, a cat, a home, and access to an impressive trust fund—and for all of it, I would forever be grateful.

But today wasn't about the associates, it was about Charles Longfellow, III, and me.

When he saw me enter the office, he jumped up from his desk and wrapped me in his arms. "What are you doing here? I was just about to sign off for the day and come to see you."

"Kidnapping you. Now let's go."

"Sure. Just let me turn off—"

"Nope. Just lock the door and come with me. There's no time to waste." I grabbed his hand and pulled him along.

We settled into my car, and I began the drive.

"Where are we going?" he asked me with an enormous grin.

I shrugged, keeping my eyes straight ahead. "It's not as fancy as what you had planned, but it's very us."

"Tell me. Tell me!" he whined playfully.

I took a deep breath and shook my head. "I won't tell you what we're doing, but I'll explain why."

"Okay, hit me."

I licked my lips before continuing. I'd practiced this a couple times but still worried it would come out wrong.

"Well, we first met at the law firm, which is why we started there today. A lot of people meet at work, but our relationship has always been a bit different as you so rightly pointed out last weekend. And even though you'd wanted to spend a relaxing, romantic day together, we ended up spending that day in a very *us* way—by throwing all our plans out the window and then helping those who needed it most. Think about it. When we first became friends, we got Brock Calhoun acquitted for murder and reunited a lost, little dog with his human.

When we first became more, we saved Octo-Cat from a kidnapper and protected his trust fund from angry relatives. Last weekend, we ended up finding five abandoned kittens and one stray dog their forever homes."

Charles nodded along, then frowned. "Yes. I guess you're right about that. Do you ever wish we spent more time doing normal boyfriend-girlfriend stuff?"

"No way!" I protested. "I love you, and I love us. Exactly as we are."

"I love you, too." He squeezed my shoulder and leaned in to plant a kiss on my cheek, then asked, "So what are we doing for Valentine's Day?"

"Haha, nice try," I teased. "Don't worry, though. We're almost there."

Ten minutes later, we arrived at our very favorite restaurant, the Little Dog Diner all the way over in Misty Harbor.

"This restaurant has always been special to us, too," Charles observed as we approached the entrance hand in hand. "Remember when we came here after catching the real Hayes murderer?"

"I do. And do you remember who came with us?"

Just then we caught sight of Nan, Mr. Gable, and my parents as they waved from a big booth by the window.

Charles turned to me with a curious look. "I thought Nan and Grant were going on the date I'd originally planned for us."

I squeezed his hand and rested my head on his shoulder for a moment. "Remember about helping people in need? Those two are still too nervous to be alone together, so we're going to help break the ice. And you know another thing about us? We love to be with the people we love, so why not be with them on Valentine's Day? Well, for a little while, at least."

"We're just staying for a quick drink." My mom looked ravishing in a pink cable-knit sweater. I swear, only she could look glamorous in such simple winter attire. She gave me a tight hug and then kissed me on either cheek.

"Thank you again for setting up the ice castle dinner for us," my father said, giving my boyfriend a manly hug and several fast pats on the back.

"We're sharing," I revealed the favorite part of my plan with a smile. "My parents are doing the dinner, and you and I get the string quartet."

Charles laughed, and I jabbed him in the ribs.

"What? You think I'm going to pass-up a romantic starlight dance to all my favorite '80s classics?"

"No, I know you better than that." After a moment, he asked, "You said that we were sharing the date I'd planned. What part do Nan and Grant get?"

"They're going to have the snowball fight, of course. They need something more light-hearted to help them get comfortable dating again. It's been a long time for both of them." I eyed the new couple, glad to see they were holding hands across the booth. Maybe they didn't need quite as much help as I'd expected.

"Take a seat, you two," Nan urged, motioning for Charles and me to slide into the large booth with one hand while still hanging tight to Mr. Gable's hand with the other.

The waitress came over and handed out waters all around. “I see the rest of your party has arrived. Are you ready to order?”

“Four lobster rolls for here and two to go,” I said as my mouth began to water in anticipation.

“Oh, that’s nice, sweetie,” Mom said, “But your dad and I don’t need anything to take home.”

“So just four for here?” the waitress asked, her pen raised over the little Steno pad in her grip.

“And two to go,” I confirmed with a sharp nod.

After she’d left, I whispered to Mom, “They’re not for you. They’re for paying the rest of my debts to a certain cat and his raccoon friend.”

LEGAL SEAGULL

PET WHISPERER P.I.

Just as I was beginning to think we'd never find the last missing member of our long-lost family, a seagull named Bravo shows up with both a promise and a threat.

He claims he's been watching me for a long time—even before I gained my strange ability to talk to animals. He also says that if I help settle a dispute between warring flocks, then he'll personally take me to see the one person I've been all but dying to meet. If I refuse to help, however, he'll send an army of mercenary woodpeckers to destroy my house. Yikes!

Unfortunately, I've already promised Octo-Cat that I'll take him on a cross-country trip to visit his girlfriend out in Colorado. With Nan and I on the road, it falls to Charles and Pringle to investigate in our absence.

Will they be able to solve the case according to the flock's satisfaction? What shocking secrets has Nan been keeping from me now? And will I be able to survive more than 70 hours in the car with my complaining kitty?

The mysteries abound in our most unusual adventure yet.

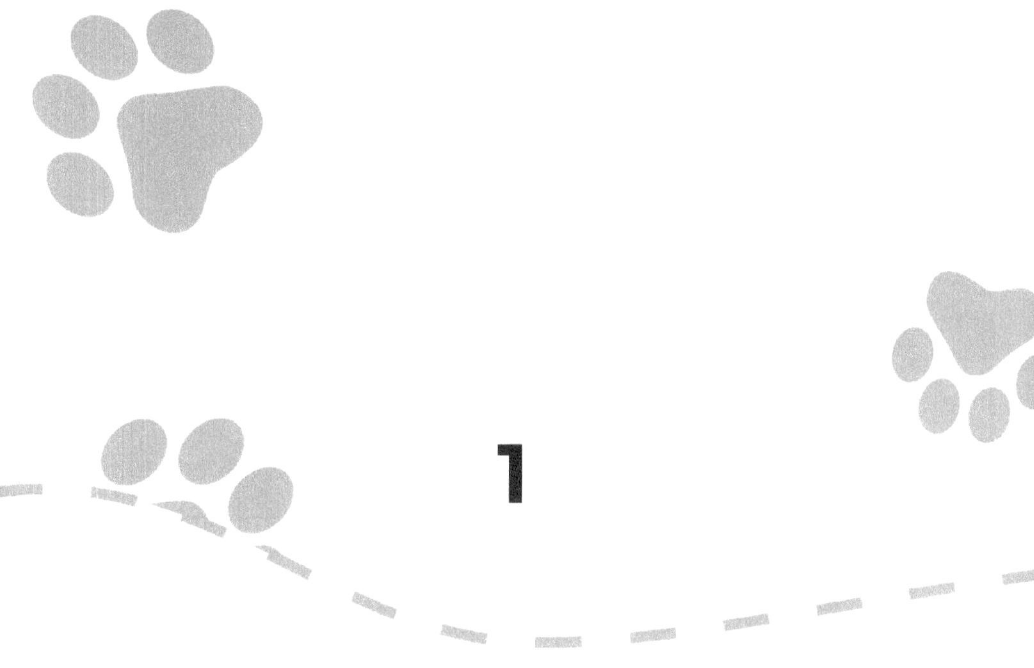

1

It all started with a coffee maker that should have been tossed into the dumpster years ago. One fated zap from that thing, and I reawakened with the strange ability to speak with animals.

Ever since then, my life has been full of four-legged chatter. You'd think being able to understand animals would mean that I'd know more about the world around me, but instead I find myself knowing less and less as I'm tossed into one mystery after the other.

I guess that's why I set up shop as a private investigator…

Oh, hi. My name's Angie Russo, and I'd be remiss not to mention that my partner in solving crime is none other than my tabby cat, Octavius Maxwell Ricardo Edmund Frederick Fulton Russo, Esq, P.I. And much to his chagrin, I've taken to calling him Octo-Cat for short.

When Octo-Cat entered my life, he brought the first of many mysteries and a giant trust fund from his previous owner, for which I am now the guarantor. It pays our monthly bills and then some—

including the giant Blueberry Bay manor house that he tricked me into buying. It's a good thing his previous owner hooked us up because we've earned exactly zero dollars for our investigative efforts to date.

My grandmother, Nan, lives with us and uses her retirement funds to pitch in, even though I tell her not to. She keeps our kitchen stocked with fresh baked goods and our walls decorated with all kinds of quirky homemade art projects—yeah, she's worked in everything from metal to hand-spun silk. She's a bit of a character, but we can always count on Nan to keep things interesting for us all.

Another roommate of ours is Paisley, the mostly black tri-color Chihuahua Nan rescued from the shelter last year. Paisley is an unfailing optimist and eternal source of joy. She makes a strong contrast to our backyard neighbor, Pringle the unrelentingly irritating and frequently villainous raccoon.

You probably won't believe me, but everything I'm about to tell you is true about Pringle. He has two treehouses with two big-screen TVs. He also has zero regard for anyone's privacy, especially mine. I've recently caught him snooping on my phone and even recording a video of me for submission to his favorite reality show. Ugh, I know. Here's hoping I don't get selected for that particular unwanted privilege.

My parents work in news, and my boyfriend Charles is the senior partner at the law firm where I used to work before giving up the glamorous paralegal life to become a full-time P.I… Or if you were to ask Pringle, "full-time unemployed."

I realize the raccoon must seem like an all-around horrible

neighbor based on my descriptions so far, but in truth, I just think he's cranky. After all, he's the only one around here who hasn't found love.

That's right.

Nan is now seeing the local jeweler, Grant Gable, and they are just adorable together. Meanwhile I've got Charles, and my parents have each other. Even Octo-Cat maintains a very serious long-distance relationship with minor Instagram influencer and former show cat Grizabella the gorgeous Himalayan.

True, Paisley is without any romantic attachment, but that doesn't bother the spritely pup one bit. Mostly because things rarely ever do.

Even though Pringle won't admit to being lovelorn, he has taken to calling his Nerf gun "Carla" and stroking it lovingly whenever he thinks no one is looking.

Things have gotten so out of hand with that Nerf gun of his that I've now inadvertently agreed to let my cat wield nunchucks to protect himself—and, in theory, *me.* This has only led to more slapstick violence and a fair number of bruised shins on my part.

He's really not good with them.

Probably because he has to keep one part in his mouth while swinging the other as he stands on his hind legs and awkwardly twists his neck to the side. I think he's actually hurt himself more than he's managed to get me and Pringle.

I also don't think either of them needs a weapon to navigate our daily suburban life, but maybe that's just me.

Thankfully, I'll be getting a break from trigger-happy Pringle this week as I take Octo-Cat on a cross-country road trip to visit his beloved Grizabella in Colorado. Yes, it's a long drive from Maine, but Nan is coming along to share it with me, seeing as Octo-Cat still refuses to get on a plane.

Also, the last time we took a train, we wound up with a murder on our hands, so driving just felt like a better way to go this time around.

We're leaving bright and early the day after tomorrow, and as much as I initially didn't want to take this trip, I'm looking forward to the reprieve from everyday life.

Let's just hope nothing too crazy happens before then...

Famous last words. Am I right?

I'd just settled into my favorite window seat with a steaming mug of coffee in one hand and my eReader in the other when Octo-Cat came sauntering into the room, a single sheet of lined paper hanging from his mouth.

"Eeeh muh et," he mumbled in my direction, his tail already flicking wildly even though I'd not yet done anything to disappoint him.

"Whatever it is, can it wait until later?" I asked. Unfortunately, I already knew what his answer would be.

He spat the paper onto the floor and glared at me with those unsettling amber eyes of his. "No. It can't wait. We're almost out of time as it is. Pick that up," he commanded with a sneer.

I set my eReader down on the bench seat and walked my coffee over to my desk, then returned to grab the paper my cat had presented to me so unceremoniously.

Octo-Cat plopped onto his butt and watched with obvious disdain, but that was life with a cat for you. "That's my list of necessities."

I turned the paper over in my hands, then shook my head. "But it's blank."

"You better get writing then," Octo-Cat said with a triple flick of his tail before launching into his long-winded soliloquy. "First I'll need my bowties, both green and blue. I also need a new one that's gold to match my eyes."

"But your eyes aren't—"

"Are you writing this down?" he snapped with a scowl that brooked no further argument.

Right.

I raced to my desk as he continued to rattle off his demands. With a red ink pen now in hand, I scrawled furiously but just couldn't keep up. "A copy of Dr. Roman's Guide to… um… Could you repeat that, please?"

My cat groaned, proving I'd disappointed him yet again. "Dr. Roman's Guide to Romance. In audio. Pay attention."

Ten minutes later, Octo-Cat had finally finished dictating his list. It filled both sides of the paper he'd brought me, and I'd even had to resort to scribbling the last few items on the back of my hand.

Well, it looked like I had my work cut out for me—and my day stolen from me.

"Are you sure you need all of this for our trip?" I asked in disbelief. "Some of this isn't exactly easy to find."

Octo-Cat nodded pertly. "I'm sure."

"But—"

"I'll be in my room if you need me." He turned tail and sauntered away.

Remind me again why I was doing this huge nice thing for him when he couldn't even bother to be the tiniest bit grateful?

It was like the more time I spent with my cat, the less I actually understood him. Maybe this road trip wouldn't be so relaxing, after all.

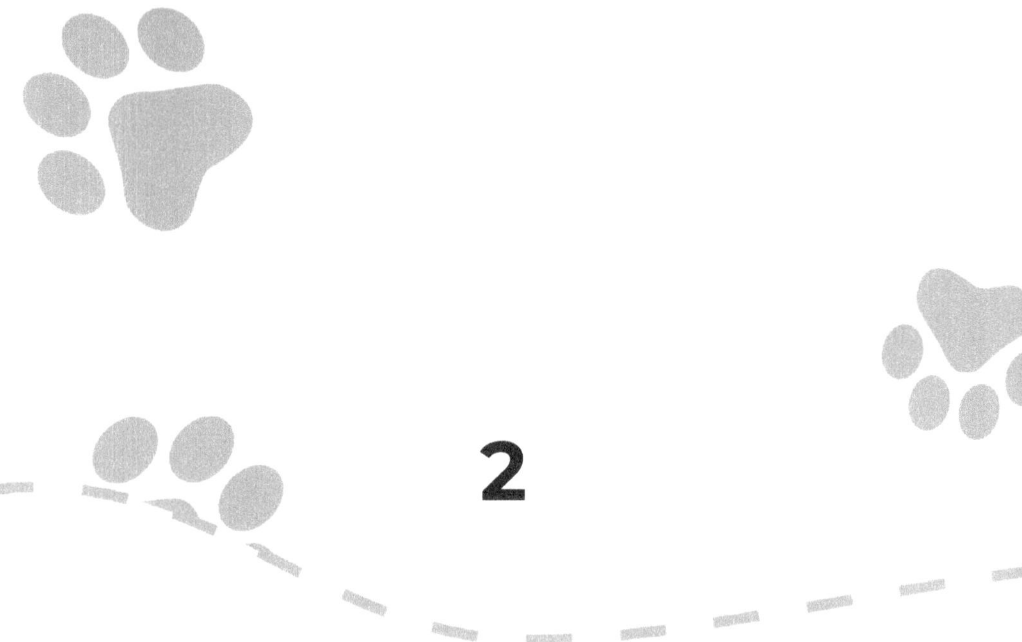

2

Fortunately, Nan agreed to take half of Octo-Cat's giant list off my hands, which meant I'd actually have a few hours to get things packed and ready for myself before falling into bed in an exhausted heap that night.

As it was, I'd already been out running errands for several hours. And since nothing could ever be easy when it came to Octo-Cat, his requirements took me to shops scattered all around Blueberry Bay.

I'd saved Dewdrop Springs for last, seeing as it wasn't exactly my favorite place to visit. In fact, it seemed every time I set foot in that wretched little town, somebody got murdered or robbed or bribed or embezzled. Fun.

Me? I just wanted to get my cat his audiobook and get home.

Of course, the title he'd requested had proven to be this season's hottest new release. How had I not heard of it before now? Probably because I didn't need any help in the romance department.

I was surprised Octo-Cat believed that he did. Normally he thought of himself as perfectly infallible. Further proof this upcoming visit with Grizabella meant the world to him. They hadn't seen each other in-*fur*son since they'd first met on the train in late November. How would they feel when they were together outside of their usual video chat setting?

As much as he annoyed me today—and, let's be honest here, *every* day—I really hoped things went well for him... Even though I was now at my third bookstore.

As it turned out, both of the big box bookstores I'd tried had been sold out of Dr. Roman's hot new release, meaning I needed to hop over the nearest independent bookstore and pray they had a copy.

When I'd called home to suggest an Audible subscription, he hung up without even speaking to me. When I called back, he groaned and slowly explained that he must absolutely have his book on CD because he didn't trust an MP3 download not to "disappear from his device when he needed it most."

Again, this was a self-help romance guide. What emergency could it possibly aid in? I knew better than to ask any clarifying questions, though.

Instead I swallowed any last vestiges of pride I'd once had and vowed to do whatever it took to keep my spoiled cat happy. That brought me to Tattered Pages, a hole-in-the-wall indie shop that had recently changed hands in favor of a much younger proprietress. I hadn't been into the shop for years, preferring my eReader to page-and-ink. I was surprised to see how much it had changed since my last visit. With a comfy lounge area, cafe, and beautifully organized shelves, I had to hand it to the new owner—the place looked great.

Maybe I would be back to get something for myself once this big road trip was over.

"Hi. I'm Dakota. Can I help you?" a woman with bright probing eyes interrupted my thoughts by offering a huge smile as she marched my way.

"Oh, hi. I'm looking for an audiobook?" My voice went up at the end even though I hadn't meant to ask a question.

Dakota scrunched her nose as she thought, then raised one index finger and pointed two aisles down. "I've got just the thing for you."

I followed her wordlessly to a selection of Jeffrey Deaver books.

"You look like a mystery reader," she informed me. "Am I right?"

Impressive.

"Normally, yes, but I'm actually here to pick up something for my, *um,* friend. Do you have Dr. Roman's Guide to—?"

"Romance. Yes, I think we have one copy left." Dakota led me to the opposite side of the store and began to rummage through a spinning wire rack. "It was here just a... Ah! Gotcha!"

She grabbed the requested audiobook out from behind another. "Messy, messy. Good thing I knew it was still here."

"Thank you so much," I said with a huge sigh of relief. My go-for work was now officially done.

Dakota waved goodbye from behind the counter after checking me out. "Make sure to come back another time and get some books for you!"

Yeah, I'd still try to avoid Dewdrop Springs as much as I possibly could, but now I could at least treat myself to a quick book shop visit next time I was in town.

Pleased with my ability to find the silver lining, I pushed through the door and out onto the street.

"No! I almost had him!" someone cried from beneath me.

I whipped around to find a fluffy orange Persian staring up at me with angry eyes. "Sorry," I murmured as I paced down the block in search of my car. I hadn't parked far, but—

"Wait, wait, wait!" that same voice followed me, growing closer with each syllable.

I stopped and turned toward her.

"You can understand me?" the cat asked, her mouth hanging open in awe. "Why can't my useless human understand me, then?"

"Yes, and I don't know," I murmured, hoping nobody was around to see me talking to this strange cat in the middle of the very public street.

"My name's Poppy, and I have some demands," the Persian informed me.

Boy, was this familiar. Octo-Cat had said almost the exact same thing to me when he first learned I could talk to him, and he hadn't stopped giving demands since.

I had no time to cater to the whims of an unfamiliar cat, so I mumbled my apologies and resumed searching for my car.

"Wait!" Poppy yelled at the top of her lungs. "Don't leave yet!"

Her pleas weren't enough to stop me a second time, though.

She growled and threw a hissy fit, but I still didn't stop. "I'm not done with you. You better come back!"

I finally reached my car and slammed the door behind me. Just as I was frantically jamming my key in the ignition, something big thumped into the windshield right in front of me.

Ergh. That cat had better—

But, no, it wasn't Poppy. Instead I was met with a wiggling white blob.

A bird.

Oh, no.

The orange Persian jumped onto the hood of my old sedan with a thud and stalked toward her disoriented prey.

Panicked, I did the first thing I could think of. I hit the horn on my car, which sent the feline running for cover.

The bird—who turned out to be a seagull—righted himself and then tapped on my windshield with his beak. "Might I have a quick word?"

Even though I still didn't have time for any distractions, I rolled my window down and allowed him to join me in the car. Maybe I could drive him somewhere safer, somewhere far away from the overly worked-up feline.

"You are a tough one to track down," the bird said once he'd settled himself on my passenger seat. "I've been all over the region chasing after you today."

"Chasing after me? Why?"

"I've always kept tabs on you. Ever since the beginning."

I felt a headache coming on. "The beginning of what?"

"Of you being able to understand us. We watch humans like you in case we ever need to call on a favor."

My mind swirled with this new information. Yes, a bird needed a favor from me, but more importantly, there were others like me. I'd always hoped, but I'd never known for sure.

"Can you take me to meet the others?" I asked, my voice shaking. I didn't have time for this, but then again, how could I possibly turn him away after the info he'd just shared?

The gull cocked his head to the side. "That depends."

"Depends? On what?"

"If you help us, we'll help you."

"And if I don't?"

"Are you really going to force me to go straight to the nuclear option?"

I nodded, afraid to speak.

The bird shook his head and wings, giving himself a ragged appearance. "Look. If you don't play nice, we don't play nice. Let's just say we have an army of woodpeckers ready to peck your house into the ground. You got me?"

"So either I help you, or you destroy my home?" I squeaked. A part of me wished I had left him to Poppy outside, but only a very small part.

"Hey, now you've got it." He spread one wing to the side and took a bow.

"I'm kind of busy. I mean, I'm supposed to go on a road trip tomorrow. I'll be gone all week."

"Then un-busy yourself," the seagull suggested rather unhelpfully and turned his back to me. Twisting his neck in a nearly ninety-degree arc, he eyed me head-on, his little eyes boring into me. "Unless, I guess, you don't want to meet your long-lost grandmother."

3

I stared at my pushy seagull visitor, unwilling to blink my eyes for fear he might disappear. "Did you say...? M-M-My long-lost grandmother?"

The bird nodded, a smug expression on his beak. "We seagulls always have our eyes on the ground. In fact, I knew who you were even before you became my assignment."

"But how?"

He shook a wing at me. "Now, now. That would be giving you the payment without first completing the job. So what do you say? Will you agree to help us?"

"Yes," I answered without hesitation. Ever since Pringle had unburied Nan's secret letter, revealing the fact that my real grandfather had orchestrated my mother's kidnapping, I'd been dying to meet the family I hadn't known existed. My grandfather, William McAllister, had already died by the time we discovered his existence, but

Mom and I had been able to connect with a number of other relatives who still lived down in Larkhaven, Georgia.

No one knew where my biological grandmother had ended up, though. No one except this seagull, apparently

"Good," he said before settling himself on the dashboard. "Since you haven't got wings, we'll drive."

I turned the key in the ignition. "Where are we going?"

"To the flock, of course. Head south by southwest."

I'd never quite mastered navigating by cardinal directions, so I simply drove straight. When I started up the car, the bird clumsily fell back onto the seat, where he occasionally hopped up to get a view through the windshield and criticize my driving.

"Not that way. South by southwest!" the seagull shouted.

I turned to the left, which seemed to satisfy him.

"What's your name?" I asked after we'd been driving for a while.

"Me? I'm Bravo. Second in command for Flock 82." Wow, this was all so official. I had no idea birds were so well organized or that they organized themselves in a vaguely militaristic way.

"If you're second in command, why were you assigned stalker duty? That doesn't seem like a job for a high-ranking bird."

Bravo clucked in disgust. "That's what I said, but Alpha wasn't having it. Said you were too important to trust to a rookie. You do your job now, and I'll be everyone's hero. Maybe score myself a new nest or even rise to challenge Alpha."

"I don't really understand how any of this works," I confessed. "Birds are usually too afraid to talk to me.

"Not too afraid," Bravo corrected. "We just find you wingless folk a bit tiring."

Perhaps I should have been insulted, but if I could fly, I'd no doubt want to see more exciting things as well.

"This is the place," Bravo said after a few more awkward minutes had passed. He motioned for me to park next to a row of dumpsters behind a strip mall.

"What now?" I asked after exiting my car.

Bravo let out a horrible shrieking caw, and suddenly an army of white descended from the skies.

The plumpest of the gulls landed right between me and Bravo and studied me with a frown curled on his beak. "Is this her?"

"Hi. I'm Angie." I offered a hand in greeting, but then immediately withdrew it when I realized he had no way of shaking hello.

"You don't look like a lawyer to me," the seagull, who I now took to be Alpha, spat and lifted one foot into his under-plumage.

I chuckled uncomfortably. Maybe it was a good thing birds didn't normally choose to chat with me. Let's be honest here, they were pretty weird. Not only that, it seemed fully possibly that even the slightest misunderstanding could send Alpha pecking toward my eyes with hostile intent. Suddenly, my demanding tabby didn't seem such a burden.

I shook my head and forced a smile. "I'm not a lawyer. I'm a private investigator."

Alpha whipped his head to the side without moving his body an inch. "Not a lawyer, huh?" he addressed me while staring daggers at his second in command.

Bravo tittered nervously. "Of course you're a lawyer. I found you at the law firm, remember?"

"I used to be a paralegal, but—"

"Stop helping," he yelled through a gritted beak.

"This is why you'll never be Alpha," the seagull leader declared.

A few ill-spirited jeers rose up from the flock, and Bravo buried his face beneath a wing. Poor guy.

"I'm not a lawyer, but I can get you one. At no charge," I sputtered, suddenly desperate to help the poor guy and not just because he knew where I could find my missing family.

Alpha stretched both wings overhead and opened his beak wide in a yawn. "Go on."

"He's my boyfriend. I can call him right now."

"Stop squawking and start walking," he told me with a stony gaze.

I took this to mean that I was to call Charles now. Dutifully, I pulled out my phone, noting it was still the early afternoon and praying Charles wouldn't be in court or with a client.

He answered on the third ring. "Angie. Is everything okay?"

"I'm fine, but I have a bit of an emergency on my hands," I mumbled into the receiver.

"Where are you?"

I walked around to the front of the strip mall and gave him the name of the first shop I saw. "In Dewdrop Springs," I added.

"I'll be there as fast as I can," he promised without asking for any more information.

"Thank you. Love you," I said before ending the call. I could explain once he arrived. That is, if I could figure out how to explain what I still didn't understand myself.

"Well?" Alpha asked, hopping over to stand directly at my feet.

"He's on his way," I said, and Bravo released a giant sigh into the wind.

"Told you I had the right one," he clucked.

"Can you maybe explain to me what's going on?" Unfortunately, I couldn't leave now that Charles was coming over to handle things—namely, because he still needed me to translate the animal-to-human communications.

"Why should we tell you anything?" Alpha demanded. "You're just the go-between."

Bravo chose that exact moment to fly to my shoulder and grab the soft fabric of my shirt as a perch. Naturally, I screamed and started waving my hands around wildly to unseat him.

"Jeez, relax," he huffed. "This isn't a Hitchcock movie, and I'm not a Hitchcock kind of bird. So relax already."

Alpha laughed and flew onto my now free shoulder. "I like you. You're funny."

It took everything I had not to frantically bat him off. At least he liked me, right?

"That movie did wonders for us, you know? All these generations of gulls later, and good ol' Hitchcock still has humans running from us in terror. We used to have to run from them, you know. Back in the dark ages of avian history."

I nodded solemnly, amazed that any creature could be more ridiculous than my cat—let alone a whole society of them. "Is that what this is about?" I asked, too curious not to try to pry it out of him once more.

"No, no, no." Bravo flew over and took a spot on my other shoulder, which meant I was now sandwiched between him and Alpha and feeling incredibly exposed. "This isn't about humans at all. Well, except for the fact we needed your help."

"You needed a lawyer," I reminded them. "Why?"

"When dealing with an inferior opponent, sometimes you need an inferior judge. No offense. That's where you and your lawyer friend come in."

Ouch.

"An opponent, huh? Is somebody suing you? Charging you with a crime?" Both options seemed equally likely—and equally ludicrous.

"Don't be silly. This isn't about silly laws." Alpha leaned forward menacingly and a mighty cry rose up from his flock. "This is war."

4

While waiting for Charles to join me in Dewdrop Springs, I texted Nan to let her know I'd be even later coming home than I'd originally suspected. Normally I would have called her for a quick chat since she was a notoriously bad texter, but Alpha's declaration of war sent his entire flock into a cawing pandemonium. I could barely hear myself think, let alone speak. Yeah, even though I was still only in my late twenties, I would probably need a hearing aid after this one. Hopefully, Charles could help them with whatever they needed quickly, and we could all go about our separate lives again.

As scattered street lamps began to pop on and neon store signs lit to illuminate the growing darkness, I became very aware that I was standing alone and exposed in a crime-ridden commercial district with only a strange flock of seagulls to protect me.

When his sedan pulled into the strip mall parking lot, I jogged over to greet him. I did that a lot these days—jogged when I could just as easily have walked. I had Nan and our new morning exercise routine to thank for that one. I loved that I now felt strong and quick, secure in my body... Well, almost. Still couldn't outrun my grandmother, though.

Charles parked and swung the door open, making a hasty exit. As soon as he was standing on solid pavement, I threw myself into his arms. Yes, it was definitely overdramatic, but tomorrow I'd be leaving on a lengthy cross-country trip and I was really going to miss him.

"What's wrong?" he asked, pulling back to study my face.

I wiped at a tear I hadn't realized I'd shed. Definitely overdramatic. "I'm fine. It's just that—"

Before I could finish, the flock came rushing over with quickly flapping wings and ear-piercing cries.

"Is this the guy? Is this our lawyer?" Alpha demanded as he circled low.

Charles threw one hand over his head protectively and used the other to hold me close to his chest. He didn't say anything, but I could feel his heart thumping wildly beneath my cheek, his breaths coming out fast and short against my hair.

Bravo laughed as he at last landed on the hood of Charles's car. "The Hitchcock maneuver, haha. Gets them every time."

Okay, that was it!

I wriggled my way out of Charles's protective grasp and turned to face the flock, wagging a finger at Bravo since he was closest. "If you want our help, there will be no more of this Hitchcock nonsense. You got it?"

"They're just messing with us?" Charles's voice came out choked. "For fun?"

I continued to glare at the birds as I nodded. "They threatened me, too. Said they'd send their woodpecker friends in to mess up my house if I refused to cooperate with whatever plan they have for us."

"I don't like this." Charles glanced from me to the birds and back again. It was always awkward for him, taking part in these conversations with animals when he could only hear my side of things, but he still gave it his best. "I'm not sure we should help them if this is how they're going to behave."

Ahh, Charles. He'd make a great father one day. He already had the tough love thing down pat.

"What?" Alpha squawked. "But you said he'd be our lawyer. He can't just say no. You already promised."

I sighed to buy myself some time, then finally responded with, "Yes, we'll help you as long as you promise to be civil from here on out."

Alpha raised both wings overhead and bowed. "Bird's honor." I wasn't sure how much I could trust his—or any other bird's—honor, but I hoped for the best.

"Angie," Charles said between gritted teeth, apparently far less appeased by Alpha's promise. "Can I speak to you in the car for a moment?"

"Be right back," I told the flock as I settled into his passenger seat. He'd turned on the seat heater for me on his way over, knowing I'd appreciate having it toasty warm when I got in.

As soon as the door clicked shut behind me, Charles spoke in a hasty whisper. His eyes reflected concern, worry—not anger or irritation. "Don't you have to leave early tomorrow morning on your road trip? Why are you taking this on now?"

He was right, of course. The timing was dreadful, but what could I do? "I didn't have much of a choice," I answered in a small voice even though I'd hoped it would come out confident to allay his doubts.

"There's always a choice. Whatever squabble these seagulls have they can solve themselves. You need to be well-rested so that you can focus on your trip and driving safely. Nothing they need could be more important than that."

I loved that Charles always had my best interests at heart, no matter how inconvenient they were for him. Unfortunately he didn't have the whole story yet. I didn't either, and of course it was fully possible Bravo had lied to get me here.

Still, I had a chance—maybe a small one, maybe a big one—to finally fill the fissure in my heart that had opened wide when Pringle revealed our family's hidden past. A part of me was missing, and these birds potentially knew how to find her. I needed to take the chance, not just for me but also my mother. She'd never known her true biological parents, and she deserved to meet the one that was still alive, to find out why she'd been shucked off under a strange veil of secrecy in the first place.

I swallowed hard, then finally raised my eyes to meet his. "They said they know where my grandmother is," I revealed, then let out a slow, shaky breath.

He cocked his head to the side, clearly confused by this proclamation of mine. "Yeah, she's back home preparing for the trip. Probably baking her fourth batch of cookies for the day."

I held his eyes, placed a hand on his shoulder, and tried again. "No, the other one."

"Your biological grandmother?" He gasped, unable to keep his voice down any longer. "But nobody knows what happened to her or where to find her."

I motioned my chin toward the window. "They say that they do."

"And you believe them?" Charles raised one skeptical brow. I couldn't tell whether he thought I was crazy for choosing to trust them when his brief encounter with the gulls had already proven they played by their own set of rules. But I'd already made my mind up. Now it was time to choose my attitude. I could pout and question everything—or I could make the best of it, no matter how awkward.

"I think I do," I answered after a brief hesitation. "But even if I'm wrong about this, I still have to try."

He grabbed my hand and gave it a kiss. A giant smile lit his handsome face as he let my hand go and turned toward the driver-side door. "Then let's go help some seagulls."

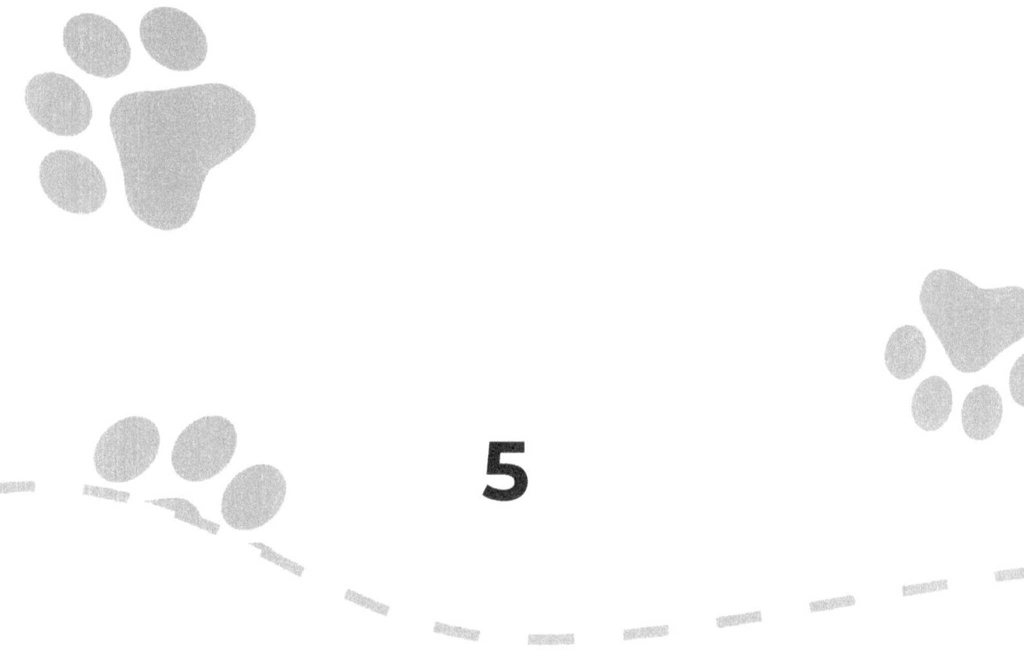

5

I clutched tight to Charles's hand as Alpha and the rest of Flock 82 led us around the back of the strip mall and into the brambles behind the pavement. Once clear of the overgrowth, we reached a clearing filled with an oversized patch of dead grass that had likely only just been exposed again after months being covered in snow.

Alpha stopped and signaled for the rest of us to do the same. "Now that we have a bit more privacy, let us begin," the leader gull announced, then flew up to perch on my shoulder.

Charles flinched but remained in place at my side, although now with a death grip on my hand.

"Go ahead. Tell us what you need," I said with a very slight nod, not wanting to startle the wielder of the sharp beak that was currently far too close to my face for comfort.

Alpha turned his head at an odd angle to stare at my face, bringing that weapon-like beak even closer. "As I mentioned earlier, this is a most urgent matter. Flock 84 has declared war, and we have ten days to secure a peaceful resolution before that declaration becomes official. We want to avoid war at all costs, because—"

"Hang on," I mumbled. "I need to be able to translate for Charles."

Alpha let out an irritated cluck but waited for me to share what I'd learned so far.

"Okay," I said once the other human was caught up. "Just pause every couple sentences as you keep going."

The bird shook out his feathers, clamping his talons into my shoulder a bit too firmly in an effort to keep his balance as he did so. "Like I was saying, we want to avoid war at all costs, because Flock 84 is much larger and better equipped for battle."

"What does a war between seagulls entail?" I asked, trying not to laugh as I pictured a pair of angry white birds fighting over a fast-food wrapper. It was a scene I had witnessed more times than I could count, growing up on the Bay.

"Silence." Alpha gave me a sharp peck on my collar bone. He hadn't applied much force, but it still really, really hurt.

I shook him off my shoulder and rubbed at the sore spot above my chest.

As I did that, Charles jumped into protective boyfriend mode. "If you hurt her again, I'll end your war before it even begins by feeding all of you to my cats!"

A panicked caw rose up, and several of the gulls took flight in an attempt to add some distance between themselves and this new guy who was aligned with their biggest predator.

"If we must respect you, then you must respect us," the gull told me. “You laughed at the thought of dozens in my flock getting slaughtered.”

I knew instantly that he was right. I’d been far too insensitive given that lives were on the line. “I’m sorry,” I said, my voice ringing out in the night like a bell. “Please do go on. We want to help however we can.”

“We have ten days to seek a peaceful resolution, and it’s up to us—the flock under attack—to declare the governing law. We chose human law, and that’s where you and your foul-mouthed little friend come in.”

I translated for Charles, leaving out the insult.

“Why would they choose human law?” he asked with a scrunched brow.

It was a good question. I wanted to know that, too.

“As I’m sure my second has already informed you, we keep tabs on you humans. Especially those of you who are gifted with the voice. All birds watch, but 82 watches closest of all. We knew we could reach out to you, a human with the voice and legal expertise. 84 will have a hard time finding someone to defend them within the allotted waiting period. Let alone to build a case.”

“Makes sense, but what are you fighting for?” I asked, hoping his answer would be the final piece needed to make sense of the flock’s needs and how Charles and I fit into it all.

“Land,” he said simply.

When he didn’t elaborate, Bravo spoke up. “Our neighboring flock, number 83, went missing several weeks ago. Assuming they’d abandoned their territory, we moved in to secure it for 82. But then 84 got it into their bird brains that the land should be theirs since they have a larger population."

"Why do you think it should go to 82?" I asked, not letting it slip that I thought the warring flock had sound logic here.

Alpha narrowed his eyes at me—at least I think he did. It was kind of hard to tell with birds since their eyes were set on either side of their head instead of straight above their beaks. "Because we were here first. Also, 83's former land sits nicely with ours."

"Here?" I asked with a squeak as Alpha flew back to claim his place atop my shoulder. This couldn't possibly be about some strip mall on the shady side of Dewdrop Springs. The rental prices here were practically free because so few ever wanted to step foot anywhere near this beaten-up town.

Alpha hopped from my shoulder onto Charles's upper arm and used his beak to climb the rest of his way up to my boyfriend's shoulder. "This is only a small part of the territory. We birds cover a lot of mileage in a day, so naturally our domains are large and encompass several human cities."

"Does your flock cover Glendale, too? That's where we live." I had no idea birds kept their own maps and territory lines, but now that I thought about it, this made perfect sense. Just as their flock hierarchy and lack of a formal judicial system also made sense.

"Yes," Alpha stated simply. "The entire bay is now ours with this new acquisition. Though, we need to avoid the war to keep it."

"And you know where I can find my grandmother," I reminded him since my involvement hinged largely on this one fact. "Does that mean she's close? Somewhere near the bay?"

"She is closer than you know," Alpha said in a maddeningly cryptic way. He shook out his feathers again, giving Charles quite the start. "Also closer than I know. Bravo is the one who tracks these matters."

"But you'll take me to her if we help?" I practically begged, needing this confirmation more than anything else in that moment.

"If you win our case, then yes."

"We will," I promised, because it seemed like the only option. "We'll win it for you."

He nodded. "Good."

"Angie," Charles whisper-yelled. "You never promise the client you'll win, only that you'll fight your hardest for them."

"I doubt you'll get disbarred over how you represent some flock of seagulls out in Dewdrop Springs," I responded with a nervous chuckle.

"If your partner has doubts," Alpha warned, giving me some serious side eye, "then we can call this whole thing off now. It's only the lives of my flock on the line."

"No, no, no!" I cried. "We'll help, and he's just being modest. He's the best lawyer in all of Maine. I promise you that."

"Angie—" Charles started again.

This time Alpha cut him off. "If you're worried about your payment, worry not. The flock will arrange something worthwhile to thank you for your efforts."

I quickly translated.

"It's not about money, or whatever passes for money with birds. I just can't make a promise I don't know if I'll be able to keep. I will definitely give your case my all, though." Charles risked craning his neck to look Alpha in the eye. "I want to save your flock and prevent the war, too. And I think you have a very strong case in your defense. I'll represent you to the very best of my abilities. I don't often lose in court, and I don't plan on losing this time."

"Then I am satisfied," Alpha said with a curt nod. "We'll meet again tomorrow to discuss your progress. I'll send Bravo."

With that, the gulls let out a collective caw and rose into the night sky, leaving Charles and I to make our own way back to the parking lot.

Ten days.

If all went to plan, I would meet my long-lost grandmother in just ten short days. I still couldn't believe it.

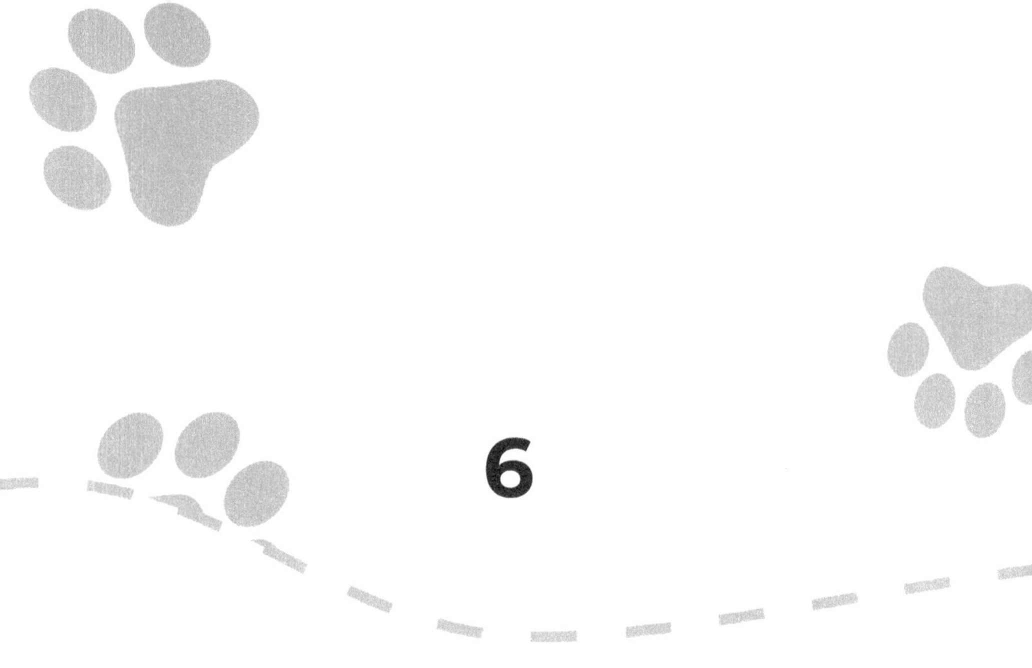

6

After being summarily dismissed by Alpha and his flock, Charles and I drove our separate cars to a little diner just outside the Dewdrop Springs city limits. He ordered a coffee, but I sprung for a hot fudge sundae with an extra cherry on top.

"So what's our plan?" he asked casually, holding the steaming mug between his hands.

Not even the sweetness of my dessert could mask the bitterness of what I realized had to happen next. I pushed my long-handled spoon as far down as it would go in the soda shop style glass and heaved a giant sigh.

"I'll tell Octo-Cat I can't take him to see Grizabella. He won't be happy, but I can take him another time. Soon, even. It's just that this is a once-in-a-lifetime opportunity, and I refuse to let it slip by. I might never meet my bio grandma otherwise."

Charles sucked air through his teeth, then regarded me with a frown. "You can't change your travel plans. It's too last minute for that. And I know you don't want to deal with how cranky Octo-Cat will be for the rest of his nine lives if you do."

I pressed my back against the firm vinyl of the booth. Charles was right, as always. There would be hefty penalties to pay for disappointing Octo-Cat, but I just couldn't see any way around it. "What choice do I have, though?" I asked.

"You go as planned. I'll work on things here." With that, he pulled my sundae to his side of the table and stole one of the cherries from the top.

"You can't talk to them," I pointed out, leaning over the table to reclaim my sundae and popping the remaining cherry into my mouth.

Charles smiled. "You use FaceTime with Octo-Cat, right? Can't we use it for the seagulls, too?"

"But what about your caseload? You've been so busy lately. I'd hate to add another thing when—"

"Angie, relax. It's okay. I want to help. Besides, my girlfriend is going out of town for the week. I'll need something to keep me busy on my off hours. Might as well be this." He shrugged and took a slow sip of coffee.

I waited for him to set the mug back onto the table. "Are you sure?"

He reached forward and grabbed both my hands, then wedged his fingers between mine. "Completely. You need this trip, and so does your cat. Besides, I already have a few case precedents in mind that should make winning this thing a cinch.

"You're too good to me," I said with a happy sigh. Especially considering he seemed to be quite afraid of the flock, but I didn't mention that part aloud.

"It's no big deal. They said they have ten days, and you'll be back by then. We can deliver the big case together."

"Sounds perfect." And it did.

Charles's features pinched as he leaned back against the red and white vinyl booth. "There's just one part I'm not sure about. They mentioned that Flock 83 disappeared, but they never said why or where they went."

I spooned a massive heap of hot fudge into my mouth and moaned with pleasure. "They're birds. Birds migrate. I'm sure it's no big deal."

Charles bit his lip and nodded. "Probably not. Still, I might feel better if I knew for sure. It could help the case, too."

"I don't know much about that, but I bet if you could get Bravo to talk to you alone without Alpha there, he'll be more forthcoming."

"I'll keep that in mind. Now tell me about what you did today before the run-in with those birds."

We laughed and chatted until I scraped the last smudge of gooey sweetness from my sundae. It was far shorter than I would have liked, but we both had big days ahead of us tomorrow.

Charles stood and extended a hand to me to help me out of the booth. "I'm going to miss you so much," he said before giving me a goodbye kiss that would need to last almost a full week.

* * *

Despite leaving early that morning with my human-do list, I arrived home after Paisley's self-prescribed bedtime of eight o'clock. The little dog, who lay snoozing by the front door, lifted her head groggily and thumped her tail against the hardwood floor.

"Are you home now, Mommy? I couldn't sleep without knowing you'd made it back safe and sound."

I set my bags on the floor and then scooped her into my arms and gave her a kiss on her forehead. "I'm home, sweetie. Go get some sleep."

She licked my hands as I bent to set her back down, then raced upstairs to find Nan, her little tail swinging back and forth the entire time.

I could always count on our Chihuahua for a warm welcome. Octo-Cat, on the other hand, did not look pleased to see me.

"Took you long enough," he spat from his perch about halfway up the staircase. "Did you at least get everything on my list?"

"Other than the stuff Nan picked up, yeah. You're welcome, by the way."

"Stuff," he said with a yawn. "I don't like you calling my things that."

He'd demanded everything from a specific brand of shrimp cocktail to that infuriating audiobook. I didn't know what else to call that odd grouping other than "stuff."

"Why are you so late?" he asked, running up the stairs in front of me as I trudged slowly after him.

"Something came up. Something with seagulls," I muttered, really not wanting to get into all that right now.

Octo-Cat arched his back and had the audacity to hiss at me. "You're not backing out on me. Are you? Because that is the lamest excuse you've come up with yet."

Oh, if only he knew how close I'd been to packing it in. He was lucky I loved him so much and that Charles loved me so much.

"Bright and early tomorrow morning. I'll be ready." I really should have lectured him on his poor manners or hurtful lack of gratitude, but I was just too tired to deal with him anymore that night.

"Good," he said, sashaying down the hallway to his bedroom and slipping through the slightly open door.

I shook my head and continued up another flight of stairs to my tower bedroom.

I was in for a very long week. Our road trip would take us thirty hours of driving each way—and that was without any breaks to eat, sleep, or stretch our legs. Thankfully I'd have Nan to split driving shifts with me, though I didn't love that she had wanted to take her tiny Audi coupe cross-country rather than my roomier old sedan.

Besides the drive itself, I knew I was in for an awkward time visiting with Grizabella's owner, Christine. She didn't know I could talk to animals and I preferred to keep it that way. This meant I'd needed to come up with a farfetched excuse that I'd already planned to be in town and would love it if she could watch Octo-Cat for me while I was off at my fake conference.

She'd bought it hook, line, and sinker. Really, she had no reason to suspect my cover story was a lie. Even though it was a harmless one, I still felt bad. Not bad enough to risk exposure of my freakish—and often troubling—ability, but still.

Despite today's hiccough with the seagulls, everything would still happen to plan with this trip, whether I spent time agonizing over the details or not. And I definitely preferred not.

I quieted my thoughts, promising myself I'd deal with each new thing as it came. The last thing on my mind before I drifted off to sleep was that I really hoped my cat knew how much I loved him, and that he would at least try to be nice to me for the duration of the trip.

Yes, I still believed in miracles, it seemed.

7

I awoke to the sound of four little feet charging rapidly up and down my private staircase. The stomping rose to the top of the stairs then paused.

"Reo-reow!" Octo-Cat cried from the other side of my door, a cat possessed. His point apparently now made, he raced back down the stairs and up again and down before letting out another echoing cry. "Reowowoweoeoweoew!"

I couldn't help but chuckle. He so rarely got the zoomies, but when he did, my sides usually ended up aching from all the unexpected laughing at his antics.

"Seems like someone's more than a little bit excited about our big trip," I called after flinging the door open.

My cat rushed into the room so fast, he appeared as little more than a brown blur. Slowing himself only slightly, he hopped onto my unmade bed and pounced on my pillow, hopping up and down on his front paws. "It's morning. Can we go now? Reo-reow!"

And he was off like a shot once again.

I glanced toward the window, which hung dark without even the slightest hint of sunlight yet peeking through. We had planned on being up early, but...

A quick check of my phone confirmed that it was hardly past four AM. The plan had been to set out at six...

Oh, well.

There really was no point bemoaning my lost sleep, nor was there any sense in trying to nab any additional shuteye before we headed out. Octo-Cat was simply too excited to accept any kind of delay.

I got dressed quickly, choosing a pair of blue polka-dot sweatpants and a T-shirt featuring a cartoon cat with his face pressed through a slice of white bread. The first time I'd worn it, Octo-Cat had insisted that the pun on "purebred" not only didn't make sense but was also offensive. Considering his past reaction to the harmless T, today seemed the perfect day to wear it. Not only would it help me stay comfortable during the long drive, but it would also enable me to exact a modicum of revenge for the early wake-up call. I smiled to myself as I swept my hair back into a messy bun and smeared Chapstick over said smile.

When I padded downstairs lugging my haphazardly packed suitcase behind me, I found Nan up and full of pep. She held out a shiny metallic travel mug, which I graciously accepted.

As I took my first glorious sip, Paisley ran into the room, singing, "Oh, what a beautiful day for an adventure!"

She yipped when she saw me, stood on her hind legs, and placed her front paws just below my knee—her signal that she wanted to be picked up.

I lowered my mug and took in the sight of her for the first time that morning. "Nan," I cried in shock. "What have you done to her?"

"That's her travel look. Don't you like it?" My grandmother patted the swirly pink scarf on her own head. It matched the one wrapped around the Chihuahua's neck perfectly. A paisley print, I realized.

On top of that, Paisley the dog also wore a pair of hot pink goggles—to help with wind-burn Nan later explained, which I guessed meant we'd be driving with the windows down for at least part of the trip. *Octo-Cat would love that.*

And, sure enough, after we all piled into the car—Nan in the passenger's seat, me driving, and the pets and luggage crammed into the sports coupe's tiny back seat—my grandmother immediately rolled down both windows.

"I should have sprung for the convertible when I had the chance," Nan remarked, much to the horror of Octo-Cat, who'd finally shaken off his zoomies and was now back to his usual crabby self.

"Are you sure we can't take my car?" I asked one last time while waiting for the engine to warm up a bit.

Nan turned to me, aghast. "Of course not. What's the point in having a nice car if you never use it?"

Well, I wasn't the one with the fancy sports car, but we would be sharing shifts, so I let that go. Our goal was to drive straight through to Colorado by alternating driving and sleeping shifts and consuming lots and lots of caffeine. I'd have preferred to actually stop at a motel for some rest along the way, but once Nan suggested making the trip a straight shot, Octo-Cat refused to have it any other way.

Tired but determined, I transitioned to drive.

Paisley let out a happy bark from right behind me, returning to her earlier song with even more volume than before. Frigid morning air rushed into the car as we picked up speed, and Paisley leaped over the center console, then scrambled onto Nan's lap, using that extra bit of height to stick her goggled face out the window.

"See," Nan clucked. "And you thought the goggles were too much."

"Can we please close the window and turn on the sun now?" my cat moaned. He'd never liked car trips, but at least now he could take them without needing to keep his claws dug firmly into my thighs for added comfort—his, obviously, not mine.

"You woke us all up two hours early. It's going to be dark for a while," I reasoned.

"Dark, fine. But does it need to be so cold?" I glanced at him in the rear-view mirror and found his unhappy amber eyes boring into mine.

Paisley let out another excited yip in response.

"Maybe we can take turns with the window the same way we're doing for the driving," I offered with a small shrug, willing myself to focus on the road ahead of me and not at the angry animal behind me.

Then something strange happened. In fact, if I hadn't been there myself, I never would have believed in.

Octo-Cat *laughed.* He actually laughed!

“The important thing is we reach my dear Grizabella as quickly as possible,” he said with a blissful sigh.

“Yeah,” I answered with a smile, hardly believing how reasonable he was being.

“Now drive faster please,” he commanded in a perfectly pleasant way.

I checked my speedometer and shook my head. “I’m already a few miles above the speed limit. Sorry.”

“Why sorry? You and I both know this car can go a lot faster.”

A quick look in the rear-view mirror revealed he was being perfectly serious, and if I didn’t comply with his demands, he’d start nagging at me again. I groaned and pressed down on the accelerator with a slight bit of added pressure before easing back again.

Oh, boy. This was going to be a long, long drive.

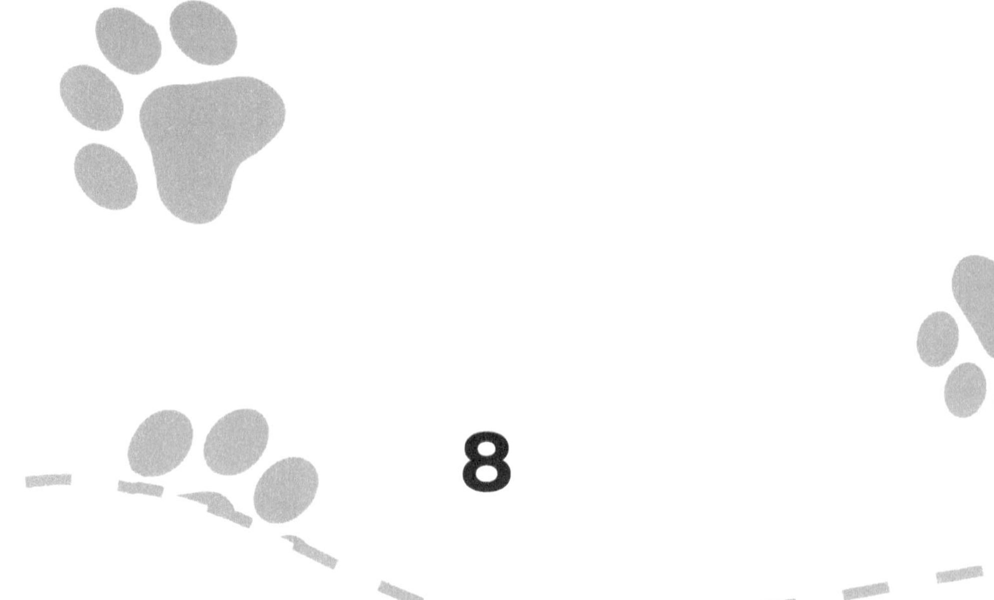

8

A couple hours into our trip, the sun had finally begun to peek over the horizon. Nan had spent most of that morning dozing softly beside me. Paisley had settled in her lap and was making cute whimpering noises as she rested. Octo-Cat, on the other hand, remained in the back seat endlessly droning on about all his plans for his week with Grizabella.

I nodded along saying nothing as was expected, since when Octo-Cat spoke, he usually did it for his own benefit rather than anyone else's.

"Mommy," a small voice rose up from beside me. I quickly turned to see Paisley had lifted her head and was staring at me with wide, sparkling eyes. "I have to go potty."

We'd just passed the perfect exit for a quick pit stop not even two minutes ago. We were also on the portion of our trip that took us through rural countryside, which meant the options would be few and far between.

"I'll keep an eye out," I said, since that was the best I could do. "I promise."

"Excuse me, I'm talking here," the tabby in the back seat growled and then continued with his long-winded soliloquy.

"I don't think I can hold it," the little dog squeaked, standing now and raising one paw after the other in excitement.

Nan awakened with a snort and glanced around the car with bleary eyes.

Paisley whimpered again, louder and more persistent.

“I promise we’ll stop as soon as the next exit pops up. It won’t be too much longer, okay?" I hoped this little white lie ended up being true.

"I can't hold it. I can't hold it," Paisley squealed.

I knew better than to push our luck, lest Nan land herself with a lap full of doggie pee. So I pulled the sports coupe to the side of the highway, grateful there weren't many people out at this early hour. Rush hour hadn't even begun yet.

"Be very careful," I explained before opening my door and allowing Paisley to trot after me. "And don't go where I can't see you!"

Nan had already fallen back asleep in her seat, which meant it was up to me to keep track of both animals.

Octo-Cat sauntered out and began to walk up the shoulder of the highway. I let him do his thing. Mostly because if I corrected him, he’d be extra sure to do the exact opposite of what I wanted.

Instead, I turned back to watch as Paisley squatted and sighed with pleasure upon relieving herself. “It feels so good.”

“Dogs are such disgusting creatures.” Octo-Cat marched toward me with his tail standing straight and tall. "Well," he said, cocking his head expectantly.

"Well, what?" I responded with a sigh.

"Where's my litter box?" He stopped and plopped his rear on the pavement, regarding me with a sneer. "You can't expect me to use the litter box without *the litter box."*

"I am not assembling your box for a pit stop. It doesn't come out until we reach Colorado.”

"So you expect me not to relieve myself in all that time? Impossible."

“You can relieve yourself. Just not in the box. I have nowhere to throw the litter once you're done, and it’s incredibly wasteful to get it out for a single use. And I'm not driving with an open litter box in the car, so forget that right now.”

"And what do you expect me to do?" he asked with a huff.

Paisley trotted back over and gave Octo-Cat a big lick on the face. "I can teach you how to potty outside, Octavius. I don’t mind at all.”

"No, thank you," he said with a shudder.

I crossed my arms and stared at him down the bridge of my nose. "Are you going to go or not?"

"Not," came his terse reply.

"Fine. Then let's get back in the car."

Once we’d all piled back in, Octo-Cat’s excited talk of his plans with Grizabella turned to bitter complaints about my unwillingness to accommodate his litter box needs.

"Will you just stop it already?" I asked after a solid ten minutes of this. "I'm sorry I upset you, but there's nothing we can do about it now."

"I would think you had a little more respect by now," he scoffed. “After all we’ve been through! After all I’ve done for you. You can’t just—”

"Oh!" I interrupted, having landed upon an idea I rather liked. "That audiobook you sent me all over Blueberry Bay looking for... Let's listen to it."

His voice softened. "Oh, yes. Shockingly, that is a good idea from you."

I rolled my eyes as I shoved the CD in and turned up the volume.

"Dr. Roman’s Guide to Romance," the narrator said in a deep, authoritative voice that felt completely wrong for this kind of book. "Chapter one. Learning to Love.”

"Love is a beautiful agreement between two souls, and it’s also one of the best things life has to offer," the narrator droned. "Romance is but a small part of the broader picture of love, although many find it to be the most rewarding."

"He's right about that," Octo-Cat said with a happy sigh. “I am a cat forever changed by the love of my darling Grizabella."

I rolled my eyes again. Thank goodness Charles and I weren’t like this.

"Romance is all about celebrating love, and to do that you first need to have love in your life.”

I groaned. "Do you really want to listen to this guy?"

"Ssshhhhhh," Octo-Cat hissed. "This is good stuff here."

I tightened my grip on the steering wheel and gritted my teeth as the speaker—Dr. Roman himself, it turned out—continued to prattle on about how love was a many splendored thing and other such clichés. Seriously, how was this book a bestseller?

Before long, Nan perked up. "What are you listening to?" she asked.

"Only the single most intelligent human to ever live," Octo-Cat answered even though Nan couldn't understand him.

I translated this as, "Octo-Cat's new audiobook." Injecting as much sarcasm into my tone as I could manage while still paying proper attention to the road, I added, "Dr. Roman's Guide to Romance. Apparently he's the single most intelligent human to ever live."

Unaware of the compliments and insults we were bandying about, Dr. Roman continued, "Unlike love, romance is not ever a noun. It's always meant to be a verb. Romance doesn't just happen. It's something you must work to actively create in your life." He paused to let this great wisdom sink in.

"Can you believe this guy?" I asked quietly, hoping the cat wouldn't overhear. "He doesn't even have a basic understanding of the parts of speech. How can you believe a word that comes out of his mouth?"

"He's right, actually," Nan said, nodding thoughtfully. "I never thought of it exactly like that, but it's true. Why just last week, Grant and I—"

"Ssshhhhh," Octo-Cat hissed again, and we all fell silent listening to Dr. Roman's words fill the car.

Was I being unfair to this book, or was I simply cynical about romance? Charles had always been the more romantic of the two of us, and I'd always been more than happy to let him take the lead. Did I owe it to him to try harder?

Ugh.

Whether or not I liked Dr. Roman, the truth was we were all going to be stuck in this car together for quite some time. I could at least listen to what Dr. Roman had to say. Especially considering Nan and Octo-Cat now hung on his every word. Even little Paisley sat with both ears erect as she happily squinted her eyes in that special way Chihuahuas do when they are completely content with life.

I listened without complaint as Dr. Roman delivered his list of seven must-haves for creating romance, and I said nothing when he launched into his guided meditation for romantic mindfulness. But by the time he started in on the aphrodisiac effect of certain foods and beverages, I'd had enough.

"Let's stop for coffee," I said, then let out a giant, demonstrative yawn.

"Shhhhhh," all three of the others hissed at me.

Even though they were talking to me, it was Dr. Roman's voice that quieted as a ringing sound poured out of the car's speakers.

Nan pressed a button on the radio and Charles's voice filled the car. "Hey, how's the drive going?" he asked.

"I hope you don't mind, dear," Nan said, "but I hooked your phone up to the Bluetooth because I knew your fellow would be calling before too long. Looks like I was right."

I smiled, so incredibly grateful for the distraction I could have cried. "Totally fine," I told both Nan and Charles since it applied to both of the things they'd said. "We're making good time. How are things there?"

Charles sucked in a sharp breath.

And that was all I needed to know good news wouldn't be coming.

9

"The flock is here," Charles whispered into the phone. "They're in my front yard. Dozens of them."

"What?" I shouted, eliciting a fresh string of complaints from the crabby tabby in the back seat. "Why?"

"I don't know. I can't exactly talk to them on my own," Charles pointed out, and of course he was right.

"Do you want me to turn around? We've only been at it a few hours. I can come back. You don't have to deal with this on—"

Even before I finished that offer, Octo-Cat flew forward from the back seat, scaring the life out of me. When he landed on my lap, claws and all, I swerved into the next lane. Thank goodness, the road was still mostly empty on this stretch.

"Easy there, girl," Nan said, stroking the dashboard of her car lovingly.

"Is everything okay?" Charles asked, his worry echoing around the car's cushy interior.

"No, we're fine. But I guess I'm not turning around."

“You better not be," Octo-Cat warned, digging his claws into my thighs once again to emphasize his point.

"Do you want to put me on FaceTime or something?" I offered meekly. “So that I can talk to the seagulls for you?”

“It’s okay. I mean, it’s definitely unnerving, but I think they're just keeping an eye on me," he said.

The tap turned on, and the sound of fresh water rushing into his empty coffee pot gave me a wicked craving for my favorite caffeinated beverage. Oh, how I wished I was there with him rather than on this obnoxious road trip.

"They must've followed me home last night," Charles continued. "I'm getting that they don't trust me."

"I don't know much about birds," I admitted as we passed a semi-truck on the left. "They've never been willing to talk to me before now, but my guess is they just want to make sure you don't forget about them." I shrugged even though he couldn't see the gesture.

"Well, it makes me uncomfortable," he informed me. "Whenever I look out the window all their beady eyes snap to me. They’re sizing me up. It's unnerving, really."

"I'm sorry." And I truly *was* sorry. "I shouldn’t have asked you to—”

"No," he cut me off. "I want to do this for you. For your family. I’m just not sure I totally understand what's expected."

I opened my mouth to argue, but Charles still had more to say.

"I researched case precedents last night before going to bed. You know, just in case those things matter to seagulls, and I did find a few cases that could work. Winning this for the flock should be pretty simple, but whether or not we can win isn't what concerns me here."

"It's having the whole flock camping out in your yard," I finished for him.

"Yeah. It doesn't seem right. Why don't they trust me? What do they expect me to find?"

"You don't think they told us the full truth about the war?" I asked.

"Or the disappearance of the other flock," he confirmed. Coffee now gurgled and brewed on Charles's side of the conversation.

"Do you think there's something important we're missing here?" I prompted while my mouth salivated for the hot bitter rush of that coffee.

"I definitely think it's worth checking out," he agreed. "I know they're just birds, but still I'd like to know the truth."

"I wish I were there to help," I moaned. "It feels wrong to be so far removed from the situation, especially since you wouldn't even be doing this if it weren't for me."

I still hadn't told Nan about Bravo's offer to introduce me to my long-lost bio grandma, so I chose my words carefully while speaking to Charles now. "I'll be back before you have to go to trial."

"These birds are definitely going to keep me on task until then. I honestly worry about what they'll do if they think I'm ignoring their case. It almost feels like they're some kind of avian mafia here. Ugh.

If only there was some way to find that missing flock," he said thoughtfully.

“Actually, there *is* a way," Octo-Cat piped in from the back seat.

"Hang on," I told Charles. "It seems Octo-Cat has an idea."

"Not an idea," he corrected with a haughty snort. "The solution.”

He wasted no time in continuing, "I don't know all the details—or really any of the details—about this seagull stuff. You know, since *somebody* didn’t deem this new case important enough to tell her partner about.”

I held my tongue to avoid another pointless argument. But when had there been time to tell him? I was out until all hours working on his honey-do list last night, and today I’d been focused on driving while he filled every spare moment with either talk of Grizabella or lackluster advice from Dr. Roman.

"Anyway, as much as I hate to admit it," Octo-Cat continued. "Our top spy stayed home."

"Our top spy?" I asked. It was rare Octo-Cat admitted that anyone could do anything better than him, especially a task he enjoyed as much as spying.

"Yeah, the raccoon."

"Oh," I mumbled. "That's not a bad idea."

"Of course it's not a bad idea. It came from me."

"What?" Charles asked. "What did he say?"

"Pringle," I explained in one single word.

"What about him?" Charles wanted to know.

"Well, he can talk to the birds for you and he loves gossip. I'm sure you don't even have to ask for his help. You just have to talk about the problem near him and he'll go explore it on his own."

"Is that what you want me to do?"

"Yeah, I think it's a good idea. Especially if it puts these questions to rest for you."

"Okay," he agreed, taking a slurp of coffee that made me incredibly antsy in my coffeeless state "I'll go over to your place after work and see what I can do."

"Great. If you want, you can FaceTime me once you're there. I'll tell Pringle what we need him to do."

"I love you," Charles said before taking another noisy sip.

I told him I loved him too and said goodbye. When we hung up, Dr. Roman's voice immediately came bursting back through the speakers. No, no more. I needed at least some kind of break from him, so I turned the radio off.

"Hey," Octo-Cat protested.

"Hey yourself," I said. "I just need a minute so I can focus on finding an exit."

"Does this mean you're finally going to set up my litter box? Because I've been holding it, and I hate holding it."

I refused to dignify that question with a response since I'd already made my position on the travel litter box more than clear. And a few miles later I found an exit that boasted a gas station, if not much else.

Hey, gas station coffee was good enough for me, especially since I didn't know how quickly Nan's car ran through fuel and didn't want to take any chances there.

"Can you top us off?" I asked Nan after pulling in beside the pump closest to the door. I was out of the car and rushing inside before she could even answer.

A few minutes later, I returned with a steaming Styrofoam cup full of the good stuff clutched greedily in my hands.

"We should stop for some breakfast," Nan suggested, finishing up at the pump.

"I'm not sure there's anything on this exit."

"Well, something will turn up eventually," she said with a smile, and so we took a twenty-minute detour until at last we found a small diner that looked like it had been converted from a mobile home.

We ordered scrambled eggs and sausage to go, then sat outside with the animals in the parking lot as we tried to enjoy our meal.

"So what's going on with those seagulls Charles was talking about?" Nan asked when we'd both eaten through about half of our containers.

"Oh, they need help with a territory dispute." I tried to wave her off and changed the subject. "How about Dr. Roman, though? Do you really like his guide to romance?" I asked with a giggle.

"It's as good as any other guide out there, I'm sure," she said. "But why are you going out of your way to help these birds now? Couldn't this have waited until you were back from the trip? Is there some kind of deadline?"

"According to their laws, we don't have much time before a war starts up," I explained casually. "So I agreed to work on their terms in hopes of preventing that war."

"But why?" she said, studying me with glistening eyes.

"I..." my words trailed away.

"It's okay, dear. Whatever it is, you can tell me. I'm a big girl. I can handle it," Nan said with a half-cocked grin.

"It's just, they said they know where..." I didn't know how to word this, exactly. Nan was my grandmother. And yet I longed to know the woman our family had lost so many years ago. "Well," I started again, taking a different approach. "You know how birds are. They see everything, and they know the lay of the land, and…" I continued to sputter nervously, getting nowhere fast.

"Is this about your other grandmother, dear?" Nan said softly, reaching over to squeeze my hand. "It's okay if it is."

I nodded but said nothing.

"Well then, we better help these birds because I'd like to meet her, too."

10

The rest of the day eked by at a snail's pace. I also felt like an ant who'd had its legs trapped in molasses. Well, whatever kind of insect I'd become, I was moving and moving and yet getting nowhere.

By this point, we'd more than half finished Dr. Roman's audiobook. Nan had taken over the wheel about an hour ago, but still I couldn't sleep. Somehow, against all odds, Octo-Cat had also stayed awake this entire time. His eagerness to reach our destination was far past being cute… and dangerously close to the point of me putting him in his carrier just to calm him down and give the rest of us a break.

When my phone rang, I jumped in my seat at the chance to answer it. I'd have liked to read a book or play some games, but I always became carsick when I focused my gaze anywhere but on the road ahead.

"Angie?" Charles said when I forgot to offer a hello.

"Yes, I'm here. Sorry. What's up?" I leaned forward in my seat eager to hear his report.

"I'm just about to leave the firm and head to your place." He hesitated. "That is, if you still want to speak with Pringle."

"Yeah, yeah, of course I do. How was your day? Better than it started out?"

He hesitated again, sending my worry into high gear. "Kind of. At least the entire flock didn't follow me to work."

"But some of them did?" Why had I ever agreed to help these annoying birds? Yes, they had some serious leverage over me, but I hated that they were practically stalking Charles while I was too far to do anything to put a stop to it.

"Yeah. Well, one of them, anyway."

"That's probably Bravo. He's kind of in charge of this whole legal thing."

"He's been sitting at my window all day. Watching. Waiting. I don't like it, Angie."

I didn't like it, either, but Charles needed me to remain calm and handle the situation. "Put him on, please."

"Just a second."

I listened as Charles wrenched the window open and whistled for the bird to join us.

"You're on speaker," Charles informed me a few seconds later.

"Bravo?" I asked, doing my best to keep my voice calm and even. Authoritative.

"The one and only," the seagull confirmed.

Okay, the flock worked according to rules and hierarchies. If I could appeal to that, perhaps I could get him to back off. "Why are you stalking Charles?" I demanded. "You hired us to help, and now you have to trust us."

"No can do. Alpha has given me express instructions to keep a close eye on everything, and that's exactly what I plan to do."

"And I'm asking you very politely not to. Charles will work better if you cut him some slack." I took a shallow breath, resisting the urge to sigh heavily into the phone.

Unfortunately, Bravo remained steadfast in his refusal. "Alpha's orders are final. Your mate's going to have a white shadow until it's go time."

A white shadow? I didn't like the sound of that at all and was starting to understand why Charles was so suspicious of what had led to this whole territory dispute in the first place.

"Okay, well, I tried," I told the bird, and then, "Charles, take me off speaker."

"Okay," he said with a huff. "So, what now?"

"Close the window," I whispered into the phone. "I don't want Bravo to hear this next part."

I waited as the window slammed shut with a thump.

"This is getting weird, right?" Charles whispered back.

"I think it started that way, but it's definitely weird." I paused and took a moment to figure out a plan. "I'm going to call you back. Let it go to voicemail. I'm going to leave a message for Pringle. Make sure Bravo's not around when you let him listen to it."

"But how can I do either of those things? Getting Pringle to listen to me and keeping Bravo away?"

That was a good question. I ran through my options, silently wondering just how well birds could hear. Would Bravo be able to listen in through a closed window? I didn't know, but I still had to take a chance with this. After all, the alternative was doing nothing to help poor Charles through this mess.

"Um, I'll call back twice and leave two separate messages," I decided. "One to get Pringle inside, and one to tell him what we need. As long as you don't let Bravo into the house, that should give you the privacy you need. You still have the key I gave you, right?"

"I do," he answered.

"Good. Head straight to my place. Pringle is probably in one of his treehouses, but he might be off collecting secrets from the neighborhood. Can you call me back when you find him?"

"What about the voicemails you're planning to leave?" Charles wondered.

"Those are just a fail-safe. Call me, and I'll make sure to stop whatever I'm doing—be it driving or sleeping or whatever—and I'll give you my full attention. Hey, do you mind hanging around my house for a while if he's out?"

I could practically hear the cringe in his voice as he said, "Better your place with one seagull than mine with the whole flock." I really wished I was there with him, and not just because this road trip was driving me crazy.

"Good point. You know you can stay at my place if you need to."

"Nah. They'll just move bases, plus Jacques and Jillianne will be furious if I'm not home by bedtime." He was right, of course. His two Sphynx cats were even more strangely entitled than Octo-Cat.

"Okay, I'll call right back," I promised, hating to let him go but also knowing I needed to move things along here. "Remember not to pick up. Love you. Bye."

We hung up, and I took a few deep breaths before hitting redial. When his voicemail picked up, I raised my voice just south of a shout. "Pringle! Pringle! Charles is looking for you. Come over and talk to him. I've left you a top-secret message that will self-destruct in ten minutes whether or not you listen to it. So hurry up and follow him inside. Further instructions await you there."

Click.

There. I'd appealed to his sense of drama. He wouldn't be able to resist that.

I texted Charles between calls: "One down, one to go."

When my second call was routed to voicemail, I laid out the basics of my plan and how it would involve the nosy trash panda.

"Agent Pringle, thank goodness you've accepted our call for help." I reached deep down and pulled out every spy movie cliche I could think of. The raccoon had once thought of himself as a noble medieval knight, but his predilections tended to change based on whatever TV shows and movies he preferred at the time. Right now, he was on a Tom Cruise/ Arnold Schwarzenegger/ Bruce Willis binge, so spy tropes it was.

"We fear our mission might have been compromised and that our supposed allies aren't giving us all the information. We've got a dirty flock and the impending threat of war. Already one flock has gone

AWOL, and we need you to find these key witnesses and extract the true nature of their disappearance."

As I continued to rattle off everything we knew in the most dramatic way possible, I started simply throwing in the names of popular action flicks. The cornier I could make this, the more our little raccoon spy would like it.

"It's going to be *Sum of All Fears* around here if we don't stop this *Lethal Weapon* from detonating. I'm counting on you to be *The Terminator* of these lies before somebody *Dies Hard*. Are you ready to join us on this *Mission Impossible*, *Agent 007*? Good, then await my next call for your assignment."

I hung up quickly. If either Nan or Octo-Cat was paying attention, it was only a matter of time until one of them burst out laughing and spoiled the ruse. Yes, I knew that last part of my plea had made very little sense, but I also knew it would get the raccoon excited and ready to do whatever it took to solve the case.

Operation Raccoon Spy, here we come!

11

Charles texted half an hour later to say he couldn't find Pringle anywhere, but that he'd stay as late as he could without upsetting his two feline overlords back home.

While waiting to see if he would need me, I eventually nodded off. I didn't wake up again until the dead of the night.

Nan was wide awake as she took her turn behind the wheel, and she was listening ahead in Dr. Roman's audiobook while the pets napped curled up together in the back seat. Octo-Cat would not be happy about that.

"Oh, you're up?" my grandmother asked, turning her head to glance at me briefly as she clicked the stereo off.

I stretched what little I could belted into my seat, then wiped the sleep from my eyes. "Did Charles call?"

"He did, but I let him know you were dead to the world."

Wow. I really must have been if I hadn't heard the phone ring.

"Do you want me to take over for a while?" I offered despite still feeling quite sleepy. We could always find some coffee to activate my awakening sequence, if needed.

"I'm fine, dear. I don't need quite as much sleep as I did when I was young."

I smiled instead of pointing out that she'd slept clear through most of the day. "Okay, then I guess I'll try to grab some more rest of my own. Wake me up when you're ready to switch, okay?"

"Not a problem," she promised and hit play on the audiobook again.

It only took a couple of minutes for me to drift back into a deep slumber—well, at least deep considering I had to do it while sitting up and buckled in. Driving was just about the most exhausting activity you could do while sitting on your butt the whole time. If I dreamed, it wasn't something worth remembering because the next thing I knew somebody in the car was screaming.

"Oh my whiskers! I've never seen such a beautiful place! We have to go! We have to go!" Octo-Cat crooned as I opened my eyes and blinked hard.

Noticing I was now awake, my cat doubled down. "Angela, tell the old woman to get off at this exit!"

Paisley barked in an extra hyper, extra high pitch, the way she did whenever she was too excited to form actual words.

My head pounded as I tried to figure out where we were and what time it was. The night sky still hung dark above us, the road empty, and yet all of my companions seemed to be wide awake.

"Angela, take the wheel! We're almost to the exit! We can't miss it!" my cat continued to caterwaul.

I glanced over to Nan who appeared to be flagging behind the wheel. Her hands hung loosely over the steering column as she drove with her wrists at ten and two.

"Nan!" I cried. "You should have woken me up!"

"Huh? What?" She turned to look at me for just the briefest of moments, but it was enough.

Thump, thump! Thump!

The car jerked off the road and into the ditch at the shoulder.

Paisley let out a panicked yelp.

Octo-Cat hissed.

And I held on for dear life.

Then the airbags deployed, waking up my senses and grounding me in our terrible new reality. *We'd crashed!*

Nan sobbed beside me. "My poor, poor baby. What have I done to you?" Once again she was talking to her car.

It would be up to me to take stock and make sure nobody was hurt.

"Paisley?" I called, knowing instantly that she was most at risk given her less than five-pound frame.

"That was scary," she whimpered from behind me. "I fell on the floor, but it only hurt a little."

I breathed a sigh of relief, then took another deep breath before asking, "Octo-Cat? Are you okay?"

"I am not happy about this turn of events, Angela," he growled. It wasn't his usual peeved-off growl, but rather something low, deep, and incredibly intimidating. *Oh no. What now?*

When I turned around, my neck twinged in pain, but I was able to see that he was still sitting on the seat with his claws sunk deep into the leather upholstery.

Bits of cushion popped through where his claws had snagged the seating. I picked up a blanket from the floor and tossed it over the seat so Nan wouldn't notice. She was already worked up enough without seeing this particular display.

"I am outraged!" my cat informed me from beneath the blanket before popping his head out a moment later. He left his body covered as he lectured me for this latest indignity. "When I requested we make a pit stop, it was so that we could see the largest aquarium in the state. Not for whatever *this* was."

"The largest... in the state? Where are we?" I wondered aloud. I knew we were somewhere between our home in Maine and Grizabella's in Colorado, but where?

"Michi-bun," Paisley provided. "At least that's what Nan said when we passed a big sign a while ago. Welcome to Michi-bun."

Michigan. That put us a little less than halfway into our journey, which also meant that despite our best attempts, we were making terrible time.

I shot daggers at my cat, realizing that for all the anger he had toward me right now, I had far more reason to be upset with him. "All this screaming and fuss was about an aquarium which wouldn't even be open at this time of night. Seriously? You have an aquarium back home!"

"It's not the largest one in the state, though. I want to see this one."

"Not a chance." I whipped back to face front. Ouch, my poor neck. "You'll be lucky if we even still get to see Grizabella at this point."

"Noooooooooooo!" he screamed, launching himself into my lap, claws still extended. "You can't do that to me."

"Ouch. Bad kitty!" I spat as I grabbed him off my lap and returned him to the back seat. My neck twisted in pain.

"Nan," I nudged, noticing her still hunched over the deployed airbag, stroking the car's dashboard. "Are you okay?"

"I'm fine, but my poor girl is a wreck."

"It'll be okay. This is what insurance is for," I offered with what I hoped was a reassuring smile. "We need to focus on getting some help. Should I look up a tow place on my phone?"

"No," she said with another sniff and a sob. "I have a friend in the area. She'll come and get us."

"Okay, but you should probably call now. We don't know how much damage has been done to the car or how long it will take to get it road-ready again."

She shook her head and a fresh rivulet of tears ran down both cheeks. "I'm so sorry about this, dear. I should have asked you to take over, but I didn't think I was that tired."

"It's okay. Really. Accidents happen," I said, although I couldn't ever remember when one had happened to me. "We're all fine. That's what counts."

Nan unbuckled her seatbelt and got out to observe the damage.

I followed suit, my feet sinking into the spring mud with a squelching sound.

"I don't know what happened," she muttered, staring at the immobilized vehicle with a dumbfounded expression. "I wasn't even that tired. I—"

What had happened couldn't be changed. Now it was up to me to keep Nan from descending into a vicious spiral of guilt.

"You don't have to explain," I assured her, coming to stand at her side. "I understand, and it's going to be okay. But we need somebody to come get us. Here. Give me your phone."

She reached into her front pocket and took it out, then handed it over to me.

"Thank you. Now what's the name of your friend who's going to come get us?"

"Melissa," she said with a small sigh. "She usually goes to sleep pretty early, but she gave me her night owl husband's number for emergencies."

"Well, I'd definitely say this qualifies." I thumbed through the contacts until I found *Melissa* and then *Melissa's Husband.*

I'd wait until later to ask Nan why she had the number of some guy way out in Michigan as an emergency contact. Because whatever her reason for taking such a strange precaution, she'd definitely been right to do it.

12

Nan's friend appeared about forty minutes later with her whole family in tow. "Climb in," she said, pointing to the cluttered back rows of the giant SUV. "Sorry about the mess."

I got in beside a little girl who was fast asleep with a glistening bead of drool dribbling off one pouty lip.

"Couldn't leave her at home," Melissa said, watching me while Nan stood with Melissa's husband inspecting the damage from the accident. "Nan called me, but I don't actually drive, so we all had to come."

"I'm not getting in there. It smells like dog," Octo-Cat informed me from outside. His nose wrinkled in disgust, and once again, I was more than a little relieved that other people couldn't understand him.

I sighed instead of answering. He knew I couldn't talk to him in front of people who didn't know my secret, but that never stopped him from complaining, endlessly complaining.

"Aren't you worried your cat will run away?" Melissa asked, glancing from him to me with a worried expression. Both tall and thick, she was a big woman, but the biggest part of her was the earnest smile she wore as she greeted me.

"He'll be fine," I said for both of them.

That was when Paisley ran over, tail wagging wildly, to say hello to the new arrivals.

"Oh my gosh!" Melissa cried in such a high-pitched voice it made my ears rings. "Who is this sweet angel baby?"

"That's Nan's dog, Paisley," I supplied.

"Well, of course it is." Melissa scooped the happy Chihuahua up into her arms and let Paisley lick her face. I noticed that her baggy T-shirt read *Crazy Chihuahua Lady* in big blocky letters. No wonder she and Nan were friends.

"Oh, you are the sweetiest-beatiest," she squealed. Both she and Paisley seemed to shake with happiness. Was this woman so obsessed with Chihuahuas that she had even started to act like them? Funny.

"I like her," Paisley said with a happy bark.

"She looks just like my Sky Princess," Melissa informed me with that ever-present smile. "You'll meet her when we take you back to our place for a rest while your car is being worked on. See..." She motioned toward the banged-up sports car. "This is why I don't drive."

Nan returned with Melissa's husband, and they climbed into the SUV.

"C'mon, Octo-Cat," I called and clicked my tongue.

Thankfully, he decided it was better to listen to me than to be left alone on the side of the road and complied.

Melissa leaned forward from the back row and bumped my shoulder. "Wow, he really listens. Almost like a dog."

"A dog!?" Octo-Cat shrieked. "That's it. Let me out of here. I don't want to spend another second with this crazy woman."

"Hush. It's fine," I murmured, the weight of my fatigue weighing heavily now that I was sitting back down.

Melissa gasped but said nothing for the rest of the drive back to her home more than half an hour away.

When we arrived, we were greeted by the loudest chorus of barking I'd ever heard in my life. A moment later, five dogs ran outside to say hello.

"You have five dogs now?" Nan asked with a chuckle, scratching some kind of mixed breed with multi-color eyes behind the ears.

"Seven, actually," Melissa corrected. "The Chihuahuas are inside because they're not strong enough to push through the dog door on their own."

"She's insane," Octo-Cat choked out. "Certifiably insane. I refuse to step paw into that house."

"It's already the middle of the night," Nan said with a sigh. "I do appreciate you coming to our rescue, but I hope we don't have to wait until morning to get someone to look at the car."

"C'mon, there's at least twenty mechanics within ten miles of us. I'm sure someone will be open and able to take us," Melissa's husband said after he'd returned from taking his daughter to bed.

"I'll be back," Nan told me before climbing back into the front seat of the enormous SUV and disappearing.

"So..." Melissa said, her eyes wide and mischievous. "You're Nan's granddaughter, right?"

Leave it to Nan not to properly introduce us. "That's me. My name's Angie."

She dropped her voice to a whisper as we climbed the twisty steps toward the front door. "Are you the one who can... you know? Talk to... well, you know?"

Anger flared in my chest, but I did my best to swallow it back down. Was Nan seriously entrusting random people across the country with my biggest secret? It seemed like she wasn't even all that close with Melissa, given how surprised Melissa had been to meet Paisley and how Nan couldn't even remember exactly how many dogs these people had.

"You don't have to say anything," Melissa said with a conspiratorial grin. "Your secret's safe with me, by the way. I would never tell anyone. Well, except for my husband and daughter, of course. I tell them everything."

Great. So at least three other people knew, and one of them was just a kid. First or second grade, tops. Kids had no filters. Not exactly the best people to trust with secrets.

Melissa flung the door open with a "ta-da," and I glanced into the dark house, expecting to see her dogs lined up to greet me.

What I actually saw was far, far worse...

Octo-Cat must have crept up the stairs behind us because he now let out a mighty growl and jumped—literally jumped—into a thin tree that lined the front stairs.

"It's my worst nightmare come to life," he howled.

I wanted to tell him that we wouldn't be here long, that he had nothing to worry about, but I honestly didn't know how badly busted Nan's car was or whether Melissa's husband was right about being able to find a mechanic at this hour. So instead I left him clinging to the tree as Paisley and I followed Melissa into the house and shut the door behind us.

Hopefully his worst nightmare wouldn't also prove to be mine.

13

What are you doing in my housssse?” hissed a Maine Coon cat, who looked a lot like Octo-Cat except he was at least twice as big, twice as fluffy, and twice as intimidating.

After demanding I explain my presence, he marched straight up to Paisley and batted her in the face. He didn’t growl or take out his claws, but the maneuver still felt extremely aggressive.

“*Ttccch!*” Melissa said, and the cat skittered away, choosing a place midway up the staircase to keep an eye on us.

“This is my house. I am the king!” the cat said, wagging his tail wildly.

I watched him wearily, worried he might make another move to dominate Paisley if we weren’t careful. Thank goodness, Octo-Cat had chosen to stay outside. This was one fight I knew he wouldn’t be able to win.

"I decide who comes and goes, and I did not approve your entry," he meowed. "If you want to stay, you must give me a treat stick."

"Oh my gosh," Melissa said with a gasp, raising a hand to her heart. "He's talking to you, isn't he? Merlin's talking, and you're understanding! What is he saying? What does he want?"

I was hesitant to admit that her cat was coming off like a major jerk, but I was even more hesitant to talk about this at all. This person was still little more than a stranger to me, and yet she knew the most intimate, private thing about me. This wasn't right.

"Well?" Melissa asked with that wide smile of hers.

I sighed. "He wants a treat stick."

She chuckled. "Well, of course he does. Come with me, and I'll show you the procedure."

She then walked me through the exact way Merlin preferred to be offered his special treat sticks, including where to stand when I was opening it, how fast to walk toward the cat tower where he preferred to take the treat, and precisely how long to hold it in my hand before dropping it for him to do the rest of the work.

Man, for not being able to speak to his humans, this Merlin sure knew how to communicate his needs.

"I'm going to let the dogs in now, okay?" Melissa announced, once we'd completed the offering to her cat.

I hadn't realized they weren't with us, but the second she opened the sliding glass door, I realized just how quiet the house had been without them.

Paisley immediately rolled onto her back and let the others sniff her as she wagged and wiggled. A fat corgi sniffed her so vigorously that he flipped her over by accident.

"This is great," Nan's little dog cried. "I've always wanted to go to doggie daycare."

I sighed. Well, seeing as my secret was out anyway, I may as well talk back to her. "It's not daycare. It's just—"

Paisley jumped to her feet with a bark so loud, I took a step back in shock. "It's the dog from the mirror! *Bark, bark, bark!*"

Sure enough, a nearly identical mostly black tricolor Chihuahua came galloping over. She barked once and then began to kick up her back legs in a comical display of scratching and snuffling that was most likely meant to be intimidating.

"No, you're the dog from the mirror!" she barked at Paisley.

"Sky Princess," Melissa scolded. "Come here."

The little dog whined and struggled for a moment before settling into her human's arms.

"Pick me up! Pick me up!" Paisley begged, standing on her hind legs and pawing me while she whimpered.

The moment I did, both dogs resumed barking and accusing each other of being mirror dogs again.

"Oh, boy. It's a good thing my daughter is such a deep sleeper, otherwise I'd be afraid they'd wake her up," Melissa said with a roll of her eyes. "It's way past bedtime for this crew, too. Let me tuck them into their crates, and then we should have some peace and quiet."

Once that was done, we settled in across from each other at the kitchen table. Melissa offered me a cold can of Diet Coke from the fridge, which I gratefully accepted.

"So how are things with you?" she asked as if we were old friends. "I can't imagine it's easy living with someone as colorful as your nan."

I chuckled at this. Even though her prying made me uncomfortable, it didn't seem nice to respond by saying that I couldn't imagine living with a small zoo in my house the way she did.

Just then, a loud thump whomped into the window, and I jumped in my seat. "What was that? I thought you put all the dogs to bed?"

Melissa pushed her chair out behind her and stomped over to the kitchen window. "Seriously, dude! At this time?" she practically shouted. Looked like her cat wasn't the only one around here who'd gone crazy.

She groaned and returned to me with a bemused expression. "That was Murder Robin," she explained as if that clarified everything. It didn't.

I stopped myself before taking another sip from my soda, just in case she was about to tell me something so shocking I wouldn't be able to swallow properly.

Finally, she offered more. "He's been coming here every spring and summer for the last several years. He spends all day thumping up against our kitchen windows, and all night hurling himself at our bedroom window."

"What? Why would he do that?"

She shrugged. "Birds are weird. You'd think he'd just find somewhere new to roost, but you know how territorial birds can get."

I nodded as I considered this. So, this crazy bird would rather sustain an injury by fighting a battle there was no way he could win than to... simply migrate into a new home?

That was weird, but it also made me think.

If birds were this crazy territorial, then why would the flock that previously held the Dewdrop Springs territory back home just up and disappear? Alpha, Bravo, and the others had seemed totally unbothered by the fact that they'd gone, but it wasn't normal for birds to leave their homes without a very good reason. And judging by Murder Robin's actions, "very good" was definitely relative.

This suggested that Charles's suspicion was right. Something fishy was going on with the seagulls. Hopefully Pringle could uncover the truth before time ran out.

Now all we needed to do was find him and convince him to help...

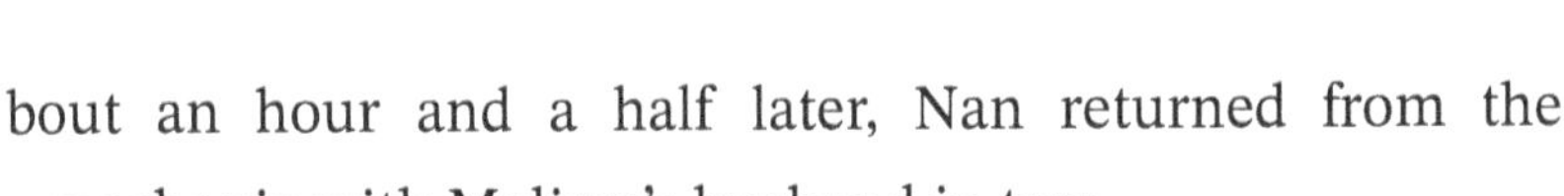

14

About an hour and a half later, Nan returned from the mechanic with Melissa's husband in tow.

"They fixed my girl up as best they could," she said with a far-off glance that may or may not have hid tears threatening to spill. "One of the tires blew out, but the engine is fine. They swapped it out and said I'll have to get the upholstery in the back seat fixed once we're back home again."

"That's good, right?" I asked, more than ready to be on our way. Melissa was nice and all, but she was Nan's friend—not mine. Besides, I was worried about Octo-Cat skulking off by himself in the unfamiliar woods outside.

"It'll drive fine," she said with a dejected sigh. I knew how much that little sports coupe meant to her, but it would be completely fixed soon enough. Besides, maybe now she'd agree to stop off at a hotel so we could both rest properly between shifts.

"Then let's go. I'm wide awake now." I smiled back at Melissa, hoping she wouldn't find my eagerness to get back on the road offensive. "Thanks so much for your hospitality and for the company."

She gave me a quick hug, which surprised me as I was not exactly the hugging strangers type. "I'm so jealous of you," she whispered into my ear. "What you can do is so cool. I'd love to talk to you about it more sometime."

And then pulling away, she finished at full volume, "Nan knows where to find me online. Oh, before you go, let me load you up with some treats for you and the pets."

And about twenty minutes later, we were back on the expressway.

"Are you sure we shouldn't just head home?" I asked as I took a swig from one of the cold brew coffees Melissa had sent with us. "We've been through a lot already and we're still only half-way there."

"You may think you've been through a lot," Octo-Cat shouted. "But you didn't have to wait around outside back there. Consider yourself lucky that the other guy wasn't an outdoors cat, otherwise things would have gotten really ugly."

"Stop complaining and have a treat stick," I said with a smirk. "Um, can you toss him one, Nan?"

Unsurprisingly, Octo-Cat enjoyed this strange Slim Jim like treat just as much as Melissa's cat Merlin had. And it took him a bit longer to eat this thing than one of his smaller treats, which meant it gave us a few minutes of blessed silence every time we tossed him a new one. Honestly, this discovery alone was worth the unplanned detour.

"We may as well keep going, seeing as we have a long drive ahead of us either way," Nan said after unwrapping the kitty treat stick and chucking it into the back seat.

"Get some sleep if you can," I told her, setting the bottle of coffee into the cup holder and returning both hands to the wheel. "I'm wide awake for now, but I promise I'll get you up the moment I feel too tired to keep going. We can decide then if you're going to take over or if we should stop and rest for a while."

"Fair enough," she agreed, then leaned her seat back as far as it would go and left me to my own thoughts.

I had enough to think about to keep myself occupied for a while. Not only was there the seagulls' original case but also the mystery of what had happened to that other flock. And we still needed to find Pringle and convince him to spy on our behalf.

On an unrelated note, Nan and I needed to have a very long talk about her revealing my ability to talk with animals to anyone really, but especially to strangers over the Internet. I shuddered to think of the dangers her loose lips could mean for me in the future. Sometimes my octogenarian grandmother acted like a little kid, I swear.

How could she not know that random people on the Internet weren't to be trusted with the intimate details of our lives?

Yes, we'd gotten lucky this time, seeing as her friends in Michigan had proven to be helpful—and while a little animal-crazy, at least they weren't full-on psychopaths.

But how many others had she also told?

As much as I wanted to jump into this topic with Nan right now, I also knew it would be better to wait until we'd finished our trip and were back home. We already had one accident under our belts, and I wasn't eager to add another.

Because Nan had already hooked my phone to the Bluetooth in her car, I was easily able to pull up my favorite 80s love ballads playlist and send it piping through the speakers. The emotional, up-tempo songs kept me company while the others slept in bursts and fits, each occasionally waking up to chat with me for a few minutes before drifting back to the sandman.

When the sound of my phone ringing drowned out the music a couple of hours later, I was so surprised I almost didn't realize what was happening.

Nan snorted in her sleep, leaned forward to press a button on the stereo, and then settled back in her seat.

"Hello? Angie?" Charles's voice called out, unsure.

"Yes, it's me. Hi!" I tightened both hands on the wheel.

"It's not too early. Is it?"

"No, I've been up for hours." I considered telling him about our accident and the detour that had followed, but I didn't want to worry him when there was nothing he could do from back in Maine. I'd catch him up on our random Midwest adventure later. We had enough to focus on right now as it was.

Charles let out a soft sigh. "Good. Well, I decided to wake up early and swing by your house before heading to the firm, and it's a good thing I did, because I found Pringle."

My heart sped up a little at this announcement. At least one thing was now going our way. "You found him? Did he listen to my message? Is he there now?"

"Yes, yes, and yes," Charles responded with a laugh that made me yearn for him. It was strange how someone I hadn't even known about a year ago had now become such an integral part of my world. "Do you want to talk with him?"

"Yes, but hang on. I'm going to pull over to the side of the road. Can you wait a few minutes then call me back on FaceTime?" It was always easiest to talk to animals if I could also see them, and I definitely needed every advantage I could get when it came to negotiating with the greedy trickster of a raccoon.

Yes, we needed his help, but I also knew that it would come with a price. His help always came with a price, which is why he had two custom treehouses, two big-screen televisions, two rapid-firing Nerf guns—one of which was named Carla—and countless other doubles of the types of belongings you would never think a raccoon even needed in the first place.

He had two of practically everything because, in Pringle's mind, if it was worth doing, then it was worth overdoing. I was definitely thankful he and Nan couldn't speak directly to each other, at least not without looping me in as a translator. Together, they'd not only live the most charmed, extra existence possible, but they'd also blab my secrets to the whole entire world...

That is *if* they hadn't done so already. And that was a massive if.

My stomach churned at the memory of how cavalier Melissa had been in discussing facts she shouldn't have even been privy to. *One thing at a time,* I reminded myself and let out a ragged breath.

We hadn't even made it to Colorado yet, and already I couldn't wait to be back home.

15

I had to wait a couple minutes for Charles's return call after pulling over to the shoulder of the highway. Nan woke up and offered to take the wheel, but I figured it would be best to have this call while fully stopped. I'd have hated for her to get distracted and crash the car a second time.

When at last he called again, Charles seemed to be out of breath. "Sorry... for the... wait," he said between gasps for air. His face was red from exertion and he wore a pained expression.

"What's going on? Is everything okay?" I tried to keep the worry from my features. After all, he could see me, too.

"Yeah, it is now. That bird caught up with me, and I had to fight him off with a broom." The redness began to fade from his face and he smiled, but I still had concerns.

"What?" I shouted.

"Eck, too loud!" Octo-Cat moaned behind me, but I pointedly ignored him.

"He tried getting in through the pet door, but not to worry. I got him back out again."

I was most definitely worried but also knew I needed to speak with Pringle before he grew impatient and scampered off to do something else. If he got away now, who knew when we'd be able to find him again? Charles was already working at a disadvantage not being able to speak to the raccoon or seagulls directly, after all.

"If you're sure you're okay," I said with a frown, and then, "Hand the phone to Pringle. He'll know what to do."

The camera maneuvered quickly, showing me an impromptu tour of my own living room from odd angles. A few seconds later, a masked face with beady eyes filled the screen.

"Commander, that you?" he asked with a voice that sounded more 1940s gangster than it did spy operative. My gimmicky presentation had clearly resonated with him, which meant it would be far easier to get him to follow orders.

"Affirmative." I leveled my eyes and pushed my mouth into a straight serious line.

"I got your message before it could self-destruct," he said in a garbled whisper, then glanced to both sides before turning back to me. "You said you had an assignment for me?"

"10-4." I didn't know what that meant, but it sounded right. "Uh, are you ready to hear the details?"

Pringle winked. "Darling, I was born ready... Hey, don't roll your eyes at me!"

Drats. That was the one downside of FaceTime. I couldn't keep playing this ridiculous role while also keeping a straight face. "Permission to speak plainly?" I asked in a desperate ploy to keep us on task, then held my breath as I waited for him to acknowledge my request.

The raccoon sighed, then nodded. "Granted."

"We need your help finding out what happened to that missing flock."

A slow, wicked smile stretched across the raccoon's face. "So I hear. I can help, but it'll cost you."

Of course it would. Pringle had never done something out of the goodness of his heart. Not once. But at least he was relatively easy to convince if the price was right.

"Fine," I said, but I wasn't in much of a place to negotiate with him from the side of the road, mid-trip. "We'll figure out your payment when I get back. Okay?"

He jerked his head sharply to the side and thrust his nose into the air. "Not okay. If you want my help, we make our contract now."

I sighed and rubbed at the bridge of my nose. "What do you want?"

Again he smiled wickedly. "Actually, I was hoping for—"

"Wait!" Charles interjected and then presumably foisted his phone from the raccoon's grasp because a moment later his face filled the screen. "He's asking for payment, right?"

Whether he figured this out from my end of the conversation, our previous dealings with Pringle, or both, Charles clearly understood that I was in the midst of negotiating.

"Yup. Got any ideas?" I sure hoped he did because I had nothing.

Pringle's fingers writhed in front of the screen and he shouted, "I already know what I want. Give it back!"

Charles, of course, didn't know what he was saying, and even if he had, probably wouldn't have agreed to it, anyway. He rose to his feet, out of reach of the raccoon, and continued, "The seagulls offered to arrange something as a thank-you. Remember?"

Oh, that was right! Seeing as neither Charles nor I were even remotely interested in whatever dumpster fire the birds gifted us, it made sense to offer it to Pringle. It might just save us from having to agree to something pricey that a raccoon had no business ever owning, like a motorcycle or a robot. And given his odd predilection for doubling up whenever possible, he'd likely demand two, if given the chance.

"Good idea," I said with a smile. I loved how my boyfriend not only accepted my strange ability but was a true champ at rolling with the punches. "Give the phone back to him now."

Pringle appeared a few seconds later with a huff.

"Now as I was saying before I got so rudely interrupted..." He paused and glanced up with a scowl—at Charles, I guessed.

"Hold it right there," I said before he could continue, then waited for him to clamp his mouth shut to deliver my offer. "A secret spy mission calls for something extra valuable. Wouldn't you say?"

I had his attention now.

"Go on." The words rolled out smooth and glib.

"We've been promised a secret treasure." I widened my eyes to punctuate this revelation.

"A secret treasure. *Interesting.*" Pringle rubbed his chin thoughtfully. "What is it?"

"Nobody knows. That's what makes it so exciting."

The raccoon narrowed his eyes at me. "Hey, you're not trying to pull one over on me, are you?"

I shook my head adamantly. "No, of course not!"

"Hmmm..." Pringle rubbed at his chin some more. His lips began to move as he mouthed words, but no sound came out. Finally he smiled and said, "Okay, sold."

"Excellent."

He switched from business mode to action mode so quickly, the change was almost visible on his face. "Now where can I find that flock?"

I filled him in on all the details—or at least as many as I could without losing his attention—and suggested he start by heading over to Dewdrop Springs. "I'm on it," Pringle promised before dropping the phone to the ground and scampering off.

Crash! The sound of the phone colliding with the hardwood floorboards sounded like a peal of thunder on my end of the call.

"My phone!" Charles cried from his side.

I couldn't help but laugh as he retrieved the fallen gadget and searched it for any signs of damage.

"Not funny," he said but laughed along with me. "I sure do miss you. Have a great time, but hurry home, okay?"

I agreed, and we said goodbye. A huge part of me wished I'd never agreed to this trip in the first place. But I saw Charles live and in person several times each week. Octo-Cat only ever got to speak with his girlfriend over the Internet. They needed this trip to keep their relationship strong. As obnoxious as my cat had been this entire trip, at least he was happy. That made my short-term discomfort worth it, especially if the two cats had a great time this week.

"I'll need a payment, too, and you can't trick me like you did the raccoon," Octo-Cat informed me from his place in the torn-up back seat, proving that he couldn't go longer than a few minutes without complaining about or demanding *something.*

I didn't turn to look at him, because I knew it would send a new pain twinging down my neck. Stupid car accident. Maybe Grizabella's human could recommend a good chiropractor while we were in Colorado because I needed to do something to treat this pain, and I really didn't want to have to endure another long drive and a whole week of waiting before getting it.

"I'm not paying you anything," I muttered and stretched my arms out in front of me with a yawn.

He tsked and declared, *"Ah, ah, ah.* Finder's fee. It was my idea to bring him in, wasn't it?"

Darn it. I really couldn't argue with him on that one.

16

Somewhere amid the rolling hills of Iowa, we finally settled into our drive. In fact, I didn't even argue when Octo-Cat asked to listen to his audiobook a second time.

"I just want to make sure I'm one hundred percent prepared to woo and wow my love, Grizabella," he explained with a contented sigh.

And it could have been a byproduct of just how boring it was to drive on the expressway for thirty-plus hours at a stretch, but the things Dr. Roman was saying actually started to make sense the second time around.

Romance is a verb because it requires action.

On the surface level, Charles battling the seagulls on my behalf wasn't exactly romantic. But the more I thought about it, the more I realized it was the best gift he'd ever given me. In just about a week's time, I could be standing face to face with my long-lost biological grandmother, and it would be because Charles had stepped up to help.

I owed him one heck of a souvenir from Boulder, although I already knew nothing could come close to what he'd already freely offered me and my family.

"Nan," I asked after internally debating whether I should broach this topic at all. Ultimately, I knew it would eat at my insides until I finally let it out. "Are you sure you're okay with me reaching out to my other grandmother?"

She was the one driving now, and as much as I didn't want to upset her by talking about difficult topics, I just couldn't get this particular one off my mind. If anyone could understand the need to let it all out, it was my nan. She had a habit of letting it all hang out—for better or for worse—and her choosing to share my secret with her online friends was even more proof of that. Still, as angry as I was with her for that, I would never voluntarily hurt her feelings. I needed to know I had her blessing for whatever happened next with my bio grandma. I needed to hear her say it was okay and to believe her when she said it.

Nan clenched the wheel so hard her knuckles turned white. Not a good sign. "It was wrong of me to keep her from you for this long. I just hope you and your mother can one day forgive me for that."

"We already have," I promised, placing a hand on her shoulder so she could feel all the love I had for her, still and always.

She sighed and adjusted her grip on the wheel, returning her knuckles to their usual pale flesh color. "You, maybe. But it will take your mother a bit longer, I'm afraid."

"I'll talk to her," I insisted, my voice strong and sure.

"No," Nan snapped, which startled me.

"No?"

"She's right to be angry. In fact, I'm surprised you aren't more upset with me, dear."

"You did a bad thing, but you did it for the right reasons." The truth was I just didn't have it in me to be angry with her. At least not for the long term. I'd already worked through all those feelings and was ready to move forward. Nan, however, seemed to carry a heavy burden of guilt that had only gotten heavier as the years passed.

"Maybe at first," she agreed, tightening her grip on the wheel once more, "but I acted selfishly all the same. When she came searching for Laura in New York and your grandfather and I chose to run away rather than meet her face-to-face."

"But how could you know what she wanted? Or whether she'd press charges? Heck, even why Grandpa McAllister lied to you in the first place?"

I still remembered that autumn evening when Pringle had offered the stolen letter that revealed Nan wasn't my grandmother by blood. She'd been tricked into taking my mother at her oldest and best friend's request. Once I learned about this, Charles and I tried to track the old man down, but it was too late. He'd already passed, leaving the reason behind his actions a mystery that only the wronged mother—my real grandmother—could illuminate for us.

While terrible, none of these revelations made me love Nan any less. She'd raised me. She'd given me nearly thirty years of true unconditional love, had always been my biggest support and my closest friend. Maybe our family started as a lie, but it had grown into something much more.

I longed to meet the missing woman who shared my DNA, to give her some kind of closure and offer back a small part of what had been stolen from her, but not if it hurt the one person who mattered most in my world—Nan.

"I didn't know," she said hardly above a whisper. "But I also didn't try very hard to find out. I fell in love with your mother from day one, and that was that. I would have done anything to keep her with us."

"We'll find out soon. Bravo will make sure of it. He says he's been following her for even longer than he's been following me, and he's had his eyes on me ever since I first met Octo-Cat. When he leads us to her, we can ask why William would have done what he did. I'm sure he had his reasons, whatever they were."

Nan shrugged, but the tension in her form remained. "I accept whatever happens next, and I'll support you and your mother as you repair your family."

"She can't replace you. That's not why we want to meet her."

"I know." Nan flashed me a sad smile, then returned her focus to the road. How I wished I could hug her right now, but my words would have to be enough until we made our next pit stop.

"I love y—"

"I've gotta make!" Octo-Cat yowled at the top of his lungs,

completely ruining the emotional, heartfelt moment. "I've gotta make! Pull over, pull over! I need my litter box, and I need it now."

I groaned and rolled my eyes. Leave it to the cat to make everything about himself every second of every day. "Nan, can you stop?"

She chuckled. "I may not know what he's saying, but I can definitely tell it's urgent." She changed lanes and pulled to the shoulder without delay.

"Do you need the pee pad?" I asked as I unbuckled myself.

"No, I need my litter box," he insisted, his voice cold with fury. "And if you don't give it to me, I'll go right here in the car, and you'll have to smell it the rest of the trip."

Wonderful. While I normally wasn't one to negotiate with terrorists, Nan's poor car had already been through enough.

I was also emotionally drained from the tender conversation we'd just had.

So I gritted my teeth and set up Octo-Cat's box with a thin layer of litter. We could toss the soiled bit at the next rest stop and pick up a fresh bag once we reached Colorado if needed.

At least we were more than three-quarters of the way there. Then again, we were only three-quarters of the way there! We still had several more hours to go, even though it felt like it had been at least a week since we set off yesterday morning. Seriously, we hadn't even reached our destination, and already I'd had more than enough of this road trip.

Admittedly, he'd come a long way since our first couple of drives together. He could even handle the trip without being dosed with sleepy medicine. Those things helped, but being locked in a tin can with him for hours on end would never be pleasant, no matter what precautions we made.

All this meant that next time Octo-Cat wanted to see Grizabella, she could come to us. And if he wanted to go anywhere else, we'd be flying—and that was that.

17

I slipped into the driver's seat for a couple quick hours, then Nan got behind the wheel again as we made our final approach into Boulder.

Charles texted a few times to check in on us and give me updates about his day. Basically Bravo continued to be glued to his side no matter where he went, and Pringle hadn't yet returned from his reconnaissance mission. I didn't particularly like either of these facts, but I also couldn't say I was surprised. At least I'd finally be in a stationary location and easier for him to reach if he needed my help.

We were so close now, and I for one couldn't wait to get out of the moving death box that I had called home for the last two days. Yes, our accident, while minor, had definitely riled me up.

And I wasn't the only one facing newfound anxieties...

Once we'd reached the city proper, Octo-Cat began hissing and panting in the back seat. His tongue lolled right out of his mouth as he struggled to take short, shallow breaths.

"Oh, goodie!" Paisley squealed with delight. "Octavius is pretending to be a dog. Look at me! I can show you how, big brother. *Heh. Heh. Heh.*"

I glanced over and found that her small pink tongue was now also lolling from her mouth as her whole body wriggled with excitement.

Octo-Cat, on the other hand, looked like he was going to be sick.

"Paisley, give him some space," I instructed.

The little dog moved to the other side of the bench seat and quirked her head. "Why? Is something wrong with him, Mommy?"

"Can't..." the tabby gasped dramatically. "Breathe..."

I pushed my seat back as far as it would go, turned on my side, and pulled Octo-Cat to my chest. Holding on tight, I righted the seat again and set him carefully on my lap.

"Do we need to stop?" I asked, watching him closely as he continued to wheeze and gasp.

"N-n-no. Just... Nerv... ous."

"He's got the love butterflies!" Paisley announced with a bark. "Just like the romance doctor said!"

I scratched Octo-Cat behind his ears, feeling fondness for him swell in my chest. He didn't often show his vulnerabilities, but whenever he did, I loved him all the better for it.

"Is this true? Do you have the love butterflies?" While not exactly how Dr. Roman had described that jittery feeling associated with romantic love, it was how we had translated the content for Paisley. She'd immediately understood and explained that she felt love butterflies every single second she was near me or Nan or Octo-Cat. Our little love bug.

Octo-Cat simply nodded in response to my question.

"You have nothing to worry about," I assured the lovesick cat now. "Grizabella already adores you. And you've put in so much extra work listening to Dr. Roman's book, making that huge list of everything you needed to show her the perfect vacation, plus I happen to know for a fact that nobody can love her like you can."

He closed his eyes and pushed his ears back against his head. He took a few moments to steady his breathing, then opened his bright eyes again and asked, "Are you sure? Grizabella is so glamorous, and I'm just a normal cat. I even think I gained a few ounces since our last meeting. Now I'm just a stupid flabby tabby."

I wanted to laugh at the rhyme—especially since I often called him *crabby* tabby behind his back—but I controlled myself as I continued to stroke his soft fur. Because of his added anxiety, he'd begun shedding like crazy, and a little storm cloud of loose hair hovered over us.

"Grizabella chose you for your heart. Plus I may be biased here, but I think you're the best cat in the whole entire world."

He looked up at me, his amber eyes wide and glistening. "But am I the best cat who's ever lived?" he asked seriously.

"Y-yes?"

"Are you sure?"

He caught me off guard, but I recovered nicely, smiling as I assured, "Positive, and I know Grizabella would agree."

Octo-Cat sat up in my lap, his breathing now fully back to normal and his tongue safely tucked inside his mouth. "You packed my bowties, right? I want to wear the blue to match my lady love's eyes."

"I have them both right here in my purse. Would you like me to help you put the blue one on now?"

"Yes, please."

Wow, he almost never said *please* and usually only said *thank you* sarcastically. Maybe he was practicing good manners on me so that he'd be ready to play the perfect gentleman for Grizabella. Or maybe he simply realized how much I did for him and how grateful he was to have me in his life.

Okay, yeah, it was definitely the first thing, but still.

I fished the silky blue bowtie out of my purse and fastened it around his neck. Even I had to admit that he looked incredibly handsome in this get-up.

"You look all grown up, Octavius," Paisley said, when Octo-Cat leaped into the backseat to rejoin her.

"I am all grown up. And so are you." He sneered, then broke into a good-natured smile. "But I know what you meant. Thank you."

"Grizzly-bella is going to give you soooo many face licks," Paisley promised with a wink. "She won't be able to keep her paws off you, you hunka-hunka burning love!"

Octo-Cat hung his head and chuckled, then whipped it back and let out a full-bellied laugh.

I translated for Nan, and then we joined in the laughter, too.

The things that came out of these animals' mouths sometimes! I wouldn't change either of them for the world. No, not even Octo-Cat and his incessant complaining. Changing that would be changing him, and I was a firm believer that we always wound up with the people and animals we needed to have in our lives.

Just like Octo-Cat and Grizabella had met and fallen in love on that one strange train trip that got neither of us to our intended destination. But they had found each other.

And now months later, the feline lovers would have their first romantic trip together. What a world.

During this whole exchange, Nan had doggedly pressed on toward our destination. And now the busy commercial district gave way to a quieter suburban street. The houses here were much more modern looking than the giant manors back home, but they had been well kept and boasted tidy lawns and colorful flowerbeds. It felt like the kind of place where you could raise a family and raise them well. Even though I would forever be a Maine girl, I instantly liked Colorado. And we hadn't even gotten out of the car yet.

"You have arrived at your destination," the GPS announced as we pulled up outside a brick split-level with red shutters and a white picket fence.

Christine came out to meet us while Grizabella waited in the bay window that overlooked the yard. "Welcome, welcome!" she called, saddling first Nan and then me with a gigantic warm hug.

"Grizz has been so excited all day," she said, beaming at us as if we were all long lost friends reuniting for the first time in ages. "I couldn't tear her away from that window, and I tried!"

"That's sweet," I said with a chuckle. "It's almost like she knew we were coming, huh?"

Christine's brown scrunched. "Well, of course she knew you were coming. You told Octavius and he told her."

"I don't get what you—"

"Oh, no need to play coy with me." She waved her hand dismissively as if I were the one speaking out of turn. "Your nan told me all about how you're the modern-day Doctor Dolittle. But don't worry, your secret's safe with me."

Nan did what? And here I'd naively assumed she'd told her friends in Michigan as a one-off thing. Looked like we'd be having our big conversation much sooner than I'd originally planned.

18

Octo-Cat ran straight to the front door, plopped his butt on the welcome mat, and waited for the humans to be done with their requisite greetings. His impatience provided a good excuse for me to get away from Christine and her desire to talk about my not-so-secret ability.

I charged ahead. She, Nan, and Paisley joined me on the porch, and then Christine pushed the door open.

Octo-Cat raced inside like a shot.

There, on the other side of the threshold, sat his lady love, a beautiful Himalayan wearing a Swarovski crystal encrusted collar and sporting a perfectly groomed coat. Her sparkling blue eyes matched Octo-Cat's bowtie perfectly, and despite the difference in their pedigrees, it was easy to tell they belonged together.

She gracefully moved to her feet, glided forward, and rubbed her flat face all over Octo-Cat's neck and chest. Both purred so loudly, no one would have been able to get a word in if we'd dared try.

"Oh, my darling Grizabella!" Octo-Cat cried, accepting an enthusiastic lick on the cheek, much as Paisley had predicted.

"Octavius, sweetest," she chimed, lifting her fluffy tail straight into the air and giving it a happy quiver. "It has been far too long."

Paisley trotted over, her tail wagging her entire body as she approached. "Hi, Grizzly-bella! I'm Octavius's kid sister. Nice to meetcha!" She inserted herself right between the lovelorn cats, and I was certain Octo-Cat would hiss and swipe at her for the intrusion.

Instead he put a paw on her back and drew her in for a hug. "Darling, you've met Paisley on our video calls."

"Nice to meet you in person at last, little sister," Grizabella said with a small bow of her head. "Come. I'll introduce you to my brothers and sisters."

All three trod into the screened-in back porch where six other show quality Himalayan cats sat sunning themselves contentedly.

"This is Juliet, Viola, Ophelia, Oberon, Othello, and Hamlet," she said by way of introduction. "They're all still active on the circuit. I'm the only one with the distinction of being retired." She laughed at this, and my pets joined in even though I'd be willing to bet that neither of them understood the joke—I didn't either.

"C'mon," Christine said, leading us back toward the entryway. "Let's get you unpacked while these two lovebirds catch up."

"Eck!" Octo-Cat screeched. "Being called a bird is even worse than being called a dog."

"She means well, sweetest," Grizabella purred at his side. "But we can't all be blessed with the perfect human companion like you. Can we?"

I stopped in my tracks and jerked my head toward Octo-Cat in complete and utter shock.

"Yeah, I said it," he growled and curled a lip at me. "And I can just as easily un-say it. Now get out of here while I'm still feeling generous."

After that accidental confession of his, I didn't stop smiling for the rest of that day. Despite all his complaints, Octo-Cat not only loved me, he thought I was the best human ever. That meant a lot, considering how difficult he was to please even on his best days.

Once Nan and I had unpacked, Christine offered us tea and cookies. More than once she tried to bring the conversation back around to my gift for talking to animals. And each time I deftly deflected. I needed to speak with Nan about her willingness to share my private business with near strangers before I included Christine in any such talks.

Charles continued to text throughout the day to update me on the non-progress of the seagulls' case. All he had were the precedents he'd immediately found regarding squatter's rights in Maine. Unfortunately, he still knew next to nothing about what had happened to the missing flock whose territory was now up for dispute.

Given that Pringle failed to return to my property the night before, we also had no idea whether he'd found something of value or whether he was even still okay... For all we knew, he could have taken a wrong turn and wound up as roadkill. If that had happened because of something I'd asked him to do, I would never forgive myself.

But right now I needed to stop worrying about what could happen and focus on what already had.

Mainly that Nan was sharing my secret with the world... *Why?*

We both begged off early that night, tired from the long drive and eager to sleep in actual beds again for a change. Christine's guest room comprised two twin beds, the perfect setup for the conversation we needed to have.

At last, I broached the topic once we'd both changed into our pajamas and settled beneath the hand-made quilts that adorned the matching beds.

"Nan? Why does Christine know about what I can do?"

"It just seemed easier to let her in on it," my grandmother confessed after turning on her side to face me. "Otherwise this trip would have been quite awkward trying to hide the truth the whole time. And I know Octo-Cat would have driven you crazy with his complaints if we had to spend our nights in a hotel instead of here with his girlfriend." She shrugged again. "I guess this just seemed like the best option for everyone involved."

Her answer did not comfort me. In fact, it seemed as if she believed she'd done me a favor. That was definitely not the case. I didn't want this to turn into an argument, but I did need to make sure she understood.

I tried approaching from a different angle. "Okay, then why did you tell Melissa and her family?"

Nan's face twisted into a grimace, proving I'd gotten through to her this time. "Oh, that. I'd forgotten I had. It just came up in conversation one day. Sorry about that."

"Why are you telling people at all? Shouldn't this be my secret to share?" I watched as her face fell.

She blinked hard. "Oh, dear. You're right. Of course, you're right, and I'm sorry if I overstepped. I really didn't tell that many people, and I made sure none of them lived anywhere near to us. I know how awkward that would make things for you if people we saw every day at the supermarket or the bank or post office knew."

I sucked in a slow, shaky breath. Confrontation was never easy, least of all with Nan. I needed to say this next part with gentle words but a firm tone. "But, Nan, I don't want anyone to know, other than the ones I've trusted enough to tell myself."

"Of course not, I'm so sorry. I guess..." She sighed. "I guess I just spent so many years hiding this big important truth that once it was out there I couldn't help but share *everything*."

I smiled to show her I understood, and that even though I definitely didn't like her actions, I'd already forgiven her for them. "You may have overcorrected there."

"You're right, and I'm sorry." She pulled the quilt up close to her chin and offered a sad smile.

We both lay silent for a couple moments until Nan suddenly popped up in bed and turned to face me with wide eyes. I could practically see the cartoon lightbulb appear over her head. "Tell you what. First of all, I hereby solemnly swear that I won't tell another soul. You have my word."

I let out an enormous sigh of relief. "That's a good start. Thank you."

She clasped her hands together in her lap and giggled. "And if it ever comes up again, I'll just tell people that I've gone senile. You can toss me in the worst nursing home you can find, and that will be that."

I gasped. "Nan, you know I would never do that!"

"Okay, fine. I'll toss myself in."

"You're not going to a nursing home."

"Well, no, because I'm not going to share your secrets anymore. See, it works out for everyone?"

"Love you, Nan." I said, snapping off the bedside lamp with great satisfaction. If only all conversations went this smoothly, we'd be living in a very different world.

19

Octo-Cat and Grizabella began the following day by feasting on jumbo shrimp from a crystal goblet and lying together in a sunbeam most of the afternoon. At night they snuggled up in front of a roaring fire and took turns giving each other tongue baths.

On the third day of our visit, the two kitty lovers strolled through the flowerbeds and ate some grass from the back lawn.

And on the fourth day, they both had upset tummies. This, however, did not stop Octo-Cat from wooing his love by hunting a robin and delivering its carcass for her enjoyment.

Day five is when the anguished mewling began. They both knew their trip was almost up and hated the thought of being separated again so soon after they'd been reunited.

When we began our drive home on day six, poor Octo-Cat was beyond devastated. He hardly spoke at all—not even to complain—

the entire drive home. But we couldn't add even an hour's delay to our return trip, given the upcoming trial by seagull that awaited us back home. I needed to be there to help Charles deliver his case, or the flock would assuredly wreak unholy terror on us. After all, they'd promised.

Paisley made sure to cuddle and groom Octo-Cat in turns, being the friend he needed but hadn't quite felt up to asking for. Nan focused on the drive and the new audiobook we'd picked up in town. This one was a sweeping historical saga that actually ran longer than our entire drive time, if you can believe that.

Once home, I had just enough time to take a good two-hour nap before Charles arrived to collect me so we could drive together to the seagulls' dumpster in Dewdrop Springs.

I gathered my hair in a messy ponytail and pulled on a polka-dotted maxi dress to wear with my thick boots and a coat, and we were off.

"Are you ready for the biggest case of your life?" I joked, happy that it was just me and him in the car and that this drive would only be half an hour instead of thirty-five.

"I'm not ready at all," he confessed with a heavy sigh. "Pringle never came back."

"What?" I stared at him as if I'd be able to read the explanation on his face. "But it's been over a week."

Charles tapped his fingers on the steering wheel, a nervous tic of his. "I know. That's why I'm so worried. Do you think something happened to him?"

Dread flooded my gut. For all his faults, Pringle was my friend. A colleague, too. I hated to think that something may have happened to him.

"I'm sure he's okay." I forced a smile and placed my hand on Charles's arm to steady his anxious rapping at the wheel. "He probably just got distracted and lost track of time. That's all."

"So what do we do without his evidence? I know none of the facts beyond what we were initially told, and something feels off about the story they told us. If their case is so cut and dry, why do they need us in the first place? Why did that one bird stay on me day in and day out while all the others waited in my yard?"

I knew he would feel better if he had answers going in, but unfortunately there was nothing to be done now. All I could do was try to comfort him and pray this would be finished quickly. "I know you want to do a good job and that you want to be on the side of truth and justice here, but you can only do so much. Present your argument, and then let the birds figure out the rest."

"I know you're right. Of course I do, but my intuition keeps gnawing at me. Something's not right."

I rubbed his arm soothingly and changed the topic. Talking about all the pieces we didn't have would only make defending the seagulls' right to the land that much more difficult for him.

We pulled into the empty strip mall parking lot and found the entire flock waiting for us. Once again, they led us back to the clearing in the field, and there a second even larger flock waited.

"Are we ready to begin proceedings?" A one-legged seagull cawed. I tried not to stare, but he caught me looking, anyway, and shrieked, "Our human guests must show proper respect for the court!"

My poor ears. “Ouch, ouch, okay. Sorry,” I muttered as they continued to ring.

Bravo landed on Charles’s shoulder. “Go get ‘em, tiger.”

And Alpha took up a perch on mine. “You better pray he doesn’t mess this one up.”

Gulp.

“So where’s your flock’s lawyer?” I asked the one-legged gull.

“I am the judge here!” he cried even louder than the first time.

“I will be presenting the case on behalf of Flock 84,” a young female bird announced, extending one wing in greeting.

“All rise,” Judgey McJudgerson said while glaring at us.

I bit my lip to stop myself from pointing out that we were all already standing. Given how loud his caws could be, I definitely didn’t want to do anything else that could upset the one-legged banshee.

He glanced at Charles and me then to the bird lawyer and began, “We are gathered here today in holy legality to discuss the dispute between flocks 82 and 84 over the territory previously held by Flock 83. Are there any objections? If so, speak them now or forever hold your peace.”

Um, why had the seagulls selected human law to decide this case when they clearly knew so little about it? I couldn’t tell if I was in a courtroom or at a wedding altar. As ridiculous as this all felt, I also knew that the best way to get through to any animal was to act natural and play by their rules.

So I stepped forward, swallowed hard, and said, “I object.”

All eyes zoomed to me, including Charles’s.

"Sweetie," he whispered at me. "What are you objecting to? The trial hasn't even begun yet?"

I didn't know, but I also didn't want to lose the opportunity to object if that wasn't going to be allowed later on.

"Please state your objection for the congregation," said the bird judge or minister—honestly I didn't even know anymore.

I cleared my throat and spoke up loud and clear. "I object because this is a case about seagull rights and should, uh, thusly, not be decided by human laws."

He cocked his head to the side. "Interesting. Do go on."

"Hey, kid!" Alpha squawked in my ear. "What are you doing to me here? Did you forget our deal?"

But I refused to back down. Something about this case had left Charles unsettled. If our situations were reversed, he never would have forced me to go forward with this. I wanted to meet my bio grandma, yes, but knowing she was out there and close by could be enough of an advantage to find her on my own.

"Since the disputed territory belongs to Flock 83, I propose we let them decide whether 82 or 84 will acquire it in their absence."

"But Flock 83 disappeared. Nobody knows where they went," Bravo said from his place on Charles's shoulder.

I raised both eyebrows. "And don't you find that a bit curious?"

"Angie, what are you doing?" Charles whisper-yelled as he grabbed onto my upper arm. "This case is open and shut. Let me tell them about the precedents, and we can all go home happy."

I shook my head hard. I hadn't known where I was going with this when I first claimed my objection, but now I knew exactly what needed to be done. “No,” I said firmly. “You wouldn’t be happy. Not without knowing.”

“Listen to your mate,” Alpha hissed at me. “Do what we hired you to do, or you’ll be sorry.”

“No, you’re the one who will be sorry!” Pringle shouted, charging onto the scene with a fuzzy brown chick on his back—a baby seagull, I realized.

Exactly three thoughts ran through my head at that moment:

Pringle was alive!

He had discovered something important!

And it would be a lot longer until I got to meet my long-lost grandmother…

20

"What is the meaning of this?" the judge bird demanded of the raccoon. Spotting the little one, however, he immediately changed his tone. "Oh, hello there, chicky. This is no place for youngsters, I'm afraid."

"I may be young of age, but I am old in experience." The baby gull's voice came out high and squeaky and so, so cute. "I have seen things, escaped things, that no bird should ever witness."

"Throw her out of here. We have a very important trial to run, and we need to do so without any more delays!" Alpha declared, swooping down from my shoulder and landing before the judge.

Pringle stood on his hind legs and clutched the fluffy chick to his chest defensively. "Quit your yapping and listen to my friend Abigull here. It's because of her I'm going to get my treasure."

I held my breath and waited. Whatever Abigull revealed next, I knew it would decide what happened in this field today.

Alpha spread his wings wide and charged at the raccoon. "We don't have to listen to you, you filthy—"

Pringle bared his teeth and hissed, which had Alpha immediately changing course and flying to the nearest tree for cover.

"Go on, Abigull. This is a safe place," the judge nudged.

She hopped out of Pringle's hands and onto the ground, then began her harrowing tale. "I was hatched in Flock 83. I loved it there with my family and had just started practicing leaving the nest. One day I came home after exploring and found that everyone had gone away. Every single bird. I cried out for my momma but couldn't find her anywhere. Then I saw that guy." She stopped and motioned toward Alpha with her beak. "I saw him pecking around, so decided to follow him for a closer look. That's when I found him talking to a cat. I couldn't hear what they were saying, but the next thing I knew the cat had a dead seagull in its mouth and was shouting 'pleasure doing business with you!' I still wasn't a very good flyer, so I ran and hid. And I've been hiding ever since. Well, until Pringle found me."

"Oh, sweetie," I murmured, my heart breaking for her.

The one-legged bird scuttled over to Abigull and put a wing over her small body. "A horrible, horrible thing this surprise witness has revealed to us today."

She sniffed and leaned into his side. "I've been so afraid."

"You did the right thing by telling us," the judge assured her. "It would seem that Alpha of Flock 82 slaughtered 83 with a feline accomplice in order to gain their land. But we won't let that happen."

"Guys!" I shouted when I saw a small patch of white launch away from a tree and into the sky above. "He's getting away!"

"Oh, no, he isn't!" Bravo cried and catapulted after him. "C'mon 82. 84, too. We can't let this stand."

Everyone but the judge, Abigull, Pringle, Charles, and I departed to bring the war criminal to justice. I doubted his end would be a pleasant one.

"You were right," I told Charles, shaking my head. It had all happened so, so fast. "This whole time. You assumed foul play, and you were absolutely, undeniably right."

He smiled and pressed a kiss onto my forehead. I thought he was going to comment on my clever pun, but instead he said, "You were going to risk not meeting your grandmother for me."

I laughed. "Yeah, well, romance is a verb, you know?"

His eyes squinted in confusion. "No, I really don't know. I believe you, though."

"Thank you for your help, Pringle." I reached down to offer the raccoon a high five. "You really saved the day."

He sniffed and held his snout high. "Maybe. It's a shame what happened to all those birds, though."

"Still, you've more than earned your treasure." Then I realized… "I'm not so sure Flock 82 is going to be eager to give us the payment they promised, but I'll make sure you're paid for your time. What do you want? A motorcycle? A robot?"

Oh, man. Why was I giving him ideas?

Pringle's eyes became huge with all the exciting prospects. "Well, actually—"

CA-CAW! Bravo announced his return with a shrill cry as he swooped back to the earth. "The others have this well in hand."

I didn't know what to say to that, so I simply nodded.

"Your name is Abigull, right?" he said to the chick who still stood huddled beneath Judge's wing.

She ambled out to face him with a salute. "Sir, yes, sir!"

Bravo bent down and gazed directly into her eyes, then straightened and said, "I know it won't replace the flock you lost, but I invite you to join 82 if you would like. I'll raise you as my own and make sure no one ever hurts you again."

"Wow. But aren't you the new Alpha?" Abigull whispered reverently.

"Alpha? No, I'm not going to take that name. Call me Bravo. That's who I am and who I will always be. I may be in charge now, but it doesn't mean I need to act like a jerk about it."

"Okay, Bravo," the chick said, then pressed her fuzzy gray body into his.

I teared up watching them.

Even Pringle seemed to have something caught in his eye.

Charles wrapped his arms around me from behind and rested his chin on my shoulder.

"You tried to help me see that Alpha's orders were too much. But I denied your help and stuck blindly to his commands. I could have stopped all this. I could have saved—"

"No," I insisted. "None of this is your fault. As soon as you knew what was going on, you fixed it. You'll be a great leader to your flock, Bravo. I'm sure of it."

"I haven't forgotten our promise to you," the bird said, hopping along the grass. "Follow me back to the dumpster, and I will present your material payment. The flock will have a lot to figure out with the loss of 83's land, but it's only fair we don't benefit from our corrupt leader's actions. Once my birds are safe, I will take you to meet your grandmother. I wish I could take you sooner as a thank-you for all you've done, but none of us expected what happened. It will be a huge transition for our flock, plus I need some good quality time with my new daughter."

Abigull gave a happy chirrup.

I bowed my head. "That's all I can ask for. Thank you so much. I'll be ready whenever you are."

Judge chose to remain in the field and wait for the return of the others.

The rest of us made the short trek to the dumpster in the nearby strip mall parking lot.

"Oh, I can't wait to see my secret prize!" Pringle rubbed his hands together and jumped up and down as Bravo dove into the smelly trash receptacle and began to rummage about.

When he emerged a few moments later, I expected to see a dirty fast-food wrapper or maybe a plastic doohickey on display. But instead Bravo held a sparkling diamond solitaire ring clamped firmly in his beak. "Now which one of you gets this?" he asked, looking from me to Charles to Pringle.

"Mine!" the raccoon screamed gleefully, scurried up the side of the dumpster, and snatched the beautiful piece of jewelry.

"Well, that was unexpected," Charles said with a laugh as he looped an arm around my waist.

I smiled but didn't say anything.

Yes, it certainly was unexpected. Not just the treasure being something of actual value, but this entire day, the truth about the horrible fate that had befallen Flock 83 and presumably Alpha as his punishment.

But the most surprising part of all had been the way I felt inside when that glittering engagement ring came into view. My breath hitched, my heart skipped a beat, and I definitely got love butterflies.

It wasn't from fear, though, rather an unwavering certainty.

If Charles had been the one holding that ring, I would have definitely said yes.

WHAT TO READ NEXT

Ever since Angie Russo woke up from a near fatal run-in with a coffee maker, she's been able to talk to—and even worse, understand—one very spoiled tabby named Octavius.

This collection includes *Grizzly Grievance, Persian Penalty,* and *Deer Duplicity*. Read along as Octo-Cat and Pringle stow away on what's supposed to be a romantic trip for Angie and Charles, as long-lost family members are reunited and bring mysteries of their own to solve, and a murder investigation that could lead to Angie winding up in jail.

The *Pet Whisperer P.I.: Books 13-15 Special Collection* is now available.

Get your copy so that you can keep reading this series today!

SNEAK PEEK

GRIZZLY GRIEVANCE

I'm Angie Russo, and lately my life has been one train wreck after another. And, yeah, I do mean that literally. First my cat and I found ourselves aboard a derailed train about six months back, and then just a couple weeks ago, my nan crashed her sports car on the highway with us in it.

I've started to fear various modes of transportation just as much as I've feared electric coffee makers for a while now. In my life, both have only led to trouble.

And that's how it all started, too.

I got zapped by an old coffee maker and woke up with the strange new ability to talk to animals. And those talking animals have led to most of my problems, like the aforementioned vehicle wrecks. I've also dealt with more than anyone's fair share of murders, thefts, kidnappings, and other nefarious crimes. Then again, I guess that's what I get for setting up shop as a private investigator.

Still…

I could really do with just a week or two where nothing life-altering comes around and rocks my world.

I can't even remember the last time I enjoyed a good old-fashioned Netflix binge or spent the full day in bed reading. Also, I almost never get paid for my investigative work, which begs the question: Why do I keep signing myself up for more and more?

My partner at Pet Whisperer P.I. has zero issues saying no. Of course, he's not the one doing any of the talking. He wouldn't miss napping in a sunbeam or giving himself a slow, leisurely tongue bath for anything… Oh, did I mention my partner is a cat?

He's a standard tabby with an oversized attitude, but don't tell him I said that. His full name is Octavius Maxwell Ricardo Edmund Frederick Fulton Russo, Esq, P.I. (a name he freely and regularly adds to). I prefer to call him Octo-Cat. He's not a fan, but at least he's stopped arguing with me about it.

The trust fund his previous owner left him pays all our bills, and those rare moments when he offers me genuine displays of love and affection are the brightest spots in my day.

We also live in our—or rather his—giant manor house alongside my nan and her rescue Chihuahua, Paisley. Pringle the nosy reality TV addict lives in a treehouse in our backyard; he's a raccoon. And then we have Charles, my big-time lawyer boyfriend, to round out our motley crew.

Our latest adventure took Nan, Octo-Cat, Paisley, and me on a cross-country trip to visit my cat's girlfriend, a former show Himalayan named Grizabella. On the way, I learned that Nan has been blabbing what is meant to be a secret ability to random friends of hers on the Internet.

While that was going on, a militarized flock of seagulls bribed me into helping with their turf dispute, a case that mainly fell to Charles and Pringle since the rest of us were out of town.

And even though we held up our end of the bargain, the seagulls needed more time to deliver on theirs. I trust them, though. Any day now, they'll lead me to my long-lost grandmother and I'll finally learn the truth about my lineage.

Until then, I've been doing my best to focus on other things. It hasn't been going well…

Mainly because my cat makes non-stop demands, and I'm just too tired to argue with him anymore. That's why I'm driving more than thirty minutes out to Misty Harbor to purchase a lobster roll from his preferred venue, the Little Dog Diner. And when I get home, he probably won't even say thank you for sending me to another far-flung end of Blueberry Bay to fulfill his latest request.

Yeah…

Have I mentioned just how badly I need a break from my life?

When I returned that afternoon with a bag of lobster rolls in hand, I found a pair of seagulls roosting on my porch.

"Bravo?" I asked as I parked my car and ambled over to greet them. "And is that Abigull? No way."

The smaller of the two birds puffed out her feathers and let out a tinkling giggle. When I last saw her a few weeks back, she'd been little more than a hatchling. Now she was almost as large as her adoptive father—and a very happy-looking bird at that.

"We've finished our search for your grandmother," Bravo informed me without further pretense. He'd promised to put me in touch with my long-lost biological grandmother in return for Charles, Pringle, and me assisting in a land dispute with another flock. And I knew he was trying his best to deliver on his end of the deal, but the more that time passed, the less I believed any of us would be able to find her.

I never should have doubted them, I realized now as an enormous smile stretched across my face. "That's wonderful. Can you take me to her now?" I moved back toward my car, but the seagulls didn't follow.

"She's not here anymore," Abigull said with a sad shake of her head.

Bravo picked up where his ward left off. "She was here in the Bay for a long time, but now we can't locate her."

"Did she...?" I swallowed hard, unable to believe the horrible timing. "Did she die?"

"Oh gosh no!" The little bird chirped and shifted her weight from foot to foot. "Nothing like that."

"I've put my best gulls on scouting duty, but so far we're unable to locate her new residence," Bravo added, all business, while Abigull seemed much more concerned about tending to my feelings.

"So what now?" I asked with a sigh. I appreciated that they'd tried but also felt terribly heartbroken that I may never get to meet my missing family member after all.

"We'll keep searching, but we'll need to expand the radius. She may have left the state. It's no problem, really. We will find her, but it's just going to take a little longer than originally estimated."

"Thank you," I said, working hard to show them a smile even though the news they'd just brought me had ruined my whole day. "Thank you for not giving up."

"Nothing can stop a bird on a mission," Bravo informed me with a narrowed gaze.

"Yeah," his adoptive daughter chimed in.

"Now we must be off." Bravo immediately launched into the sky with Abigull at his tail.

"Bye, Angie," the girl gull called as they soared away on the winds.

I slumped down onto the worn oak porch steps and sat there for a while, just me and the dwindling warmth of the setting sun.

What would I do if the flock failed to find my grandmother? I'd already questioned my remaining family in Larkhaven, searched every nook and cranny of the Internet… I'd even tried the genealogy route but had come up with absolutely nothing.

Somewhere out there, I had a grandmother I hadn't even known existed until last year. Her entire family had been stolen from her when my grandpa took their baby—my mother—and asked Nan to take her somewhere far away.

None of us knew why, and my grandpa had already passed by the time I learned of his existence. And now these two huge players in my personal history were nothing more than a giant question mark, and I doubted I'd ever really be whole again until I could find her.

***Grizzly Grievance* is available as part of the *Pet Whisperer P.I.: Books 13-15 Special Collection*.**

Get your copy so that you can keep reading this series today!

ABOUT MOLLY FITZ

While *USA Today bestselling* author Molly Fitz can't technically talk to animals, she and her three feline writing assistants have deep and very animated conversations as they navigate their days.

She lives with her child and their own private zoo somewhere in the wilds of Alaska. Molly will occasionally venture out for good food, great coffee, or to meet new animal friends.

Learn more about Molly and her books, and be sure to sign up for her newsletter at **www.MollyMysteries.com**.

ALSO BY MOLLY FITZ

Learn more about Molly's collected works, so that you can decide which book you'd like to read next...

PET WHISPERER P.I.

Angie Russo just partnered up with Blueberry Bay's first ever talking cat detective. Along with his ragtag gang of human and animal helpers, Octo-Cat is determined to save the day... so long as it doesn't interfere with his schedule.

Start with book 1, ***Kitty Confidential***.

MERLIN'S MAGICAL MYSTERIES

Gracie Springs is not a witch… but her cat is. Now she must help to keep his secret or risk spending the rest of her life in some magical prison. Too bad trouble seems to find them at every turn!

Start with book 1, ***Merlin Takes a Familiar***.

PARANORMAL TEMP AGENCY

Tawny Bigford's simple life takes a turn for the magical when she stumbles upon her landlady's murder and is recruited by a talking black cat named Fluffikins to take over the deceased's role as the official Town Witch for Beech Grove, Georgia.

Start with book 1, ***Witch for Hire***.

THE MYSTERIES OF MOONLIGHT MANOR (WITH TRIXIE SILVERTALE)

Sydney Coleman has it all—until she doesn't. No sooner does she launch her bed and breakfast, than a trio of ghosts turn up oppose her at every turn. They insist she solve the murder of their mistress, but Sydney is desperate for cash. If she can't book some guests fast, her haunted mansion is utterly doomed.

Start with book 1, ***Moonlight & Mischief***.

CONNECT WITH MOLLY

Sign up for my newsletter and get a special digital prize pack for joining, including an exclusive story, *Meowy Christmas Mayhem*, fun quiz, and lots of cat pictures!

Sign up: **MollyMysteries.com/subscribe**

Now, if you ever wished you could converse with cats, here's your opportunity! This is me officially inviting you into my whacky inner world as part of my Cozy Kitty Book Club.

For those who just can't get enough of my zany cat characters and their hapless humans, this book club will provide new content to devour and the chance to get to know my best author friends.

From exclusive stories, behind-the-scenes trivia to never-before-released bonus content, and monthly giveaways, there's a lot to love about the Cozy Kitty Book Club. Join today to find out what we're reading next!

Join: **MollyMysteries.com/club**

www.ingramcontent.com/pod-product-compliance
Lightning Source LLC
Chambersburg PA
CBHW030626310726
48979CB00003B/900
* 9 7 8 1 6 4 4 5 1 5 3 2 7 *